"PULL OVER."

Molly signaled, slowed and pulled off the empty highway. Jake reached across the seat to turn off the ignition and moved closer to her, propping his elbow on the back of her seat. "No one has ever called me a mule and a stuffed bear!"

"Is that why we stopped? Don't tell me I've hurt your feelings!"

"Don't flatter yourself!" he said, but there was laughter in his voice. "I'm going to see if you still think mule and stuffed bear after we kiss."

"We're not going to get to Missouri at this rate," she said, but her words were slurred.

His arm circled her waist and he leaned down to kiss her, deeply and long. Forever. Finally, he paused and whispered, "I'm a stuffed bear and a mule?"

"Absolutely," she said dreamily.

ABOUT THE AUTHOR

The Romantic Book Lovers Conference bestowed
their Love and Laughter Award on Sara Orwig in
1985, and fans familiar with her wonderfully
contemporary dialogue will instantly know why.
Between books this Oklahoma native, the mother
of three, enjoys go-carts and acrylic painting; she
describes herself as having ''a house full of brown
plants and a fertile imagination!''

Books by Sara Orwig

HARLEQUIN SUPERROMANCE
57–MAGIC OBSESSION
212–A CHANCE IN TIME

HARLEQUIN REGENCY ROMANCE
2–THE FAIRFAX BREW
4–REVENGE FOR A DUCHESS

These books may be available at your local bookseller.

Don't miss any of our special offers. Write to us at the
following address for information on our newest releases.

Harlequin Reader Service
901 Fuhrmann Blvd., P.O. Box 1397, Buffalo, NY 14240
Canadian address: P.O. Box 603,
Fort Erie, Ont. L2A 5X3

Sara Orwig

GYPSY FIRE

Harlequin Books

TORONTO • NEW YORK • LONDON
AMSTERDAM • PARIS • SYDNEY • HAMBURG
STOCKHOLM • ATHENS • TOKYO • MILAN

Published December 1986

First printing October 1986

ISBN 0-373-70241-8

With love to David . . .

CHAPTER ONE

ON A BALMY SPRING Monday afternoon late in May, Jake Cannon whipped his black car off a six-lane Michigan thoroughfare. Exiting to a side street, he slowed to drive past rows of offices in an older section of Detroit. Ahead, surrounded by a well-tended expanse of landscaped ground, a tall glass building contrasted with the weathered wooden office beside it.

Jake drove into the narrow parking lot on the one-storey United States Post Office. All the parking slots were taken in front, so he turned the corner to stop along the west side of the building. He drove almost to the end of the lot, parked, and climbed out, glancing briefly to his right.

A stretch of grass separated the two structures. Near the east door of the Brantz Building, a concrete drive widened to accommodate a few cars for parking; two black vehicles stood there, sunlight glinting off the shiny tops.

Jake recognized the blue diamond logo above the doors of the glass office complex—it was headquarters of Blue Diamond, Incorporated, one of the largest computer firms in the United States.

Near the front, a gardener spaded around yellow tulips and pink hyacinths while a brown car slowed and parked at the curb. Jake turned the corner and headed down the street to the east, where two more modern structures made of steel and dark glass dwarfed older buildings.

His interest shifting to the business at hand, Jake entered the warm interior of the post office. Sunlight poured through the windows, revealing the dust on the floor, and the cobwebs in the corners of the plastered walls. Beside a scarred brown table, Jake pulled out folded sheets of paper and envelopes from his coat pocket and began to write, bending his dark head over the table. Sunlight caught midnight highlights in his black hair while his gray eyes focused on the words he penned hastily:

Regina—
I'm in a post office and have to run. My secretary is on vacation or she would have typed this. Here are brochures for your parents' trip; these tell briefly about the restaurants and sights in Detroit and Windsor, Canada. Sorry I won't be here to show your folks around town. As I said on the phone, don't fight traffic and try to meet me when I get to Chicago Friday night. Hope this letter gets to you before I do. See you soon.

Love, Jake

He put the letter into an envelope, sealed it and wrote another brief letter.

Ben,
Tried to call and couldn't catch you in. Can't believe I'm finally getting my vacation. A whole week to loll around and fish and relax. So glad you're taking your holidays now and will join us. I'll get to Chicago and see Regina on Friday night.

I'm flying to Springfield, Missouri, will rent a car at the airport and drive to the cabin. I'll get the place spruced up before you and Jamie and my in-laws arrive on Saturday. Hope the fish are biting. Gather up your gear and come on. Cheer up and don't worry too much about your job. Jamie and I want to see you.

He paused a moment, thinking about his six-year-old daughter. Then he wrote:

See you soon. Jake

He slipped the letter into an envelope, and stepped into line to buy stamps.

TWO CARS AWAY from Jake's empty one at the very back of the lot, Molly Ashland sat behind the wheel as she addressed the letter in her lap. She picked up the typewritten sheet and added to the bottom of the page:

P.S. Ivy, I'm writing because I just got last month's long-distance phone bill and I have to watch the calls. I'll get to Houston Friday night and Garvin will meet me at the airport. Saturday morning I'll see you when I get to Dallas. I'll be glad when this weekend is over and know you will be too. Chin up. See you Saturday. Molly.

She thought about the coming weekend while she glanced at her surroundings. The alley behind the post office was paved, lined with metal trash bins and bordered by a wooden fence.

With a sigh Molly put the page into the envelope, and scanned another letter she had written at home, her gaze fixing briefly on the last words:

We need to sit down and talk again. I'm not ready to settle down. Please understand. We talked about this last time we were together and you know how I feel. I thought we were meant to be good friends—not husband and wife. See you Friday night.

Love, Molly

She sealed the second letter; then she picked up a bulky package, opened her door and hurried down the parking lot. Sparing a glance for the gardener who was turning dark brown earth in the bed beside the Brantz Building, she remembered the neglected flower bed at her apartment. It would have to wait another week. Maybe when Ivy was back in Detroit they would have time to dig. Molly turned the corner, her high-heeled red pumps clicking against the concrete walk as she hurried into the post office. There were four people in line ahead of her. The first was a woman talking to the postal clerk at the window.

While she waited, Molly noticed the man in front of her. Thinking momentarily of Garvin, she realized this man was taller, just as broad-shouldered, with a well-shaped head and an enticing mass of wavy black hair. She thought of Garvin's blond hair as she looked at those raven waves cut neatly above the collar of the man's white shirt. He was well dressed in a charcoal suit and his handsomeness made her feel a slight pang of loss over Garvin, but she was sure about her feelings.

After straightening her navy blazer, she brushed a bit of lint off her red skirt. The diamond on her finger caught the light. She would have stopped wearing it, but her finger seemed the safest place for the ring until she returned it to Garvin. The woman at the window finished and left, and Molly moved forward. As she waited, she glanced down at the package containing a birthday present to her mother and noticed she had forgotten to write a return address.

She tried to balance the bulky box and write at the same time. Jiggling the package, she accidentally bumped the man in front of her. When he turned around, she apologized. "I'm sorry. I didn't mean to poke you." She gestured helplessly. "I was trying to write."

When he looked amused, his full mouth widening in a faint smile, she thought she had met him before, and decided he was someone she knew. She smiled at him, racking her brain to remember where they had met. He was too appealing to forget. "That's all right," he said. "Can I help? I'll hold the box for you, and you finish writing the address."

His voice was deep and marvelous, reminding her of radio shows and disc jockeys; then she knew who he was. Mr. Soundmaster. He did television commercials for his stereo company, Soundmaster Stereo. She recalled one of his commercials, his deep voice saying, "Hi, I'm Jake Soundmaster..."

"You're in a commercial, aren't you?" she asked him.

"Yes." His smile widened a fraction.

"I knew you looked familiar. You're Jake Soundmaster." When he nodded, she bent her head to write swiftly. As soon as she was finished, she smiled at him. "Thanks."

"Anytime," he said and winked.

The wink was as impersonal as the post office, but it added to his appeal, and for an instant made her feel as if he were a friend. Another customer left, the line moved up and in minutes Jake Soundmaster moved away, putting stamps on his letters. He walked through open glass doors to the foyer, where he stopped to write on an envelope.

Molly waited while the clerk weighed her package. Then she paid and bought two stamps. As she left, she affixed the stamps to her letters. Her attention was on the letter and not on where she was going. She collided with Jake.

"Oh! I'm sorry!" she exclaimed and blushed. "I wasn't watching my step."

"I don't mind," he said with an engaging grin.

She smiled in return and waited while he started to put letters in the drop, saw she was going to do the same, and motioned politely for her to go first. She did and headed outside. At the door a large hand reached around her, and Jake pushed the door open for her.

She flashed him a smile. It was easy, because he had an interesting face. She noticed appreciative smoky gray eyes as he flicked one quick, assessing glance at her. His appraisal made her wonder if her shoulder-length red hair needed combing, if her makeup was all right. It was the direct glance of an attractive male, and it made her aware of herself as a woman. She smiled as she passed him, catching a woodsy scent of pine and laurel from his clothing or after-shave. "Thanks," she said, stepping outside. A gray-haired man who had left the post office a few steps ahead of her had paused to read a letter. The woman who had been first in line was standing talking to a friend on the walk in front.

Jake fell into step directly behind Molly as they both headed west toward their cars. Her back tingled, and she wondered if he were watching her or not. She turned the corner and when she heard his footsteps follow, she glanced at him.

He smiled. "I'm parked back this way, too."

She shrugged indifferently, feeling silly for having turned around.

"I thought you might be afraid," Jake added pleasantly.

"Not in broad daylight," she said, and forever after remembered her words. She turned, noticing it was a glorious spring day, though storm clouds seemed to be building in the distance to the south. The post office was still busy with customers coming and going and people milling around outside. Another woman drove into the lot, climbed out of her car, and picked up a package. Adjusting bifocals, she smiled as she passed Molly and said hello to Jake Soundmaster.

From the side entrance of the Brantz building next door emerged an auburn-haired man with a briefcase; another man, dressed in a tan suit, walked briskly beside him. They turned toward the black cars parked on the drive.

As if in a dream, everything seemed to happen with lightning swiftness. For the first few seconds of stunned surprise, Molly couldn't move.

The gardener, dropping his spade, stood up from behind a spirea bush and in his hands was a machine gun.

At the same time, as a man in coveralls sprinted from the brown car at the curb, two men, identically dressed with blue coveralls emerged from another red car. Another man stepped out from behind bushes to leap on the man with the briefcase while the gardener ran toward them. At that moment a man came out of the building, saw what was happening and yelled as he ran back inside.

Suddenly a shot rang out from Molly's left. While his companion knocked one of the assailants to the ground, the man with the briefcase broke free and began to run, veering toward Molly and Jake.

The gardener fired at him and Molly heard a ping near the wall of the post office behind her. A security police car screeched around the corner and slid to a stop. Two security guards jumped out, one of them brandishing a gun, which he fired. The gardener spun on his heel to return the shots.

"Oh, damn," Jake Soundmaster muttered; then they were in the center of the fracas. The auburn-haired man with the briefcase barreled into Molly and she staggered back as he started to run past. A man clamped a hand on his shoulder, spinning him around to try to get the briefcase away from him.

Someone shoved Molly out of the way. The auburn-haired man with the briefcase struggled silently to break free. Without thinking, Molly swung her purse with all her strength and struck one of the men attempting to get the briefcase.

"Let him go!" she cried, her heart pounding with fright.

The gardener with the gun yelled an obscenity at her while his partner pushed her aside, yanking her purse from her hands before hauling back his fist to hit her.

Molly saw his big knuckles, the anger in his black eyes, the scar that ran across his cheeks and the bridge of his nose. Terrified, she couldn't move, but knew she was going to be hurt.

Suddenly, Jake Soundmaster tackled the man, deflecting the blow while yelling, "Run!"

She ran. She looked over her shoulder and glimpsed Jake hitting the man while two others hurried toward a waiting car with the auburn-haired man between them, but she forgot them all as a blond man dashed after her.

She ran until a hand clamped around her arm. The blonde spun her around as he raised a gun. Her breath caught in her throat and she felt lightheaded as she looked at the ugly muzzle of the weapon.

A volley of shots sounded; the man flinched, and Molly broke free. She heard shouts and gunfire and cars roaring away while she ran toward the back of the post office. Sirens screamed in the distance, and Jake came flying past her. She saw two men push the fellow with the briefcase into a black car. One of the men looked directly at her, his black eyes squinting as he stared intently. "Get her!"

Her heart thudded with fear. She dashed around the corner as sirens grew louder. Jake Soundmaster crouched behind a trash can while another volley of shots sounded behind them. She knelt with him, breathing rapidly. They heard footsteps running nearby; then steps turned away from them. "You may have saved my life! Thanks for coming to my rescue," she said, beginning to shake in reaction to the past moments. "Were you hurt?"

"I'll survive." He glanced at her, and she saw he had a cut on his cheek. "Would you mind not following me?"

"The police are coming!"

"Yeah. Good news," he said so sarcastically that she forgot the melee and stared at him.

"You don't want to see the police?" she asked in surprise.

"Not exactly." He peered around the edge of the trash can and ducked back against the wall.

"Why don't you want to see the police?" She stared at him, curiosity mounting over his aversion to the law.

"We just witnessed the crime of the year."

"What are you talking about?"

Someone yelled, tires screeched, and gunshots flared again. Jake flashed her a glance. "You didn't recognize the man with the briefcase?"

"No."

"Oh, geez. You know me, but you don't know him. That's Karl Brantz, the multi-millionaire. That's his Blue Diamond computer company and his building—the Brantz Building. They've kidnapped him and we saw every second of it." He leaned around the trash can. "Excuse me," he said and sprinted away.

"Hey, wait!" She didn't want to be left and grabbed his coattail. In a momentary, silent struggle he tried to yank loose.

Footsteps sounded and a man in coveralls appeared at the front of the alley. "Here they are!" he yelled.

Jake yanked his coat out of her grasp and ran with Molly racing after him. He jumped on a trash can, vaulted the fence and dropped down out of sight.

She scrambled up and jumped down on the other side. Jake had come to her rescue and without stopping to reason it out, she felt safer with him. She didn't intend to get left behind, and stretched out her legs to run as fast as possible. Behind her two shots were fired; she heard a dull thunk as a bullet hit something nearby.

As she emerged from the alley she saw Jake ahead, running down the street. His tall, solid form represented the only security in a world gone crazy and she rushed after him. He turned between two red brick buildings. Molly followed, her mind not functioning, her feet just going wherever he went. He dashed into another alley and climbed on top of a trash can to go over a high board fence.

"Wait for me! Help me!" Molly cried as she followed him. He glanced over his shoulder at her, increased his speed and disappeared over the fence.

"Hey!" She heaved one trash can on top of another and went up swiftly, grabbing the top of the fence as the cans fell out from beneath her feet. She went over and dropped down beside him. After falling, she scrambled to her feet swiftly. "You don't know how to be a gentleman!" she snapped.

"At a time like this I sure as hell don't! Will you stop following me!" They had jumped into a concreted area that was enclosed by buildings. A faded and ripped sofa lay overturned against a wall. Boxes littered the area and bulging black trash bags were thrown carelessly beside doors. Jake looked around frantically. The red brick building at the north end of the enclosure had a black iron fire escape; its last step hung high above the ground.

Jake tried a door and discovered it was locked. He yanked on another, then tried another to find them all locked. On the other side of the fence, they heard someone yell.

Molly looked around at the buildings, the litter that looked permanent, and the fire escape that ended about nine feet above the ground. Jake ran below it to stare up at it.

She hurried after him, pulling on his arm. "Put me on your shoulders. I can reach the bottom rung and my weight will pull it down so you can get hold of it."

"Get your shoes off," he snapped. After hastily stuffing her shoes in his coat pockets, he boosted her up. She stood on his shoulders, feeling him weave beneath her as she grabbed at the black iron step. "Stand still!" she cried.

"How can I stand still with you on my shoulders?"

As her fingers closed around the rung, she lost her balance and fell off his shoulders.

She hung by her hands, clutching the fire escape tightly. Then she swung her foot to get a toehold; with a pull of muscles, she scrambled up. Her weight forced the iron ladder down as she had expected. Jack caught hold, and she went up ahead of him. Relieved to get out of the alley, she climbed over a concrete-and-brick parapet onto a flat, black roof. In the center was a structure, a windowless frame room on the top of the building with a scarred, weathered door.

Jake sat down, leaning against the parapet while he gulped for air. Molly sank down beside him, and he glanced at her. "You must be an Olympic runner. What do you do for a living?"

"I'm a teacher."

"Lordy, I'm out of shape," he said, staring at her.

"I teach dancing. I exercise," she said, thinking he wasn't too out of shape.

He returned her shoes, pulled off his tie and stuffed it into his coat pocket. As she slipped into the red pumps, Molly heard a helicopter sweep overhead. In seconds it hovered above them.

"Oh, hell! That's a police helicopter," Jake grumbled. He turned to look at her. "Look, you know who I am. Would you do me a favor and don't tell the police?"

"Why?" she asked, staring at him, contemplating what he was hiding from the police.

While sirens wailed loudly on the streets below, the helicopter made another circle and Jake covered his head. She put her own head down to peer at him. "You can't be a wanted man because you wouldn't go on television. Why are you afraid of the lawmen?"

"I want to get away from the helicopter," he said as he crouched and then ran for the door to the building. Yanking on the knob, he swore when he found it locked. Molly stayed right behind him. "Why don't you want to see the police?" she asked, wondering if he had some dark secret. "I thought they were the good guys."

He leaned against the door breathing deeply. "Lady, we just witnessed, eyeball to eyeball—" he paused and looked around, scratching his head as if his thoughts were barely on what he was saying to her "—a major crime. Perhaps *the* major crime of this year. I'm so damned long overdue a vacation that it's absurd; I get to see my—I'm not giving up my vacation. It's been nice to know you. Please, forget who I am or that you ever saw me. I was just a stranger. You go your way, and I'll go mine." Without another word he ran, hurrying around the central structure on the roof. After one startled second, Molly went after him and they circled to come back to the locked door.

"Dammit, there's no way off this roof except back down the fire escape and out the way we came, where it's crawling with police."

"What does your vacation have to do with anything?" she persisted, puzzling over what he had been about to say when he had stopped abruptly.

He focused on her, and somewhere in the back of her mind she registered again how gray his eyes were. "We're witnesses. You know who I am from my television appearances. If the crooks know as well as you do—there's probably a contract out on me right now."

"That's all the more reason to go to the police."

He looked at her as if she were a small child who needed the simplest problem explained. "We weren't the only witnesses, so they don't have to have my testimony. For that matter, they won't have to have *your* testimony. If I go to the police for my own protection, chances are I will be tucked away, safely guarded in a hotel room while I miss another vacation. This vacation is important. I have everything coordinated and worked out. I'll do my civic duty when I get back to town."

She blinked, thinking about her own life. "The police can't hold you indefinitely. They won't know how long it'll take them to find the crooks."

He walked to the edge of the building, looked down and moved back swiftly.

"This is a kidnapping of an important, brilliant, enormously wealthy man. It'll come to a head one way or another in a short time, and they'll hold me or you, or anyone else who was down there, until something happens on the case. If they don't protect the witnesses..." His voice trailed off and he shook his head. "There's got to be something up here to break open that door." He looked around while she dogged his footsteps and caught up to stand beside him.

"Where'll you go if you don't go to the police? You can't go home."

For an instant he seemed to remember her. He smiled fleetingly, and his voice changed to a different tone, growing wistful and tender. "Far, far away from here I have a home, a nice lake home—big, comfortable, three bedrooms, with a screened-in porch way back in the woods where no one can find me. No telephone, no television, no paved road. I can enjoy my vacation and come forth afterward. I'll be glad to help then."

"Seems as if that's shunning your civic duty."

"There were witnesses galore," he said, and his voice became brisk again. "You saw all those people. I'll bet the police already have half a dozen witnesses on their way to secluded hotel rooms."

"You're probably right there," she said, thinking it over.

"Maybe I am shunning my duty, but I need this vacation and I don't want to spend it locked up in a hotel room with some bored guard when they might not ever need my testimony at all. If they needed my word and my word only, I'd come forth. And if the police arrest the guys, I'll come forth to help identify them. Right now I can't go home or to work. Neither can you. Why don't you go to the police? You can join the guy that was behind us. The last time I looked, I saw him run toward the security guards."

She bit her lip, remembering what had happened, thinking about her plans for a weekend in Texas. An important weekend in Texas.

"I can do what I want safely because no one knows who I am," she said, thinking aloud.

He paused and turned around to look at her, running his fingers through his hair. "I may hate myself for this," he said and shook his head. His voice was filled with reluctance as if he really didn't want to say whatever he was about to tell her. "You hit that guy with your purse and he grabbed it."

She remembered; then she realized what jeopardy she was in. "I forgot about my purse! They have all my credit cards, my driver's license, my identification," she said. "They'll know who I am, and I can't go home, either."

He scowled at her. "That was a dumb thing to do. Don't you know better than to hit a man who has a gun? To hit him with a purse of all things!"

She bristled, feeling a touch of irritation. "It was a reflex action. Like following you," she said, thinking she could have done something better in both instances. All her irritation fled as she returned to the new worries. "If they have my purse—would they put out a contract on me?" she asked, trying to fathom that her life could have changed drastically in such a brief time. "I didn't think that really happened."

"It really happens. For a crime like this, there'll be many people involved, perhaps organized mobsters who can assign men to hunt for you. You better go to the police for protection. Just don't say you know who I am."

She followed him back to the door. He lunged against it, banging his shoulder, yelping with pain and standing to glare at the unyielding rectangle of wood. Then he pulled out a pocket knife, opened it, and knelt down. While he tried to get the door open, picking the lock with his knife, she thought about her life and the fact that a group of organized criminals probably wanted her eliminated.

As she mulled it over, she realized she couldn't go home or to work. If she were locked up in a hotel room, she wouldn't see Garvin to talk to him about the letter that she had already mailed; she wouldn't be able to help her sister Ivy at one of the most traumatic moments in Ivy's life. A cabin on a lake in the woods. She pictured Minnesota or Colorado. Isolation, but a degree of freedom.

She tugged on Jake's shoulder as he worked at the lock with his pocket knife. The helicopter swooped over them again and Jake swore.

"Mr. Soundmaster?"

"Yeah?" He glared at the door.

"Where's your cabin? What woods?"

He looked up momentarily, giving her a sly grin. "Sorry. That's for only me to know."

Annoyance flared again and the word *jerk* came to mind. "You could say north, south, east or west," she prompted, trying to keep her patience.

"Nope. No, indeed. It's a secret hideaway." He smiled and went back to work on the lock.

She debated her choices for about one second, realizing she couldn't try to get a flight out of Detroit, take a bus or go to any public place of transportation because some gangster could be watching for her. Besides, she didn't have so much as ten cents in her possession. And Jake Soundmaster must be an all right citizen, albeit a jerk and uncivic-minded. He had been in her living room countless times, his smiling face and deep, drawling words selling Soundmaster stereos. He had to be a *safe* guy whether he was likeable or not. She forced a smile. "Mr. Soundmaster," she said sweetly, tugging on his arm.

"Yeah, what?" he snapped, turning the point of his knife in the lock.

"I don't want to be locked up in a hotel room, either. Take me with you to your cabin. Let me stay just for a week, and then I'll go to the police."

He turned around to look at her, and she could see emotions play at his expression. Amazement, incredulity, laughter. "Sorry, lady. I'm sorry, but I won't do it. We're strangers."

"I'm Molly Ashland," she said quickly, "A twenty-nine-year-old dance instructor. My mother, Belle, lives in Akron, Ohio, and my father lives in Fresno, California. My sister Ivy is divorcing her husband, Willis Bronski. Listen to me. My sister's divorce is ruining her life."

"I'm sorry," he said, keeping his attention on the lock. She doubted he had listened to half of what she had said.

"I need to be with Ivy," Molly said firmly, staring at the back of his head and thinking, *mule*. "Please, let me go with you for a week."

"And do what? Bring your sister to my place?"

"Well, I didn't have that in mind," she said, admitting to herself that she had exactly that in mind, because Ivy desperately needed to get away from the danger of Willis's brutality. "I figured I can find a phone at a nearby town and talk to her."

Jake squinted at the lock. "The police will let you talk to her to your heart's content from a secluded hideaway. No deal."

She took a deep breath and fought to keep her voice calm. "Please. I don't want to be locked up either. I have to help my sister. I'm about to break my engagement and I want to talk to Garvin. I just sent him a letter about it when we were in the post office. I don't want him to get the letter, and then not be able to talk to me."

"Nope. Sorry," he said flatly. "I don't run a hotel or an institution of charity. Get your own hideaway."

Anger began to rise and patience waned. "I figured you were married with a family after seeing you on television, but you're single," she said, putting her hands on her hips to glare at him.

He pulled his gaze from the keyhole to look at her in surprise. "Yeah, how'd you know?"

"You're too big a jerk to have someone love you enough to marry you!"

He grinned and went back to work picking the lock while she strode away. With her temper boiling, she glared at him as he worked. Walking around the roof of the building, watching policemen on the ground in the distance, she tried to figure out where she could go or what she could do. She had no money, no checks, no credit cards. It was a helpless feeling. As she paced and worried, she spotted a heavy beam lying next to the low parapet of the building. She stopped to stare at the rough wood and then walked to the edge of the roof. Beyond the next row of buildings, she could see a police car with its lights flashing. Occasionally a policeman came into view, then disappeared. Sirens still sounded as more official cars arrived at the scene.

The police helicopter swept over the roof again, coming down so close Molly could feel the draft stirred by the propellers. The clatter of the motor was loud, and then suddenly it was gone. Molly walked back to find Jake standing up and taking his coat off his head.

"You know, you'll draw more attention to yourself by hiding like that. If I were in a helicopter and a guy knelt down and pulled his coat over his head, I'd be overcome with curiosity.''

"No doubt you would," he said in a scathing tone. He glared at the door. "Damn, I expect that door to open any minute and police to come through. Or else they'll come up the fire escape."

Molly would have been happy to see the police come and take Jake Soundmaster out of her life, but for the moment she was stuck with him and she wanted to escape as desperately as he. So she said, "I know how we can get away without going back down the way we came."

He looked at her. "How? For Lord's sake why are you just standing there watching me work to get this door open! Tell me how."

"If I do, will you take me with you to the lake house?"

"The hell I will," he said in disgust, his dark brows coming closer together in a frown. "We'll both wait right here for the police."

Mule—the man was an absolute mule! She bit her lip. She agreed with his premonitions. With every sweep of the helicopter, she expected police to come out of the door from inside the building or up the fire escape after them. She could see a car blocking the alley where they had come and if they tried to go back that way, they would walk into a nest of policemen. She decided to show Jake Soundmaster her way to escape and try to bargain later.

"Okay, I'll show you how to get off this roof. Come here. I saw a wooden beam like a railroad tie over by the edge of the roof."

When she showed it to him, he asked, "What good will that be? I'm sorry, you may be as strong as Samson, but you and I together can't lift that hunk of wood to try to batter open the door.''

"Good grief, no! That's not what we can do." She crossed to touch the beam with her toe. "We can lift the end of this up on the edge of the building.''

"Yeah, and what good would that do?''

"We can slide it to the building across the alley from us. It's not a big space. It'll make a footbridge and we can walk across.''

His gaze traveled beyond her to the building only yards away. He looked as if he were turning green. "Walk?''

"Yes. It's not far,'' she said, wondering if he were having an attack of indigestion.

He ran his fingers through his hair and stared beyond the edge of the roof. "It makes me sick to think about it. I have vertigo. I can't walk over open space.''

"Then you come help me, and I'll leave you to be one of the police's star witnesses. Help me put the end up on the edge here.''

He went over and worked grimly, tugging the end of the long piece of wood up. Veins stood out on his head; she heaved with all her strength. With a groan from him and spots dancing before her eyes, they dropped one end of the beam on the low parapet.

"Now we'll push it across the space. Don't let it tip and fall.''

"Don't talk about falling,'' he said hoarsely., "I hate height.''

They continued in grim silence, almost losing it twice, but each time, Jake grabbed it, throwing his weight on one end, and causing the other end to tilt up in the air until they finally slid it into place over the edge of the other building. Once they did, she stood up and brushed off her hands.

"There. Good job."

"Oh, lordy!" He gasped for breath. "I think I pulled something."

"Now just walk across and maybe we can get inside that building or the one next to it."

"I can't walk across open air on that beam," he said in a flat tone, staring at it as if it had sprouted fangs.

"Sure, you can," she said cheerfully, because she needed him. "You look at me. I'll go first. Just stare at my back. Don't think about being more than an inch off the ground."

"Oh, geez. I don't sit higher than the tenth row at football games."

She stepped up, pausing to look back at him. His face was ashen, and perspiration dotted his forehead as he rubbed his hands together.

"I can't do it."

"Think of your home in the woods and keep your eyes on me," she said briskly. She took a deep breath and focused her gaze on the rooftop across from her as she moved quickly across the beam. Aware of the space below, she fought an urge to look down, but she was accustomed to acrobatics and exercise bars and it actually wasn't a difficult feat. Behind her, he groaned. She jumped down and turned to see him, his arms flailing the air.

"Jump!" she yelled, suddenly holding her breath as she watched in horror. He lost his balance, lunged for the edge and fell.

CHAPTER TWO

SHE GASPED and rushed forward as his hands locked on the edge of the building. He was dangling above the alley, fully nine stories below.

"Help!" he yelled and tried to get a toehold in the brick.

She leaned over the top of the building. "I'll help you, but you take me to the lake house with you."

He looked up. "Pull, dammit!"

She pressed her advantage. "I go with you to the lake."

"Deal. Help me."

Instantly she locked her fingers on his arm. "Swing your leg up here." He did as she said, and she caught his leg, pulling his knee with one hand and tugging his clothes with the other as he gradually moved up and slid over the edge.

"Oh, lord," he gasped, sliding his hands over the roof beneath him when he flopped down. "Terra firma."

"Actually *roofa firma*," she said cheerfully. He squinted his eyes at her as if he had pinched something. "You're safe," she said and knelt down to look more closely at him.

"No thanks to you!" he snapped. "What are you, half cat?"

"I told you, I'm a dancer," she answered sweetly, her feelings toward him having been somewhat mollified. "And you promised to take me to the woods with you."

"Any other time I'd be delighted to hear you say that. Don't you have to go to work?"

"Would you want to go to work if there was a contract out on you?"

"No." Wiping his brow with the sleeve of his coat, he sat up. "I think my arms just stretched several inches. Where do you work?"

"I have my own dance studio, but I can close it for a brief vacation. I teach adults and teens aerobics and jazz, and in the afternoon I teach little girls tap, jazz and ballet."

Suddenly he grinned, and leaned close to look at her intently. "You're a dirty fighter, making me promise to take you when I was hanging by my fingers!"

"So be it," she said calmly, deciding that he was extremely appealing when he smiled.

"I'll get revenge," he warned in his deep voice, and his eyes held a challenge. She had a suspicion it was the first time he had really looked at her. "What's your name again?" he asked. "I didn't listen before."

"You're a real doll, you know? Molly Ashland."

"Hello, Molly Ashland. We've got a score to settle," he said in a husky voice that was half threat, half teasing and made something vibrate deep inside her. "You almost did me in. I don't walk on beams high up in the air. That was a damned unfair advantage you took to get your way."

"All's fair in a crisis. Shall we try to escape?" she asked. The words came out breathlessly, and his grin widened.

As he stood up, she pointed. "We can cross to the next building without any danger. The buildings adjoin and you won't have to get out above the ground."

"It's a good thing. Never again will I do something as foolhardy as I just did."

His gray eyes seemed to pull like magnets and she couldn't resist leaning closer. "Never?" she asked, and her voice dropped.

Something flickered in the depths of his eyes. "Not as foolhardy or as dangerous as hanging in space," he said, but his tone of voice conveyed a surge of interest, and she felt tension arc between them like a shooting star. Silence stretched, and she knew she should move away or say something. Instead, she looked at his mouth, a tempting mouth. How would it be to feel the touch of his lips?

"Molly—"

The helicopter's motor broke the spell, and she moved away swiftly. "Hurry! This way." They moved to the next building, found a door open, and went down a flight of stairs in an old apartment house. Odors of cabbage and stale smoke filled the air, and Molly noticed all the cracks in the faded yellow walls. The stairs squeaked with Jake's weight as they started down a second flight.

Around the turn in the stairs, they heard footsteps coming up. Jake whipped around, pushing her ahead of him, and they returned to the hall above. He tried first one locked door and then another until he found one that opened on a small broom closet. He pulled Molly inside and closed the door. It was crowded, pitch black, and his body pressed against hers, his hand slipping over her hip as they heard two men knock on a door and talk to the occupant, asking about a man and a woman.

"Watch your hands!" she whispered, trying to keep her own from brushing against him.

"In this darkness?"

"You know what I mean!"

"Shh. Pray they won't look in here," Jake whispered in her ear, his breath tickling her. In the darkness, she became more aware of Jake Cannon than of danger. He pulled off his coat, his hands and arms lightly bumping her in the process. She tried to listen to the conversation going on in the hall.

"They're looking for us all right. Do you think they're really police?"

"Who knows? I don't want to find out. Take off your blazer."

She did as he asked, realizing the police probably had a description of them and the criminals knew exactly how they were dressed. "Why would the police search for us?" she whispered.

"For our protection. Or maybe because they're curious why we're hiding and running. Or maybe they think we're criminals." As Jake pressed closer, he said, "I'm not trying to get cute. But if they yank open the door our only chance is to make them think we're lovers in a clinch. Sorry, but I'd better put my arm around you."

"I understand. Go right ahead," she whispered, listening to the muffled voices of the men in the hall. Jake's arm circled her waist; his thighs pressed against hers. He smelled nice and his breath tickled her ear again as he said, "Put your arms around me. You won't have time if they open the door. Hike your skirt up a fraction so we look sincere."

"Sure." She did as he asked, feeling his heart beat, feeling other things that made her even more aware of him. She inhaled deeply the enticing woodsy scent on his clothes. The voices stopped, a door closed, footsteps grew louder and Jake began to nuzzle her neck.

"All for the sake of escape," he murmured, laughter in his voice.

"Sure." She closed her eyes, waiting for the door to be jerked open, waiting while Jake kissed her throat. "You smell nice."

"So do you."

Footsteps grew louder. "Oh, lordy," Jake said and turned his head to kiss her fully, crushing her to him. For an instant he kissed her deeply; she was startled, feeling his swift arousal as she clung to him. He could kiss. She should have felt nothing, perhaps been repulsed because he was practically a stranger. At best she should have been mildy intrigued. But the embrace wasn't repulsive, it was definitely more than nothing and far more than intriguing. Defying logic, his kiss stirred tremors, made her heart beat faster, made her want to kiss him in return.

Jake raised his head and after a second she realized the footsteps were almost directly across from them. Jake's voice was husky, tinged with amusement. "Just in case they open our door," he said and bent his head to find her lips. She let him, telling herself it was in the interest of safety. She had to admit she was curious. Had the first kiss been a fluke? Something that dazzled because her nerves were on edge?

To her amazement, the second kiss was as exciting as the first. For a moment she was dimly aware of footsteps moving past, of a knock and voices, a deep male voice clearly saying, "We're looking for a woman with

red hair and a man with dark hair. Have you seen..."
The voices became a blur; danger ceased to exist. A
moment became suspended in time by Jake's kiss
which captured all of her attention.

Finally, the bang of a door closing penetrated and
she heard footsteps moving farther along the hall. She
pushed Jake away a fraction. "They're going on down
the hall."

"Yeah," he said gruffly, and suddenly she wished it
weren't pitch black so she could see the expression on
his face. "They're checking all that side, and then
they'll probably come down this side. We have to slip
out of here if we get a chance. Listen," he whispered.

They were quiet while the policemen moved to another door and knocked. Jake's fingers idly stroked the
nape of her neck and she wondered if he were aware of
what he was doing. She was aware of it right down to
her toes! Another flurry of knocks sounded, and Molly
guessed people weren't home in many of the apart-
ments. The next knock sounded as if it came from the
end of the hall.

"I'm going to peek out," Jake said. His arm loosened, and he leaned away. Listening again for the policemen, he waited; his lips were still tingling from
Molly's kiss. It had been a long time since the last date,
and his body had reacted swiftly and intensely to Molly
Ashland. He had reacted even more strongly to her
kiss. The lady could kiss better than she could run—a
disconcerting fact. She'd wrung out the promise to take
her with him, something he did not want to do.

He set his lips grimly, telling himself that his emotions and nerves were on edge; otherwise the kisses
would have been ordinary. Some little inner voice
sneered, but he ignored it. Molly Ashland was calam-

ity personified. And strong. She didn't look as if she weighed one hundred pounds dripping wet, but he couldn't have moved that beam by himself, and she had gone up the fire escape with the ease of a monkey. And no monkey had legs like those Jake had glimpsed when Molly was hanging by her hands trying to swing her feet up onto the iron steps of the fire escape. Her skirt had slipped up around her hips, and as preoccupied as he had been with the criminals and the law, he still had noticed she had a fine pair of legs.

Trying to get his mind back on flight, he turned the knob and prayed nothing would squeak. He peered through the opening and saw two policemen standing with their backs to him, knocking on another door at the turn of the hallway.

"Let's see if we can get out of here and avoid being noticed while their backs are turned. Quiet now and hurry."

Slipping off her shoes, holding her jacket, and glancing briefly at the two policemen, she felt as if her heart had stopped beating while she followed Jake. He led the way only a few feet before they turned the corner and descended the stairs out of sight of the two lawmen.

While she slipped on her jacket, she let out her breath. "I hope I don't have to go through that again!"

Jake shot her a quizzical look and grinned. "The kisses gave you that kind of reaction? You could've fooled me—"

"Oh, no!" She looked up, startled over his interpretation. He had stopped on the stairs and was staring at her. "Come on!" She tugged on his coat.

"The kisses were okay?"

"Will you come on! They were definitely okay!" He laughed softly, and they tiptoed downstairs again, hurrying down back alleys as the sky became overcast and rain threatened. A police car cruised past on the street and they ducked into a doorway.

"Try to walk purposefully, calmly, and let's get out of here," Molly said, feeling as if a hundred pairs of eyes were watching them.

"Sure thing," he drawled. "Calmly. You have red hair, a bright red skirt and bare feet. It would be easier to slip a fire engine unnoticed through the crowd."

She glared at him. "You're not exactly inconspicuous yourself!"

"Me?" He arched his brows. "What the hell is conspicuous about me?"

"Your sexy eyes."

Suddenly, he grinned and winked, and she smiled in return. He took her arm. "Let's go."

As they hurried away, she had to fight the temptation to look around constantly. "I feel as if we're being followed."

"Don't look to see. It'll only draw more attention. No one will be interested in us now," he said, but the words gave her a hollow feeling.

Finally Jake found a pay phone in a gas station. He called a cab and within the hour they were on the highway heading south in a rented Lincoln. Molly ran her hand over the maroon seat. "This isn't an inconspicuous car."

"I like something comfortable," he said, as if that explained and excused renting a car that cost twice as much as necessary and was far more noticeable than an ordinary, smaller car.

"Now can you tell me where we're going? Where is your lake home?"

He grinned. "Oh, no! And have you called your sister to come join us? No, you're not going to know the directions."

He stopped on the outskirts of Detroit to make a call from a phone booth. Before he stepped out of the car, he peeled two fifties off a stack of bills and held them out to her. "Here, in case we get separated."

She shook her head. "No, thanks. If I have money, you might try and put me out somewhere."

"If I were going to do that, I wouldn't bother to give you money," he said, but she had been right. He wanted to be free of her, and he regretted his promise extracted under duress, which to him was as unethical on her part as grand larceny. "Okay. Want a quarter to call home? I'm going to call a neighbor and my manager. Otherwise, they'll call the police to set them looking for me. You know we left our cars at the post office. I'm having mine picked up by a friend."

"How'll they get a key?"

"I keep a spare in a little metal box under the fender."

She tilted her head to one side as if lost in thought. "I have a key at home. I suppose I could get my friend to get my car and take it home."

"It would be safer. Here, make your calls." He held out four quarters, hoping his voice had the right note of indifference. He was not taking Molly Ashland to the Ozarks with him if he could help it, promise or no promise!

"While I call, will you buy an early edition of the paper? We might be written up in it," she said, taking the change.

"It's too soon, but I'll get one," he agreed amiably.

She smiled at him. "Just in case you might forget I'm not in the car when you're ready to go—if you go off and leave me—I'll call the police and tell them everything I know, including which highway you're on."

It was just as difficult to force a smile as it was to keep his voice light. "I promised. You don't trust me?"

"Not one bit farther than I can spit."

He wanted to shove her out of the car, take the keys and be on his way alone. Instead, he smiled and climbed out of the car to make his calls, get a paper, and buy two maps of Michigan and Missouri. As he walked back to the Lincoln, he heard thunder rumble. Cool wind bent spring grass and whipped across the lot. He looked at the budding green branches around him and his spirits lifted; in a short time he would be down in the Ozarks in even warmer weather and Jamie would be with him. Roses and summer flowers would be blooming and the days would be warm. He took a deep breath and smiled.

Back in the car, he pulled out a piece of paper and studied the directions he had received over the phone, directions telling how to find his home in the Ozarks. In a few minutes he saw Molly step out of the booth. She had the graceful walk of a dancer, her long legs stretching out in a fluid movement, and he stared at her appreciatively. At the same time, he recalled hanging above the concrete over the side of the building, and he wished she had wanted to stay behind. She was an unnecessary burden in an enticing package. He was thankful beyond measure that there had been other witnesses because he would feel better far from Detroit. Particularly if he had to keep Molly at his side.

With her red hair, she was as noticeable as a neon light. Too late, he realized he had become so engrossed in watching her, he had forgotten the directions in his hand. As she opened the door, he hastily stuffed the paper into his inside coat pocket. If she noticed, she didn't give any indication. She merely climbed in and smiled at him. "How nice of you to wait. It gives me more faith in mankind."

"I promised you I'd take you," he said, feeling mildly guilty while he started the car.

To his surprise she laughed. "Tell the truth: all the time I was in the phone booth, you were wishing you could go off and leave me."

"What would you expect?" he admitted with a grin. "This is my first vacation in six years."

"Six years?" She stared at him with raised eyebrows. "Are you in the ad business?"

"No. I own the Soundmaster stores."

"And you do your own commercials?" she asked with surprise.

"Yeah." He shrugged. "Years ago I had a yen to be an actor; I've been in some amateur theatricals."

"Your commercials are good or I wouldn't have noticed them."

"Thank you," he said, feeling pleased.

"I called a friend to pick up my car, and my assistant will close the studio. While I was in the phone booth, there was something odd that happened."

"Yeah?" he asked, enjoying the faint aroma of her perfume.

"I saw the same car go past twice."

Jake felt as if he had fallen into an icy pond. "Describe the car."

"That's why I noticed it. The driver had a hat pulled down so I couldn't see his face well and his collar was turned up. I wouldn't have paid any attention except I noticed him go past the second time."

"Oh, geez. They could have followed us from the scene of the crime." He adjusted the rearview mirror. "What kind of car?"

"I'm not good at cars. I don't know one kind from another usually, but this was big and dark green and the license had mud on it."

"Damn."

"Do you think it's someone after us?"

"I don't know. It could be or it could be coincidence. Who knows? Keep your eyes open and see if you can spot it again."

"If there are other witnesses, I don't see why they'd keep after us."

"No, I don't either, but if they're on to us, I want to know it. I'm getting off the highway and I'll get back on in a mile or two. That way, maybe I can tell whether we're being followed."

She shivered and peered into the grayness of late afternoon. "It'll be dark earlier because of the rain."

"Yeah. If we can lose anyone following now, we'll be fine."

She turned in the seat to look out the back window, and he noticed her smooth, shapely calves on the seat beside him. "I don't see anyone," she said, settling down again. In twenty minutes, they were back on the highway and some of the stiffness went out of Jake's shoulders.

"If you own the Soundmaster stores, why haven't you taken a vacation?" she asked.

"Business has been good and that makes it hard to leave."

"Seems as if it would make it easier."

"Do you take vacations every year?"

"Sure," she said, folding her long legs up under her. She touched the maps lying on the seat. "Any time I take a notion."

He could imagine how successful her dance studio was. "You must have inherited money, or you have parents to help support you or some other source of income if you close down on a whim."

"Like today. Nope. I support myself, but I have to take a little time to watch the butterflies—to have a little fun."

Her words stung as he called to mind briefly the past two years and the problems he'd had. He gripped the wheel more tightly and tried to force his thoughts elsewhere.

"What's wrong? Don't you have fun in your life?" she asked, startling him.

"How'd you know something was wrong?" he snapped, feeling a mild surge of irritation because he didn't want her to be able to discern his bad moments so easily. It made him feel vulnerable to realize that he couldn't control his emotions over his family and it showed to a stranger.

"You look as if you could chew on the tires."

"I'm single now because I'm widowed," he said, but he still couldn't make his voice sound light or normal. He wondered how many years would have to pass before he could tell about his status casually.

"I'm sorry. What hap—I'm sorry."

"That's all right," he said quietly, more in control now. "She had hepatitis and died. It happens. We have a little girl."

Seeing an entirely different man, Molly stared at him, noting the change in his tone with the words, "little girl." The love that filled his voice was obvious. "What's her name?"

"Jamie. She's six. That's why I have to have this vacation. I'll get to see her."

"That's what you started to say on the roof. You'll be with her. She doesn't live with you all the time?" Molly asked curiously, because it was obvious he loved his daughter deeply.

"No, not for the past year." The pain that filled his voice was revealed as strongly as the love had been moments before. He gripped the steering wheel until his knuckles were white. "She developed asthma after Sheryl died. I have a housekeeper, Vera Majors, I hired to stay with Jamie when I'm at work or gone from home, but after the asthma, we had to make other arrangements. My father-in-law took early retirement from the phone company and he and my mother-in-law sold their house, packed up, and bought a place in Arizona. They took Jamie along and put her in school there."

Jake sounded so hurt Molly ached for him. She reached across to pat his knee. "I'm sorry. That's tough."

He turned his head for a long glance, and she noticed the change in expression as the grim set to his jaw melted away; she realized he was seeing her as a woman again, and she took her hand off his knee. "I'm glad you're human," she said, trying to inject some lightness.

"Yeah." He chuckled. "What did you think I was?"

"An absolute, long-eared, block-headed mule."

He laughed and some of the tenseness seemed to go out of his shoulders. "Said by a woman with the scruples and the agility of a cat! You extorted a promise from me under extreme duress. The only reason I agreed to take you along was because I have vertigo. And your sister is not going to cross the threshold, understand?"

"You'd like her, and she's no trouble. Quiet as a mouse."

"You have a place to stay. Don't push your luck."

"She needs to get away desperately. Willis, her husband, has a violent temper—"

"Look, your sister may have an incredibly sad story, but I do, too. I need this vacation as badly as I need air to breathe, and I don't want it cluttered up with weepy sisters and ex-fiancés!"

Smiling as sweetly as possible, Molly settled in the seat. Time enough to bring up the subject of Ivy again. She had a suspicion that if Jake heard all of Ivy's story, he would yield. As she picked up the paper, she recalled the brief phone calls she had made to Garvin and Ivy. She had told them what she was doing and promised to call again as soon as she knew her exact destination. Feeling it best to tell Garvin her decision before the letter arrived, Molly had broken the news about returning his ring, and he had taken her announcement better than she had expected. The news should have come as no great surprise after their past few phone calls. It was a decision she had made before she had met Jake, but her reaction to him had ended the slightest doubt. Her attention shifted to the paper and she began to read.

The storm that had threatened all day broke loose and as he drove along the freeway, Jake held the wheel firmly, staring intently ahead. The wipers made a steady swish against the glass and the rear window fogged up. Jake glanced at Molly curled up on the seat beside him with her legs tucked beneath her. "What does the paper say?"

"Not a thing. You were right; it's too early."

He switched on the radio and found a Detroit station broadcasting news. They rode in silence as they listened to the national news. Then, finally, local news came on and a brief mention was made that an executive, Karl Brantz, had been abducted at gunpoint during the afternoon at the Brantz Building and that the police had witnesses.

"There—they don't need us," Jake said.

"They didn't say much about what happened."

"They're probably being cautious."

"You think it was organized crime, a mob?"

"Yep. I could be wrong, but they were armed with Uzis, machine pistols, and it went fairly smoothly—if you hadn't swung your purse..." She wrinkled her nose at him as he smiled and continued. "And the weapons were the latest...the gardener was in on the crime, so it had to have been planned in advance. Nope, looks like pros to me, and I don't want to take any chances of ruining my vacation."

For an instant she stared at him, speculating about him. He'd noticed the weapons and knew they were the latest models; he had avoided the police at all costs; he assumed the job was done by pros...was Jake Soundmaster the person she thought he was? A flickering doubt arose about the man she was traveling with to an isolated mountain area. Then she remembered the

Soundmaster commercials and reassured herself with the fact that she had been seeing him on television for quite some time. Still, she studied him, her mind a little less easy than before.

He glanced at her, and his eyes narrowed. "My eyes turn green?"

"Oh, no!" She shifted uncomfortably, realizing she had been staring at him.

"We'll drive straight through. It's a long, hard trip. We can take turns driving, so if you want to sleep, I'll wake you later."

"Okay." After a few minutes she asked, "Why don't you sell your stores and move to Arizona?"

"We talked about it, but it's not that simple. I've established a reputation and I'd be starting all over again."

"That's not so tough."

He gave a derisive snort. "How many times have you started over?"

"I don't keep count."

He looked at her briefly, and she could see his eyes in the reflection of light from the dash. Thunder rumbled and lightning flashed again. "This storm—just one more little complication," he said gruffly. She studied him until he flicked another glance her way. "What's on your mind?"

"I was thinking about your working six years, day in and day out."

He grinned. "You make me sound like Ebeneezer Scrooge. I have some fun."

"Do you go to a store every day?"

"Well, yes, but I take time off," he said defensively, his voice a deep rumble.

"To do what?" she asked, and he shifted in the seat. She was beginning to annoy him again.

"I enjoy myself."

"You're not giving me a direct answer, you know? How do you enjoy yourself?"

He debated telling her it was none of her business. Instead, he smiled and said, "Until this year, playing with Jamie, taking her places."

"You don't have any hobbies, do you?" she asked, but there was a note of wonder obvious in her voice.

"I never really stopped to think about it, but I guess I've been too busy to develop hobbies. What are your hobbies? I'll bet I can guess—weight lifting and mountain climbing."

She laughed, and it was an inviting musical sound that made him smile. "I like both of those. And dancing—"

"That's not a hobby for you. It's your profession. It doesn't count."

"I like swimming, skiing, jogging, playing Scrabble, reading, lots of things."

He shrugged. "To each his own."

"What do you like?" she asked. He shifted in the seat, staring at the road while he tried to think of an answer. "I like football and basketball. I like music. Just run-of-the-mill things."

"Will your little girl be at the lake house when we get there?"

He grinned, wondering if he could ruffle her feathers a little. "No. We'll be all alone until the end of the week. Only you and I all alone. Aren't you afraid to move in for a week with a stranger?"

Another inviting laugh came. "You're Mr. Sound-master. I feel as if I know you. You're too well known to be risky."

She sounded far too happy and confident. Suspicions arose. "If you're thinking we won't be alone because you're going to send for your sister, just forget it," he said abruptly and caught a surprised look on her face, making him realize that was exactly what she had intended. "I promised you could come. She can't!"

"She's having a real trauma and she's a quiet little thing. You'd never know she was around."

"No. You'd probably be safe with her. Why don't you go stay with her?"

"Because she's in a motel hiding from her ex-husband. She doesn't have a home now."

"I'm not giving her mine."

"Her husband loses his temper and strikes her. The first time—"

"Will you skip the gory details?"

"Will you please not fold up your long, mulish ears and just listen a moment?"

He grinned, shrugging his shoulders. "I'm not taking her in. It's my home, not a shelter."

"The first time he hit her he said it wouldn't happen again," Molly said swiftly, sure that once Jake heard Ivy's story, he would relent. "The second time he told her that, she told him she would leave him if he did it again. He did, and each time gets worse."

"What about your parents? Can't she go there?"

"No. Our stepmother doesn't like Ivy and our stepfather likes her too well."

"Oh, geez." He shifted, hunched his shoulders and glanced at her, his forehead furrowed. "You know how to ruin a person's day real quickly."

"She's desperate."

"I'll think about it," he snapped gruffly and Molly smiled at him as she reached over to pat his knee again. "Thank you. I knew you'd be reasonable."

He clamped his jaw shut and glared at the highway, but Molly felt as if he had already given her permission to ask Ivy.

"I'm not going to take her in," he said quietly, after a time.

"You think about it a little while," she said, serenely sure of the better nature she'd seen surface at times.

"I'd planned to spend Friday night in Chicago with a friend of mine and then Saturday night my in-laws will bring Jamie. And my brother will arrive Saturday, because he's taking a week's vacation. My in-laws are just spending the night and then going east on a trip they've planned. Anyway, I intend to relax."

"I'm glad to hear you have a friend in Chicago. You were beginning to sound a little like a robot, Mr. Soundmaster."

Suddenly he laughed. "Look, Soundmaster isn't really my name. That's just for commercials. I'm Jake Cannon."

Her eyes widened, and then she smiled. "I'm glad! Cannon is a nicer name than Soundmaster."

"Won't your mother worry about your going with a stranger?"

"My mother married two strangers," she said. When he gave her a startled glance, she shrugged. "Well, she knew them a little better than I know you, but not much better."

Out of the corner of his eye, he could tell she was openly studying him. "Now what's going through your mind?" he asked.

"I'm trying to imagine what kind of woman she is."

"Who is?"

"The friend in Chicago. I'll bet she's friendly; she's a blonde who likes to read. She's probably in advertising or sells stereos and you two can discuss business."

He chuckled, amused by her description as he thought of Regina. "You're wrong. Poor judge of people, Molly." He drew out her name; his voice was deep in the quiet of the car and he remembered when he had held her in his arms in the closet. "Molly," he said again in a huskier tone, glancing at her. Her big, green eyes were wide and her lips were parted, and for an instant he forgot every shred of irritation she had caused and wished he didn't have to keep his attention on the road and his hands on the wheel. Shaking his head as if to clear it of ridiculous notions, he returned his attention to the gray strip of paving ahead of him.

CHAPTER THREE

THEY RODE in a comfortable silence, rain coming down, a feeling of intimacy suffusing the narrow confines of the warm car. He lowered his voice to talk, speaking quietly. "We have a long drive. Go ahead and sleep if you want. I'll wake you when I get tired."

"Frankly, I'm famished. I'll pay you back every cent, but I have to eat."

"Don't tell me you're one of those women who has to stop every ten minutes."

"Only every few hours. I'm famished."

"We just got started," he said, deciding she was going to be a bigger nuisance than he had expected.

"We can get a bite along the turnpike and eat in the car."

"Okay." After a moment he asked, "Do you mind music?" He turned the dials of the radio.

"Goodness, no!" she answered, startled that he would ask after his disregard of her feelings earlier when they were on the rooftop and he had been willing to leave her behind. He moved the dial until he found a classical station and then he settled back to drive, smiling at her.

"You like opera?" she said, not bothering to hide her surprise this time.

"Yeah. You sound shocked."

"You don't look like the type."

"Mules and opera shouldn't mix, huh?" he asked cheerfully.

"You'll have to admit it's a strange combination."

"What kind of music would you have thought I'd like?"

She looked at him a moment; his firm jaw, the slightly crooked nose, his high, prominent cheekbones and slender face. He glanced her way and his attention settled on the road.

"I'd think you would like jazz. Duran Duran, Arcadia, in an earlier time the Beatles, that sort of thing."

"Just goes to show what a judge of character you are," he said blithely.

"Uh-huh. And what do you think I like?"

He looked at her, his gaze sweeping in swift appraisal that went from her head to her knees. "Jazz. Billy Joel, Duran Duran, Huey Lewis, Barbra Streisand."

"Wrong, wrong, wrong! Speaking of misjudging character... I like David Allan Coe, Lee Greenwood, and Merle Haggard."

He groaned. "I was on the verge of offering you equal time with the radio, but I withdraw my offer. Country!" he said with contempt. She smiled and laid her head back against the seat, closing her eyes.

After thirty minutes he said softly, "Molly, are you awake?"

"Sure," she answered and sat up.

"It's still over twenty miles to the next restaurant, and I'm getting so damned sleepy I can hardly keep my eyes open."

"Let me drive," she said. He whipped off the road and ran around the car to change places, then quickly settled down with his arms folded across his chest.

"You'll have to tell me where we're going."

He pulled open a map and unfolded it. Turning on the overhead light, he said, "We're on Highway 75, heading south. Just north of Dayton, Ohio, we'll turn west on Highway 70 until we get to St. Louis, Missouri. We're going to the Ozark Mountains in southern Missouri." She looked up at him; his face was inches away, his lashes dark above his cheek as he drew his finger along the highway marked on the map. His voice had changed when he had said, "Ozark Mountains," and she guessed it might be a special place where he and his wife used to go. She wondered if it would conjure up sad memories once he arrived. He looked up with a curious frown when he saw she was watching him.

"You haven't been there for six years, have you?"

"No, I haven't. The first Soundmaster store did a whale of a business that second year and I bought the house because Sheryl wanted it. We used to talk about moving south, to Kansas City, Missouri or Tulsa, Oklahoma, but then the stores got established and that was that."

He talked softly, his gaze traveling over her features in the dim light of the car. As they sat with their knees pressed together, both holding the map, their arms touching, she became intensely aware of him. While he talked, his words slowed a fraction and his tone dropped. "You just stay on this highway for the next few hours and you'll be all right."

When she bent her head over the map to look at it, he reached down to pick up her left hand, and turned the sparkling diamond with his thumb. "That's some ring. You're giving it back?"

"Yes." She kept her gaze on his fingers holding hers. She was acutely aware of him, and remembered their kisses earlier. He kept turning the ring.

"You're not compatible?"

She looked into his eyes. "We're compatible, but I'm not ready to settle down. I'm too young."

She saw the flicker of surprise and a faint smile. "You're in your early twenties?"

"I'm twenty-nine," she said easily.

"Ah, come on—you're twenty—" he tilted his head to one side to study her "—twenty-four."

She laughed and shook her head. "Really, twenty-nine."

"Twenty-nine isn't too young to get married."

"It is for me. I want to be sure," she said, noticing that he went eons without blinking. He was looking at her in a steadfast manner that was disconcerting because it was so intent it became sensual. His gaze lowered to her mouth, and the sensuality tripled. She could all but feel his lips on hers.

"How long have you known him?"

"Almost two years. We've been very good friends," she answered perfunctorily, her attention caught like glue—held by a compelling look and a husky voice.

"That's a fair amount of time."

"I come from a long line of disastrous marriages and mixed-up lives and I don't want that to happen to me," she said, but it was getting more difficult by the second to talk. The car was steamed up; the dome light was shedding a tiny glow; the heater was warming them; and she was squeezed close to him. His focus alternated between looking into her eyes and watching her mouth as if he were debating whether to kiss her and his expression made her blood flow with heated lethargy. It made her words thicken into a slight drawl, and it made her want to be kissed.

"I suppose the kiss in the closet was in the interest of self-protection," he said softly, leaning a little closer. She noticed his skin was smooth except on his jaw, where tiny, dark bristles were beginning to show.

"Definitely," she whispered, wanting to kiss him.

He tilted her chin up, his eyes took on a sleepy quality, and his voice was the stroke of velvet on her nerves. "This one won't be in the interest of self-protection."

She didn't want to get involved physically with Jake Cannon because it might complicate the next week terribly, but she closed her eyes in anticipation, curious if his kiss would seem as good as before. Maybe the last time her nerves and the situation had caused her reaction. This time...

His mouth opened hers, his tongue made desire ignite, and this time was better than last time. She heard the rustle of the map, felt him crush her to him and pull her onto his lap. He shifted her around while he kissed her long and hard until she wasn't aware of putting her arms around him or clinging to him. Finally, she pushed away to look at him. "I won't ever be able to view your commercials with the same detachment again."

He smiled and ran his finger along her cheek to her ear. "That's okay with me."

She felt stunned because his kisses were even more exciting than before. She was caught in a strong current of physical attraction and she fought it. Jake Cannon wasn't her type of man and she didn't want to be attracted to him even briefly. He was busy with his life; he was different from the men she liked and dated. She sat up and scooted away, frowning as she moved.

"What's wrong?"

"That was a very casual kiss, I want you to understand."

In spite of keeping a solemn expression, he looked as if he were biting back a laugh. "Why do I have to view it as casual? I would have called it—" he paused and his voice lowered, "—a *great* kiss." The words seemed like the caress of invisible fingers making her tingle in response. "Why does it have to be casual?" he persisted.

"Would you want to be attracted to me?" she asked, trying to ignore her fluttering pulse.

He chuckled and arched his brows. "You ask as if you had the bubonic plague. Big green eyes, sweet-smelling red hair—"

"We are not the same type," she said with all the firmness she could muster, leaning forward to punch his chest with her forefinger. "Do you want to complicate the week? Only a short time ago you were doing everything you could to get rid of me."

"That was before the last kiss."

"Now just answer honestly, do you want to be attracted to me? Do you want to complicate this week?"

He smiled at her and sat quietly as if in deep thought. "To be honest, you're right. Absolutely. But—"

"No. As I said, we're not the same type. I date men who like to do exciting things. You have no hobbies."

"I'm not like Garvin."

"Right. You're a workaholic. That's no way to enjoy life."

"If Garvin's your type, why aren't you marrying him?"

"Are you trying to get smart with me?"

"You're right. We're definitely not the same type," he said with such cheer it grated on her nerves. "What type do you like—wait! Let me guess."

A truck whipped past, causing the car to rock slightly as the air vibrated. "We better go," she said, pulling the map back onto her lap and smoothing it out. "I take this highway and then what do I do?"

He grinned. "I'll tell you then. I'm not telling you our exact destination until we get there. I don't want a weepy sister on my hands."

"You go from being a very nice guy to being sort of—mulish!"

He chuckled. "So be it. I want my peace, because I've earned it." As she pulled onto the highway, he settled back and said, "As I was saying, let me guess your type. Garvin's blond isn't he?"

"Yes. A good guess, but that doesn't prove anything."

"He lifts weights, he runs, he water-skis and he thinks twangy western music is the greatest."

"You're right," she said, feeling a flicker of irritation that he could accurately surmise what Garvin was like.

"He's also artistic, probably plays some instrument, played football in school sometime in his past and loves dogs."

"How did you guess?" she asked. Though trying to keep her attention on the road, she was startled at the precision of his description. She glanced at him briefly to find him watching her with amusement.

"I'm getting to know you well."

It doubly annoyed her that he could figure out what Garvin was like while she had been wrong about the woman in Chicago. She drove in silence for a time and then said, "Tell me about your friend in Chicago. Since I misjudged terribly—what's she like? A jogger and cook in a restaurant, maybe?"

He laughed. "Nope. She's a high school librarian."

"And what does she like?" When he was silent, she glanced at him questioningly.

"I don't know." He shrugged. "She's busy like I am."

"Well, where do you go when you're together?"

"Out to eat and then—" he stopped abruptly.

"And then?" she persisted, her curiosity growing.

"It's personal," he snapped so quickly, she suspected it wasn't personal at all. She imagined it was something he didn't want to admit.

"You surely share something else in common besides food and sex."

He coughed and said, "It's none of your business, and I don't care what you and Garvin what's-his-name do! You're right. You and I aren't compatible," he said coolly.

"You do something with her that you don't want to admit. Hmm."

"Stop imagining things!"

"I can't help it. A grown man and you won't talk about—"

"After we eat we both have things to do. I usually have some bookkeeping, and she has paperwork for the library. Now, does that satisfy your curiosity?"

She tried to refrain from smiling and attempted to keep her voice pleasant. "On a date—and the dates must be special occasions because you live far apart— you do *bookkeeping* and *paperwork*. We're definitely not the same type!"

"To each his own. Pumping iron isn't exactly the most exhilarating way to spend a date either! Or listening to twangy music. And as for my being a workaholic—some women call it being dependable!"

She laughed, her feelings slightly mollified. Bookkeeping! On a date Jake Cannon must be as dull as used sandpaper, she told herself. But another inner voice argued that his kisses weren't. "A workaholic," she insisted, "bookish—bookkeeping on dates—we're different as a butterfly and a stuffed bear. I like to do things."

"You are a nomadic gypsy who shuns responsibility."

"That's not so! I'm going to help my sister."

"You're scared of commitment; you've known this guy two years and almost are headed to the altar when you get cold feet. You're a thistle in the wind; you close your business when the whim strikes you; you go off with a stranger. Pull this car over a minute."

"What?" She glanced at him, worried that he might be angry enough to put her out on the road.

"Pull over."

She signaled, slowed and pulled off the empty highway. He reached across the seat to turn off the ignition, and moved closer to her, propping his elbow on the back of her seat and leaning his head on his hand. Her heart thumped; she didn't know if it was from his proximity or the uncertainty of what he intended to do.

"No one has ever called me a mule and a stuffed bear!"

"Is that why we stopped? Don't tell me I've hurt your feelings!"

"Don't flatter yourself!" he said, but there was laughter in his voice. "I'm going to see if you still think mule and stuffed bear after we kiss. You didn't mention either one after our last kisses.''

"We're not going to get to Missouri at this rate," she said, but her words were slurred and her mind was elsewhere. Her heart now thudded for a definite reason.

His arm circled her waist and he leaned down to kiss her, to kiss her passionately, deeply and long. Forever. Her thoughts ceased to function and she wrapped her arms around his neck. Finally, he paused and whispered, "I'm a stuffed bear and a mule?"

"Absolutely," she said dreamily. "You called me a gypsy and a thistle."

"A thorn in the flesh is more like it!" he murmured and kissed her again, pausing to add, "A cocklebur underfoot!"

He kissed her throat and she tilted her head to kiss his temple. "I think I should be angry," she whispered.

"Instead—?"

Rain drummed on the car as his lips sought and found hers again. It was another five minutes before she pushed against his chest. "If your ego is satisfied, we better drive on," she said lightly.

His eyes opened slowly and focused on hers. He answered gruffly, "Yeah, sure."

Her heart slammed against her ribs over the hungry need she saw in his expression. In one of his mercurial changes, he had gone from fun kisses and teasing banter to something earnest that tugged on her heart and senses. Shaken, she moved away and started the motor. They rode in silence, the bantering gone as emotions churned. His kisses did stir her more than anyone else's; he was so different, yet she was as drawn to him as a tulip to sunlight. She stared straight ahead, wondering what was going through his mind while the wipers clicked steadily, splashing drops off the windshield. "If you fall asleep, where did you say I turn?"

"Highway 70 to St. Louis, 40 to Springfield, Missouri," he answered, and his voice still sounded sober. She glanced at him and drew a sharp breath. He had turned to face her, and sat with one leg crossed, ankle on knee while he answered solemnly. "Outside of Springfield we'll take a state road, then we turn off on a dirt road."

"You're sure you know how to get there? Six years is a long time."

"I know." He tapped his head as if indicating the knowledge was there. "I got my manager to read directions to me when we stopped to phone before we left Detroit."

"I hope the rain stops by the time we reach Missouri."

"It can't be raining all across the country," he said, turning to settle lower in the seat.

"You should have bought a lake house closer to Detroit."

"Yeah, I know, but at the time who could foresee the future?" His voice took on a wistful quality that made her glance at him. Lost in memories, he seemed to have forgotten her presence. "All this year I've dreamed of the lake house. It's big and comfortable with a wide rock fireplace in the front room and in the kitchen. It has a screened-in porch and you can sit out there at night and listen to frogs and crickets and look at the moonlight on the lake. Trees are all around, but you can see the lake through the trees. The kitchen has modern conveniences, a dishwasher and a freezer. Upstairs is a big, soft bed—''

He broke off abruptly. His tone changed, becoming flat and brisk. She suspected he was trying to hide pain. ''It's only a short distance out the back door to the lake and a sandy beach. We have a canoe and a flat-bottomed boat with an outboard motor.''

''It sounds lovely,'' she said, deciding he had the most expressive voice. Emotions played in his words like music from a piano. ''Why did you stay away so long?''

''It's too damned far.'' His voice changed again, the cold, impassive tone returning. ''I'm going to put it up for sale while I'm there.''

''That seems a shame.''

''I never get down there, and now with Jamie's asthma problems, life is more complicated than ever. She has a lot of medical expenses but thank heavens, the stores enable me to take care of her properly.''

After a few minutes of silence Molly asked him, ''Why'd you wait so long to go back to Missouri? Because of the distance?''

''No. Of course, distance makes it necessary to plan, but mostly I haven't gone back because I couldn't leave the stores. Sheryl and I talked about it a lot, but there never was a good time. I opened a new store each year. Then two years ago Sheryl got sick and time was gone. I haven't wanted to go back until now. I feel as if I have to get away for a few days or some mainspring will pop.''

While he talked, she set the cruise control and relaxed, listening to him.

''It's a grand place,'' he said, his voice slowing. ''For months I've been planning on this. To have Jamie with me again, to just row around the lake, to walk in the woods. Spring comes earlier there than in Detroit, and now it'll be almost hot weather. Summertime. The trees will be green; hopefully, the water warm enough to swim. You'll like it there.''

He sounded so wistful, she couldn't keep from asking, ''Are you sure you want to sell it?''

''Yep. It's an expense and it isn't practical. I let Sheryl talk me into it. Silly thing to do.'' He became quiet and in minutes he was asleep. In half an hour he slumped over and his head came down on her shoulder. In another half hour he sank down farther, shifting, folding his long legs so that his head could rest on her thigh. Through drops of rain, headlights caught the glint of the sign announcing a restaurant. Then the restaurant's lights loomed in sight. With a sigh of resignation, Molly glanced down at the man asleep in her lap, his arm draped negligently across her legs. She hadn't ever known a man quite like him. Stubborn, fun, and breathtakingly appealing at the same time. She passed the restaurant and tried to ignore the pangs of hunger that assailed her.

On the radio, a deep male voice sang; an opera continued playing as she drove south. She listened, bored with the music and foreign words until a male voice came from the radio that sent a tingle across her shoulders. For the next half hour she had to concede that the music was marvelous and she began to listen until the sounds changed and once again she lost interest. She began switching stations to find music she liked and listened until the station went off the air for the night.

She was curious about exactly where Jake and she were headed and when she could call Ivy and tell her where to go. She had no doubt Jake would relent, because underneath his stubbornness was a warm heart. He wasn't as thorough a grouch as he had seemed on the rooftop either. She smiled, feeling a swift rush of excitement as she remembered his kisses, the husky words said in her ear, the silly names they had called each other. Her smile broadened as she thought of his words for her; thistle, thorn and cocklebur. Yet Mr. Cannon didn't mind kissing the thorn, thistle and cocklebur! She signaled and pulled off the road, letting the engine idle as she watched to see if he continued to sleep.

She slipped her hand cautiously beneath Jake's coat and into his breast pocket. Her fingers touched a pen, behind it a folded paper, and she withdrew both carefully, then opened the paper to read in the light of the dash. She flipped up her skirt to write on her white half slip, copying the map that showed how to get to his house in the Ozark mountains.

Her attention shifted from the map to Jake. Lashes lay feathered above his cheekbones; the cut was a dark line on his cheek, and stray locks of wavy, black hair curled over his forehead. His breathing was steady and deep. She fought the urge to reach down and brush a lock back in place. And she fought another urge to bend down and brush his cheek with a kiss. Puzzled about why they had such an intense reaction to each other, she used both hands to carefully return the folded instructions to his pocket.

Hours later, she had to shake him. He came up, rubbing sleep from his eyes.

"I'm getting tired," she said.

He blinked and stretched. "Sure. I'll drive. Holy smoke!" He leaned forward to look at his watch in the light of the dash. "It's almost four in the morning! You should've called me."

"I didn't mind until now."

"You haven't eaten either."

"I don't care any longer." She signaled and pulled off the road to change places with him. He ran around the car in the rain, then slammed the door, and started up. In half an hour he turned the car into the lighted parking lot of an all-night restaurant. After ordering a hamburger, Molly excused herself, telling Jake she had to go to the ladies' room. She went first to the ladies' room, then to a pay phone, where she dropped in a quarter Jake had given her and placed a collect call to Ivy. She heard her sister's sleepy voice. "Yeah?"

"Ivy, listen, it's me. I only have a few seconds to talk."

"Is it after four in the morning?"

"Yes. Look, I saw a map. Do you have a pencil? I can tell you how to get to Jake's Ozark house."

"Did the guy say I could come?"

"No, but he will. He's nice underneath a gruff exterior."

"Huh! I don't ever want to meet another gruff male exterior. I hate staying alone in this motel. I'm scared Willis will find me." She began to cry and Molly squared her shoulders.

"I'm sorry. Are you all right?"

"Yes." While Ivy cried, Molly leaned out of the phone booth to look for Jake. "Look, I'm sorry, but I have to get off the phone," Molly said. "Get a pencil."

"Yeah, sure. Just a minute." In seconds, Ivy was back. "How can I get there, Molly?"

"Can you buy a ticket to Springfield, Missouri?"

"Gladly."

"Okay, rent a car there and it's about a two hour drive to his cabin. Here are the directions."

Molly pulled up her skirt, and turned the hem of the slip to read the directions. A shadow fell on the booth, and she looked up to see Jake's nose pressed against the glass as he peered down at her slip. She dropped her skirt at the same time he yanked open the door.

"I have to go, Ivy. Bye!" Molly said and hung up, trying to wriggle her hips and get her skirt smoothed down.

"What the hell was that?" he snapped.

"Nothing. I called—"

"Nothing, my eye!" His arm slipped around her waist, tightened, and his hand locked firmly, holding her still while he flipped back her skirt to look at the hem of her slip.

"Lady, are you all right?" a man asked, approaching them.

Jake straightened up and turned around.

"The lady's fine," he said.

Molly smoothed her skirt, and emerged from the booth, brushing past Jake and smiling at the stranger. "I'm just fine," she said with composure. "My friend is interested in lace. He has a lace fetish." She went ahead into the restaurant, turning to look over her shoulder at Jake and bracing for his anger.

He still stood by the phone booth, fists doubled on his hips, but he was laughing, shaking his head, and watching her. His smile was infectious and she smiled in return, waiting as he joined her.

"I ought to wring your pretty little neck."

"But you won't," she said sweetly, "because in spite of your mulish tendencies, you're really a nice guy."

"Sweet talk from a little serpent in the grass. When did you copy my map? While I slept?"

She slid into the booth across from him and smiled. "You don't really object to Ivy, do you?"

"I object like hell! Fat lot of good it will do me traveling with Miss Molly Sneak!"

"We'll discuss it after you've eaten," she said.

"You know, you could've gotten me into a fine mess of trouble, telling that guy I have a lace fetish!" he said, but the bite in his words was vanquished by his grin.

"You could've handled it. You handle all trouble that comes your way ever so smoothly."

"All except a bit of trouble with red hair!"

"You're doing all right there, too." She smiled at him as the waitress interrupted their conversation.

Once again in the car, Molly sank back against the passenger side, feeling drowsy and comfortable as Jake slowly pulled out of the lot. Her gaze swept the cars parked at the curb by the restaurant, glancing at license tags from various states until she saw one smudged with something dark, making it unreadable. A big, green four-door car with a spattered license tag was parked in a row with other cars. Molly stiffened and sat up to grip Jake's arm.

"Jake, look," she said in a whisper, feeling cold fingers of fear tickle her nerves.

CHAPTER FOUR

"SEE THAT CAR. I think it's the same green car I saw go past twice while I was in the phone booth in Detroit."

He swore and put on the brakes, staring at it. "You're sure?"

"No, but it's big and green and the license is unreadable."

"Damn." He stepped on the gas and they whipped out of the lot. "We can't lose them here, but maybe we can down the road."

"If they don't stop us first," she said, all drowsiness fleeing. "Why would we be that important? There are other witnesses."

"I don't know, but if it's a big enough organization, they may be trying to get to everyone who saw what happened in front of the Brantz Building."

They drove in silence and to Molly's relief, no lights appeared behind them.

"You don't know for sure. If someone's after us, I'll lose them later," Jake said. "We'll just have to be more careful."

His words frightened her. "I thought when we left Detroit, we'd be safe."

"Yeah, I did too. We'll lose them. As long as they don't follow us to the lake, they'll never find us. We'll be way back in dense woods."

"At the moment that doesn't sound reassuring."

"Molly, no one heard you when you were in the phone booth giving directions to Ivy, did they?"

"You'd know better than I do—you were the one on the outside."

"Yeah. I didn't see anyone except a guy at the post card rack. Damned if I know why they'd follow us from Detroit!"

Something had been nagging at her all afternoon and she finally mentioned it. "Jake, I saw several of them close at hand. I can describe them down to scars and eyelashes."

"Oh, geez. I remember one, but I was too busy defending myself and you to notice their appearance. But if they're following us to tidy up all loose ends—this is a big deal. Definitely pros."

After a few minutes he reached across the seat to squeeze her hand. "Go to sleep. I'll be careful." Gradually the warmth and vibration of the car lulled Molly to sleep. She felt his hand moving her and then she curled up on the seat, her head slipping down to Jake's shoulder as she slept.

She took another turn driving, another turn sleeping, and as the hours passed, her muscles cramped from riding in the car so long. She stirred and came awake again just north of Springfield during the late afternoon. She sat up sleepily, noticing with relief that the rain had stopped. But puddles still dotted the highway and glinted with a silvery sheen on some low meadows. However, the skies were bright blue now and the sun was warm. With eagerness she took in the green landscape. Green leaves shone on tall oaks, and banks on both sides of the wide highway and the grassy median seemed verdant expanses; wildflowers bloomed in a rainbow of colors on the roadside. Molly gazed in delight at her surroundings. "Isn't this pretty! Breathe that fresh air!"

"Yep, and if we're lucky, we'll have some hot days. It'll be great!"

Her spirits lifted momentarily, and then she remembered the threat of danger from the night before. "Have you seen the green car?"

"No, but I'm watching. We'll drive around in Springfield as a precaution."

When they got off the highway in Springfield, Jake drove through town for over half an hour to try to make sure they weren't being followed. He stopped and disappeared inside a department store in Battlefield Mall and Molly stepped out into the sunshine with relief. She worked at knee bends and leg lifts to loosen her muscles until a voice halted her.

"What the hell are you doing?"

She turned around to see Jake standing watching her. She smiled at him. "Exercises. My muscles feel creaky."

"You'll draw attention to us."

Startled, she glanced around, but she didn't see anyone watching them. Her inspection gave Molly brief illusion of safety. She stood up, smoothing her red skirt.

"Look, I have my money and credit cards. You can't spend a week in the woods dressed like that." While he talked, he walked around to put packages in the trunk of the car.

"Here's a credit card. Keep track of your expenses, but go get yourself some clothes."

"Thank you." She smiled at him. "There are moments when you're a very nice, considerate person."

He grinned. "Yeah. Come on and get some jeans. I bought a pistol."

Molly hated guns. She asked, "Do you know how to use it?"

"Of course."

"Well, I don't. I don't like guns."

"No, I know. You take on criminals with your purse. You better get a new purse along with jeans and shorts and sneakers. Get a swim suit. We'll go to a supermarket next and you can get a toothbrush and that sort of thing."

He looked beyond her, his gaze traveling over the parking lot.

"Do you see the green car?" she asked, studying a row of cars.

"No, but be careful, and let's get out of here as soon as we can. I'm going to turn the Lincoln in and rent another car or Jeep."

She fought the urge to turn and look around again. "If they changed cars, they could be right beside us and we wouldn't know."

"That's right," he said grimly, holding open a glass door to the one-storey mall. Sunshine poured through the skylight shining on the green leaves of trees in a planted area. Benches and greenery decorated the length of the long hallway; lights were bright from shops around them. Jake patted her arm. "Be careful. I'll meet you here in—how long? Try and make it short."

"Twenty minutes."

"You can't get a purse, jeans, some shorts and shoes in twenty minutes!"

"Thirty minutes at the most. I move quickly."

"Oh, yeah," he said in a resigned tone. "Make it forty minutes. I don't like to sit and wait."

She rushed to the nearest large department store, trying to watch the crowd, aware there could be danger right beside her. Along with lingerie, a cotton nightie and robe, she bought jeans, a sweater, shorts, several T-shirts, a sweatshirt and sweat pants, and carried them all to a cash register without trying them on. She did try on a swimsuit, taking more time and care with it. Though she didn't want to examine her motives too closely, she recognized that she had in mind what Jake's reaction might be to the suit. Then she tried on sneakers quickly and purchased a pair along with an inexpensive purse. Next, she went to sporting goods and bought an inexpensive barbell and a jump rope. She hurried to meet Jake and was glad to see that she had reached the designated spot first.

While she dropped her packages onto a bench, she scanned the crowd and noticed a pair of intent, dark eyes as a man hurried toward her. It wasn't a casual glance; he stared at her without wavering, and she backed up a step, feeling her heartbeat jump.

"By golly, you are a fast shopper!" Jake said cheerfully from behind her.

She reached back and gripped his arm, watching as the man instantly veered into a shop.

"That man! I know he was going to do something until you appeared."

"What man?"

"He went into the shop. See the black-haired one in the yellow shirt!"

"I don't see him, but we're getting out of here. You head out. Let me see what's going on. If I need help, there are security guards in the mall."

Jake started toward the shop and the man in the yellow shirt ducked out the door and disappeared around a corner into another part of the mall.

Molly rushed outside while she watched for the man. Jake caught up, his arms loaded with packages. "Let's go!"

Urging was unnecessary; she almost ran. As soon as Jake opened the car door, she dumped her packages onto the back seat, and climbed in front quickly. As Jake pulled out of the lot, she twisted around to see if they were being followed.

"Before we leave Springfield, we're going to spend a few hours making sure we've lost whoever is after us, but first we have to get some groceries and supplies. Are you sure you might not have imagined the guy was going to approach you?"

"I can't say for sure, but I felt he was. He didn't seem like a casual shopper."

"Yeah. He beat it out of there when I started after him. Of course, he could have been your garden variety thief who saw you as a possible mark."

"Maybe. Should we go to the police?"

"I've come this far. I want my vacation," he said, the stubborn note creeping back into his voice. "Look, I'll be glad to take you to the police. Just don't tell them about me."

"Oh, no." She sat down and smiled at him. "I want to be able to talk to Garvin and Ivy."

"It's time for the calls. You'll have to phone while we're here. There won't be a phone available after we leave Springfield except at a general store in a tiny town, and if you phone there, half the population will listen to your conversation." Slowing, he turned the car into a lot and parked in front of a grocery.

"I'll need to get two quarters from you."

"Don't call the guy collect to break an engagement! Whoo! You have a heart of stone," he said as he fished change out of his pocket.

She frowned, wanting to snap at him that she had already broken the news to Garvin and she intended to fly to Houston as soon as possible. Instead, she lifted her chin and merely asked, "You want to pay for the call to Garvin?"

"You can pay me back. Write down your expenses and what you owe me, but don't call him collect!"

"Jake, Ivy needs to get far away from Willis," she said, knowing this was her last chance to plead Ivy's case. "I told you she's filed for divorce and she's hiding in a motel in Dallas. She's quit her job because she's scared to go to work for fear Willis will be there. He's abusive and has threatened her. He took her car and locked it up, and she's out of work now. She has nowhere to turn and she's afraid if she stays there, he'll find her." She talked fast, disliking the look of resignation that came over Jake's face, because she didn't want to spoil his vacation. But Ivy was in danger from Willis. "I'm sorry to interfere in your vacation, but can she come?"

He hit the steering wheel lightly with the palm of his hand. "Oh, geez. I need a vacation and peace and quiet."

She waited in silence, praying he would say yes and hating to have to ask him.

Finally, he sighed and nodded. "Okay, but can we make it a day or two from now?"

"Oh, thank you!" she said and reached across the seat to hug his neck. She moved back quickly, surprised at the flush that darkened his cheeks and the curious smile that curved his mouth. "You're staring," she said, suddenly embarrassed.

"I'm not accustomed to your enthusiasm. You throw yourself into whatever involves you at the moment, don't you?"

"Maybe so," she said, wondering if, in his eyes, that was a plus or a minus. "Ivy will wait a few days to leave Dallas because of legal matters. I wasn't going to see her until the weekend anyway. "Thank you, Jake."

"Yeah, sure," he said with another sigh. "I better get the groceries. There's a pay phone. Go make your calls while I watch for trouble. Then we'll both shop."

"Okay."

"Oh, here's the map. You pull up your skirt out here and traffic will come to a standstill."

With a smile, she took the paper from him. He caught her hand in his. "Wouldn't you like one of these fifties? You can pay me back."

"No thanks, the quarters are fine."

"Doesn't it bother you to go around without money?"

"No," she answered with surprise. "Why should it?"

He shrugged, his eyes focusing beyond her. "I'd hate it. I went too long without money in my pocket," he declared in a hard, flat voice. "I don't ever want to be that way again." His gaze shifted to her as if he'd suddenly remembered her presence. He smiled. "Be careful."

As he walked to the newspaper vending machines, she stared after him, wondering what kind of childhood he'd had to make his voice sound so bitter. Deciding Jake Cannon was more complicated than most people she had known, she strode to the phone.

Standing in warm sunshine, she dialed Ivy's number, and watched cars pass on the street while she waited for the operator to put through the call.

"Ivy? This is Molly. Can you talk?"

"Yeah. What was that weird call from you at four this morning?"

"I had to go all of a sudden. Now I'm in Springfield."

"Molly, you think you ought to go off to the woods with a stranger?"

"Ivy, he's not a stranger. He's been in my living room every week for the past year—on television."

"You're not making much sense. I think the excitement of the kidnapping unhinged your mind."

"Listen to me, I don't have many quarters to pay for the call; I have to make this short. Here's the rest of the directions. Can you come this weekend?"

"Yeah, of course I'll come. I've already called about plane reservations. I'll fly to Springfield like you suggested. I should get to the cabin by noon Saturday."

Molly detected a funny sigh. "Don't cry. Get a pencil and we'll finish the directions." Shortly, she hung up and phoned Garvin.

"Molly, I want to drive up and talk to you," he said, giving no indication of his feelings. He was remarkably different from Jake, who could express his emotions far more easily.

"I know we need to talk, but I'll be way back in the woods and this guy who owns the home is very touchy about having his vacation interrupted."

"I'm touchy about having my engagement broken. Can I drive up there tomorrow? I'll be off work then and I can leave tonight. Even if we just have a couple of hours, I need to see you. I'll pick you up and we'll go off by ourselves. I won't disturb that Soundmaster guy—is he married?''

''No, he's widowed and his little girl and in-laws and his brother are coming.''

''Okay. Can I pick you up about noon?''

''I suppose so, Garvin, but my mind is made up.''

''I still want to talk to you—and not on the phone! I want to drive up there and see you.''

''All right, but be careful. Someone followed us to Springfield.''

''Why don't you go to the police?''

''I told you before—you're part of the reason. I wanted to talk to you and I need to help Ivy get out of Dallas as soon as possible so Willis won't have a chance to find her.''

''Can you give me directions to the cabin?''

She did and told Garvin goodbye. She stepped out of the booth to find Jake waiting, newspapers under his arm. ''Did you see anything suspicious?''

He shook his head slightly. ''I haven't noticed anyone watching us.''

Again, she wanted to turn and look, but she knew it seemed too obvious. Still, her back prickled and she felt exposed.

''Get your calls made?''

''Yes. Garvin's coming up to see me tomorrow. We won't bother you,'' she said hastily when she saw Jake's brow crease in a frown. ''He'll pick me up and we'll go off by ourselves to talk.''

''Okay, but the more people trailing in and out, the more chances of someone finding where we are.''

''I told Garvin to be careful.''

''Okay,'' he snapped. ''Let's go.'' While Jake shopped for food, she added makeup, a toothbrush, a hairbrush and an inexpensive powder and cologne to the cart. The day was growing uncomfortably warm so they stopped at a gas station, where each changed clothing in the rest rooms. She emerged in red shorts and a red T-shirt to find Jake leaning against the Lincoln watching cars pass in the street.

"See anything?" she asked.

He turned and focused on her. His eyes drifted down in a slow appraisal that made her blood heat. And she couldn't resist returning the assessment. He wore a blue T-shirt and new jeans above tennis shoes. Again she realized not only that he was an appealing man, but that there was a strong current of attraction between them.

"Yeah, do I see something!" he said, exhaling deeply. "Very nice!"

"Thank you," she said solemnly, beginning to feel on fire from his intent study. She had to pass him to get into her side of the car but he blocked her way, his gaze lingering on her tight-fitting red shorts. "I should have stayed long enough to try on the shorts," she said. "They're a little snug."

"No. They're perfect," he said without taking his eyes off them.

"Are you ready to go?"

He looked up as if his mind were ninety miles away. "Sure," he said, but he didn't move.

She realized then that he knew what he was doing. "Will you move?"

"I'm bothering you?" he asked in mock surprise.

"You're in my way."

He grinned and stepped aside, standing with his feet planted apart, and his arms folded over his chest while he waited and watched her. She felt as if the few yards to the door of the car had just become a parade ground and she was the parade. "You're staring!"

"I can't help it. This is a rare view," he said seriously.

"We've discussed the physical attraction that sometimes develops between us. Vibes or something. We're going to ignore it, not feed it and fan the fire," she announced firmly. Was she trying to convince Jake or herself?

"Is that right?" He grinned and opened the door for her, then leaned one hip against it, and hooked his hand on top. When she stepped closer to get into the car, he was only inches away. "I didn't know I was going to *fan the fire* by merely looking." He drawled the words in a husky tone, and her pulse jumped.

"You know what you're doing!" she tried to snap, but her snap fizzled into a breathless whisper.

His smile faded, and he looked into her eyes. What she saw in the depths of his made her heart thud. "Jake, you agreed!"

"Yeah. It was something about we're not the same type and all that malarkey. If we weren't in a public spot with people milling all around, I'd show you how little 'type of person' matters...." His voice trailed to nothing, but his eyes finished what he had intended to say as he studied her mouth.

The warm, sunny day became an inferno and Molly couldn't break the invisible, mesmerizing hold that he caused so effortlessly. Seconds ticked past and she moved, slipping into the car quickly. Too quickly. She hit her knee on the car door and scraped it. "Ouch!" She rubbed a raw spot where the skin had broken.

"Want me to kiss it and make it well?" he asked suggestively.

"Are you kidding?" When she glanced up she saw a twinkle in his eyes, and she smiled as he closed the door.

He climbed in and rested his fingers lightly on her knee below the scratch. "Are you all right?"

"Sure," she said, more aware of his fingers than her injury. Warm and firm, his hand rested on her bare leg, doing nothing more than touching her, not budging the slightest fraction, yet his touch made her nerves come to full attention, waiting...

"For someone who can walk on a narrow beam high above the ground without a ripple of difficulty, I'd think you could get into a car with ease," he said, not taking his hand off her knee.

"Are you starting something again?"

"Who me?" he asked innocently. "I was just making an observation. I'm surprised that such an ordinary thing as climbing into the car would be difficult for someone—"

"You're not cooperating! You looked at me as if I were a steak and you hadn't eaten in the last two years. Then you made suggestive comments and got me so flustered I ran into the door—"

"I didn't realize I was doing all that!"

"I'll add lying to your faults," she said in haughty tones, but the grin on his face was irresistible, and she had to laugh. "And you need to move your hand, and don't ask why!"

"All right, I'll stop flirting, but it's fun."

"And dangerous. You know what flirting can lead to," she said, feeling a giddying current of excitement resurge.

"I've got to hear this. What does flirting lead to?"

"You're doing it again!"

"It's something you and your red shorts bring out in me," he said, leaning closer and sliding his arm across the back of the seat.

"Jake, let's get out of Springfield."

He watched her for a moment that seemed suspended in time. Then he shrugged, and moved to start the car. Refusing to acknowledge the disappointment that tugged at her, Molly leaned back against the seat. For the next two hours they drove around Springfield. Finally, he rented a Jeep and left the Lincoln at a Hertz Rent-A-Car agency.

"It seems to me this Jeep will draw more attention than a plain, ordinary car," she said while they raced along a divided four-lane highway.

"We'll need it for the rough roads." He signaled, and exited on a state road. At the first farm he turned onto a dirt drive. After a few yards, he left the road, and they bumped across rocky open land to park on a bluff overlooking the highway. He cut the motor and pulled out the map she had looked at the night before while he had been asleep.

"From here, we can see if anyone turns off the highway. And while we wait, let's look through the newspapers. I bought a *Chicago Sun-Times*, a *St. Louis Post Dispatch*, and the Springfield and Kansas City papers." He handed her a paper while he unfolded another one. They rattled them in the silence, and all became still.

She scanned the words quickly. She found something first and read a brief article swiftly. "Nothing new here. Brantz is still being held. That's all. No leads in the case."

His head was bent over the print when she turned to watch him. "Same here," he said.

They read the other two papers and found even smaller mention. "I think something is going on in the case that they don't want known." He folded up the pages and tossed them into the back. "Who knows? Maybe we're too far from the scene of the crime to get news about it."

"You don't really think that, do you?"

"No, I don't. Karl Brantz is news in any locale in the U.S." He drummed his fingers on the steering wheel. "Molly, don't go off alone for the first day or two ."

"I don't know why anyone would chase us."

"I don't see the sense in it either, and that bothers me."

She sat quietly, listening to an occasional bird call; the rumble of the distant traffic was muted. She breathed deeply. "This is nice! So quiet and peaceful, you wouldn't dream anything was wrong with the world."

She was startled when she glanced at him to find him watching her. "You're not wearing the diamond ring," he said quietly.

"No. I would have taken if off sooner, but I was afraid I might lose it. And if I left it at home, it might have been stolen while I was at work. Now, it's in my purse."

"You're sure of what you're doing? You're certain you don't want to marry him?"

"Yes. More than ever, I know Garvin's not the man for me. We've very good friends—and not much more."

"Even if you have all those things in common?" He touched a wisp of hair that curled against her throat and his fingers felt like feathers that teased raw nerves.

"I'm sure," she said, concluding that his long thick lashes gave him bedroom eyes, and knowing that she was more certain than ever about the break with Garvin because another man's kisses shouldn't have stirred her beyond anything she had ever known if her heart truly belonged to Garvin.

"I'll show you where we're going." Jake spread the map on her knees and leaned close, one arm across the seat behind her, the other tracing the route with his finger while he leaned over the gear shift.

His voice softened with reminiscence. "Here's the last tiny town—a general store and maybe half a dozen houses. Hattersville." Only the map stood between her bare knees and his fingers as he continued his tracing. Tingles radiated from his touch, and she knew she was having a dangerous reaction to Jake Cannon. "People will sit on the porch and wave when you go past. Ozark folk are friendly. Here's where you ford a little creek, then another one's a bit farther. We wind up this mountain, then come down into a valley where the house and lake are." His voice was filled with eagerness and in spite of the long, tedious drive, his eyes sparkled in anticipation of the coming week.

"Will we be isolated or do you have neighbors?"

"There was a home about two miles to the west, unless it's been built up since then."

"Who takes care of your place in your absence?"

"No one."

"Well, seems as if someone should watch over it. So many years . . . vandals . . ."

"We're way back in the woods; no one will find the place. We just locked up between visits."

"In the stores in Springfield, people were talking about the rain they've had lately. How close is your house to the lake?"

"It's close, but it's safe. Maybe three hundred feet. The lake's not going to rise that much."

She studied the map, rechecking the directions she had given Ivy. "This is all forest surrounding this lake, isn't it?"

"Yeah," he said. His voice had dropped and with the one word, she could tell his thoughts were no longer on his house. Startled, she looked up to find him studying her again. His arm was behind her, and he leaned close, only inches from her. "You never did answer me back in Springfield. What does flirting lead to?"

"It leads to complications," she said, becoming aware of the closeness in the Jeep, aware of the cotton scent of Jake's new clothes. He had long lashes, perfect lips. Sensual lips.

"I've been wanting to do this since we were in Springfield," he whispered and leaned closer to her.

Any intelligent thought evaporated with the touch of his lips. She closed her eyes while desire fanned into life. She wanted to reach for Jake, to be in his arms. His arm came around her waist, holding her; the gear shift poked her leg, but she was barely aware of it. All attention was elsewhere, taken up in passionate kisses that made her want to melt. Finally, she pushed away, staring at him in a daze. "We discussed how risky this is. We weren't going to give in to the physical attraction, remember?"

"I changed my mind," he said in a low voice that vibrated through her with tiny after shocks.

"Your mind isn't working!" she whispered, feeling a sense of desperation. "Remember all the things about me you don't like—I'm a gypsy, a thistle in the wind, a cocklebur underfoot! You don't want to complicate the week. We're not the same—" His dark lashes came down as he leaned forward and his mouth stopped her words for long minutes. Eternity. Desire escalated, growing with the speed of a brush fire, alarming her enough to stir her mind into action.

She pulled back, barely able to open her eyes. "You like bookkeeping. I like jogging and mountain climbing."

"Yeah!" he said and kissed her again. She felt like a drowning person going under for the last time.

Abruptly, he released her and climbed out of the Jeep to come around the front in long strides. He opened her door and reached for her. "Come out here, Molly."

Unable to resist or protest, she stepped out, and walked into his arms. He crushed her to him, kissing her until she thought she would faint. She stopped finally, saying, "This is absurd! You have a friend in Chicago. I have Garvin—"

"My friend in Chicago isn't a permanent commitment; she's a friend. You won't have Garvin much longer because you're returning his ring."

"But—"

"This is grand, Molly, and they're just harmless kisses. Kisses we both want. You're the one who knows how to enjoy life—don't stop now," he drawled in her ear as his lips touched and nuzzled. And then he kissed her.

The gunshot made them both jump. It blasted like dynamite exploding beneath their feet. Birds squawked; the shot echoed across the hill.

CHAPTER FIVE

JAKE KNOCKED MOLLY to the ground as he exclaimed, "Lordy, the thugs have found us!"

Before she could answer, a man yelled, "This land's posted! You folks saw the signs. Get off my property to smooch!"

"A farmer!" She looked at the fellow standing pointing a shotgun in their direction. He wore a straw hat and jeans and held the longest gun Molly had ever seen. "Get going before I fill you full of buckshot!" he yelled.

"This is one of your friendly Ozark folks?" she taunted, spitting out a mouthful of dirt.

"They seemed friendly before. We better get in the Jeep. I'm sliding under it to get in on the driver's side."

"Gee, thanks. You'll leave me here for a target in your usual gentlemanly fashion!"

"So what do you want me to do? Get up and hold the door for you?"

"You get in this side. I'll slide under and drive."

"Hell, no! I drive faster than you."

"I promise you, I'll drive fast."

Another shot made her jump, and Jake swore. Yet another shot pinged nearby, and she felt like shaking her fist at Jake Cannon.

"Deal. You drive," he snapped. "Let's get out of here."

She scrambled under the car, jumped into the driver's seat, and found Jake already in on his side. Another shot was fired. "Get this thing going!" Jake shouted as she threw it in gear and pushed down on the gas. The Jeep shot forward and Molly swung in a circle, bouncing when they hit large rocks.

"Oh, geez," Jake said, clinging to the side. "Why me? Why of all people—"

As she turned the wheel, the Jeep swung around sharply. Jake's door flew open and he almost fell out. He clutched the seat and yanked the door shut while they bounced across the field.

Molly swerved onto the road, and the Jeep skidded crazily as its tires slipped in the mud. Finally, she slowed and stopped to look at Jake.

In a low voice he swore a steady stream of words while he stared straight ahead. He turned to look at her. "No wonder you move on a whim—does disaster strike everywhere you go?"

"Me! I didn't do a thing! You're the one who told me about the friendly Ozark folks! Look at me! I'm covered in mud and grass!" She climbed out and began brushing off the dirt, oblivious of Jake until he appeared before her and began to help her brush off the smudges, his hand playing lightly over her hip. She stopped instantly and looked at him, noting the twinkle in his eyes and the way his lips were pursed.

"Oh, don't you dare laugh!" she snapped, irritation as abundant as dirt. "My new shorts and my new shirt are covered in mud. I have a mouthful of grass. We were shot at..." His lips clamped together tightly, the hint of a smile about to surface, while he brushed her hip, her derriere, and ogled her at the same time.

"Cut that out!" she said, stepping out of his reach and finally laughing. She threw up her hands and turned in a circle. "What next?"

He pulled a twig out of her hair. "Let's go find my house."

"You think we're being followed?"

"Nope. I think we gave it long enough. Come on."

He climbed behind the wheel and followed the wide road, graveled in spots, muddy in other stretches where it was deeply rutted from recent rains. Oaks closed in on both sides of the road, grapevines covered fences, and sunflowers bloomed in the ditches. The world looked untouched, carefree, and Molly's spirits lifted a fraction. The Jeep bounced over ruts and stones and then the land became clearer. A farmhouse appeared and in moments a signboard. In another few minutes they spotted a sign that read Welcome to Hatters—The rest of it was rusted away where someone had riddled it with bullets for target practice.

On a short asphalt street they drove past two blocks of simple white frame houses with neat beds of flowers in each yard. Then Jake turned to park in front of the general store. "Let's get a few more grocery items. I put off some of the perishables until now; milk, butter, that sort of thing. There's a bait shop behind the store and I'll get some minnows. We can get fishing licenses here."

When they returned to the Jeep, Jake smiled. "I'm starting my vacation right now." He rattled the sacks holding the latest purchases. "Besides the minnows, I bought shrimp pieces for fish bait; I'll dig some worms later. I have stuff to clean with, food, drink—beer, wine—do you like either one?"

She nodded. "Wine sometimes, milk daily."

"I have milk, and I got a bag of ice in case I didn't leave the trays filled."

"They might not be too tasty after being unused for six years," she said dryly.

He settled back and started the Jeep. After they'd traveled the next two blocks out of town, the road once more narrowed and changed to gravel. Jake pressed the accelerator, sending a spate of gravel flying behind them. He grinned and began to sing.

"We're off on vacation! We're off on vacation!" he crowed at the top of his lungs and Molly laughed, clutching the side of the Jeep. She was amazed and delighted at the transformation in him and mildly surprised at the deep, strong voice that boomed out the words.

"We're off on vacation and we'll all have a great time!" he sang. This time she joined him, their voices rising above the roar of the Jeep. A rabbit dashed across the road and Jake swerved the Jeep to one side to avoid hitting it. Molly screamed, but then joined in his singing again. Next, he launched into an old camp song about bottles of beer and she sang that one along with him too. When they finished the song, she laughed heartily and squeezed his arm. He looked at her and smiled, his eyes twinkling.

"Jake!" she yelped as the Jeep headed toward the trees.

He whipped it around and grinned at her, slowing and pulling to a stop. Her heart jumped as she watched him. "Why're you stopping?"

"When you laugh like that, I have an overpowering urge to kiss you," he explained as he moved closer and leaned over the gear shift.

Her heart beat violently. His words made her want the same thing, but the two of them were toying with danger, because to her very bones, she felt she and Jake had an unbridgeable chasm of differences between them. "Hey, look," she said hastily, "remember, we don't want to get involved. You're a workaholic and I'm a gypsy."

"Your kisses are spectacular," he drawled in his husky voice, instantly undoing any logic she had. He tilted her chin up, and she looked into gray depths that changed to silver. His brows narrowed into horizontal dark lines above his eyes and she saw the lightness go out of his expression. His arm slipped around her shoulders, and he pulled her to him, leaning forward to place his mouth on hers.

Time and place ceased to exist. Molly slipped her hands over his hard shoulders, tangling her fingers in the soft waves of his hair, and feeling the warm column of his neck while sensations bombarded her. Desire flared, physical and intense, but along with it came the realization that the man whose kisses had been electrifying from the first moment in the closet had now become as potent as dynamite to her because she knew he could be fun. She had laughed with him, struggled to escape with him, glimpsed some of his heartbreak and worries. Now he wasn't a stranger, but Jake...

He was becoming a friend; his kisses were demanding a lover...

She pushed him and moved back breathlessly.

Jake slowly opened his eyes, staring at her. Her red hair was tousled; a stray lock fell above her eyes and others curled on her shoulders. Mud smudged her chin. His heart thudded against his ribs as he scrutinized her full lips, red from his kisses, and then her wide green eyes that almost seemed filled with fear.

"Molly, are you all right?"

"We aren't the same type and we agreed we shouldn't complicate the week."

He drew a sharp breath, feeling something constrict inside. All logical thought indicated she was right, but he wanted her. It had been so long since he had held a woman, since he had cared... The thought startled him, because as he stared at her, he realized he did care. Molly intrigued him as no other woman had since Sheryl. Molly was fun and lively... a bundle of trouble sometimes, but there were moments it took his breath away to look at her. And when he kissed her...

He lowered his eyes. Her breathing was rapid, her breasts strained against the cotton shirt, and for a moment, he imagined what she looked like without the shirt. He ached with desire, wanting to reach for her, and knowing he couldn't. His glance drifted lower over the trim shorts, her slender bare thighs and her long, smooth legs. He fought the temptation to stroke those legs. Abruptly, he turned to the wheel, started the Jeep and accelerated. With a lurch they were off, but this time there wasn't any singing. They topped a hill, and he heard her gasp before she cried his name.

"Jake! Look out!"

Directly below, at the bottom of a steep incline, a stream rushed across the road, covering it in about an inch of swiftly rushing water.

"Don't worry," he said confidently, slowing, and they drove across without difficulty. Her fingers closed around his wrist.

"Can we stop? Let's wade."

He cut the motor and watched her with amusement as she climbed out.

"I haven't done this in years," she said, kicking off her shoes. She ran the few feet to the water and stepped in squealing. "It's cold!"

He watched her, aching with desire still. She pranced in the water, drops glistening on her shapely legs. He wanted to charge out and crush her in his arms, to feel her soft fullness pressed against him.

"Aren't you coming?" she called.

"No, I'll wait."

"Chicken!" she yelled. "Scared of getting wet?"

"No," he called, laughing and watching her.

"C'mon, it's fun."

She pranced in the water, and suddenly he capitulated and climbed out of the Jeep. He rolled up the jeans, kicked off his sneakers, and waded into the water, gasping as icy water stung his skin. "That's damned cold!"

"Why do you think I've been yelling!" she said, dancing in the water.

They laughed and waded and finally climbed back into the Jeep to drive on. They turned onto a narrow dirt road, actually little more than one lane. Blackjack oaks crowded the shoulders almost obliterating sunlight, and bushy undergrowth took up every available inch of ground. The noise of the Jeep's motor became more noticeable in the isolation of the backwoods, and Molly began to wonder if Jake had the correct directions. They branched to the right, next to the left when the road forked in a confusing pattern. Glancing around her, she sensed that if she were to get lost, she might never find her way out of the thick growth.

A snake slithered across the road and she clutched Jake's arm without realizing what she was doing. She turned in the seat to stare, and watched it slide beneath thick bushes. She shivered, suddenly cold, and tried to conjure up the welcoming house he had described to her. Jake shifted down and the Jeep motor revved loudly as they rode up a steep hill, slipping and leaving deep ruts behind. She heard the water before they topped the rise and realized another bit of road was disappearing beneath rushing water. But this time it wasn't an inch-high stream.

The road bed had vanished under water that spread a dozen feet across. The silvery cascade thundered as it tumbled over a drop a few yards upstream, gained momentum, and poured across the roadway. It looked almost a foot deep.

Molly clutched Jake's arm. "You can't drive through that!" she shouted above the noise of water and engine. He drove down to the water's edge and climbed out to examine it, running his fingers through his hair distractedly.

"Damn, I don't remember anything this deep."

"Maybe some farmer upstream changed the course of the stream," she suggested. "We'll get swept away if we go through it."

He studied it, observing the clear water that tumbled over a rocky bed. He could see the bottom and guessed it was twelve to fifteen inches deep. "I think the Jeep will get through that."

"Oh, no! We'll get washed away."

"I don't think so," he said. "Let's try."

"That's ridiculous!"

"Are you coming with me?" he asked in dulcet tones.

She glared at him. "I don't have a choice."

"Well, what do you propose—we camp here for the next two weeks? Maybe the water has risen because of all the recent rain, but it'll go down soon."

"Why don't we camp here today and wait to see if it goes down."

"No, sirree. My house is not far, and I can get this Jeep through that water. You're the physical one—how come you're balking at this?"

"Because, if you've noticed, only a few yards downstream it gets really deep." She glanced again to her left, where banks were spread three feet farther apart. The water's surface there was silvery and smooth, indicating depth.

"Yeah, well I'm going."

"You'd just leave me right here, wouldn't you?" she demanded, glaring at him.

He looked at her green eyes flashing fire and found himself unable to resist the temptation to tease her. "Yes, ma'am. I surely would. You weren't invited on this vacation, if you'll remember."

She stomped to the Jeep, red curls bouncing, her derriere displaying just enough wiggle to be enticing. He fought a grin as he climbed behind the wheel. Then he gunned the motor, glanced at her and yelled, "Charge!"

She screeched as they drove into the water, sending a spray flying over them. Again she yelped, and then fell quiet as the motor churned and water swept near the floor of the Jeep. He pressed the accelerator, muttering, "C'mon, baby, c'mon..."

They emerged on the other side and she let out a whoop of joy, clapping her hands. He grinned and waved his hand. "Nothing to it!"

She turned to look back at the water. "If it rains, we won't get out of here. Neither will Ivy, Garvin, nor your relatives get in."

"The stream will go down. I don't remember it ever being that deep."

She settled in the seat and brushed her hand over her T-shirt . "Was it necessary to plow into that so fast? I'm soaked."

He turned toward her, his glance drawn to the shirt that now molded her like a swimsuit, revealing plainly the lacy bra beneath. His pulse jumped because she was beautifully shaped with full, upthrusting breasts.

He clutched the steering wheel and stared straight ahead to avoid staring at Molly. In seconds, they reached a fork in the road and he slowed to a stop.

"What's wrong?" she asked.

"I don't remember the road dividing at this point." He pulled out his map and studied it, reading the directions written in his big scrawl. "Well, damn, it's not on here, and I don't remember it."

"Fine and dandy. We're lost," she said, her visions of food and a bed and being able to stretch her legs evaporating. Detroit was beginning to seem a long way back and a long time ago.

"Dammit, we're not lost! It's here—we'll go to the right, and if that's not it, we'll come back and take the left."

"If we can find our way back...okay, off to the right."

He turned the Jeep and the road was gobbled up by thornbushes, creepers and high grass. Only two faint lanes for the tires were visible, and then those disappeared for yards at a time. Weeds scraped and were smashed by the Jeep; thick trees and a multitude of leaves filtered out the light, and Molly clutched the seat to keep from bouncing around while she worried about how Ivy would ever find her way to the house.

"Jake, this is impossible! There's no road. Ivy can't find this!"

"Our tracks will leave a trail. She'll find us," he said with an optimism Molly didn't share. She silently prayed they would reach the house soon. Suddenly, Jake shouted, "Hey, look over there!"

Smiling over the exuberance in his voice, Molly looked at him, momentarily astonished at how he could be so mulish one minute and so adorable the next. And then so breathtakingly exciting! That was the dangerous part, because they were such different types. And in spite of what he'd said, she couldn't call his kisses "harmless." She followed his pointing finger and saw a huge mossy boulder nestled off the lane between the trees, grass growing high around it, jagged cracks running through it.

Jake slowed to stare at it. "We're going in the right direction. We called that the Rock of Gibraltar." His eagerness faded and he said solemnly, "The road's overgrown with weeds. I didn't think we were the only ones who used it." He threw the Jeep into gear and they drove on. He returned to singing, his voice carrying loudly in the dense woods while words in Italian spilled out. She recognized the music as operatic. He glanced at her and caught her staring open-mouthed at him.

"You know opera...I mean you can sing it!"

"I studied a little a long time ago during my freshman year in college," he said and launched back into song, but suddenly stopped abruptly. "Look, there's the house!" he shouted, leaning out of the Jeep to peer as he drove. He sat back down and hunched over the wheel as Molly spotted something gray through the trees.

"There it is! Oh boy!"

Growing as eager as Jake, relieved they had finally reached their destination, she laughed. "I don't think you should wait six years between vacations."

He grinned at her. "Clean sheets, a glass of wine, broiled steaks, peace and quiet, maybe a boat ride . . . I can't wait!"

Oh, yum, y-u-m," she said, licking her lips.

Jake glanced at her just as her pink tongue slid over her lips like a kitten satisfied with cream, an action that was unconsciously sensual. He wondered how sensual she would be in a man's arms. The thought sent a flash of hungry desire through him and his eyes again swept over the wet shirt hugging her uptilting breasts. She had a breathtaking figure and lush breasts, yet she was slender, with a tiny waist he knew he could span with his hands. And at the moment he wanted to badly. He realized it was time to start dating more. He'd had some dates, but they had been meaningless, women who had left him aching and lonely for Sheryl. He had thrown himself into work to keep from thinking about Sheryl and his separation from Jamie, and the long hours had left him little time to date.

Thinking back over the moments with Molly, he remembered dangling from the edge of the roof while she had forced the promise from him before she would help him. He grinned, recalling how cheerfully he could have shaken her when he'd finally caught his breath on the roof.

Seeing his smile, she smiled in return. Weary from traveling and the strain on her nerves in Detroit, Molly conjured up thoughts of relaxing and supposed Jake was doing the same. She leaned forward to look with eagerness at the roof of the house becoming visible before them.

Jake sang another chorus and she turned to watch him, amazed at his voice, fascinated by his sudden buoyancy. He noticed her expression and asked, "What's going on in your mind?"

"Don't stop singing."

"C'mon, you're staring."

"Sorry. You're an enigma ... you know opera and you have quite a voice; why didn't you go into music for a career?"

"Oh, lordy, I wanted employment that was solid and dependable with a monthly salary!"

She shook her head. "You're so solemn one minute, then in another you're full of enthusiasm. You sing classical songs, you do television commercials, you sell stereos, you can be so much fun and yet you can be so ... stubborn.

"In short, I'm a complicated man," he said blithely, and she smiled. "And you," he said, "are a sneaky, sexy, exciting, troublesome, gorgeous woman!"

"I think I'll forgive you for sneaky and troublesome."

As he laughed, they turned a bend and the house loomed into view.

"Oh, my lord!" he said and then they both became quiet while he drove the last yards and stopped. Molly's breath caught in her throat. When Jake cut the motor, the silence was total, wrapping around them like layers of thick cotton.

But, as though they were in a storm, shock waves buffeted them.

CHAPTER SIX

WISHING SHE WOULD WAKE UP and discover her surroundings were only a dream, Molly stared at a ghostly, darkened house with shutters hanging at angles. Two lay on the ground. The weathered boards were gray; paint had long ago peeled off. The front door stood ajar, and the screen on the porch was ripped across the front. Brambles grew on the steps; a squirrel dashed across the porch and jumped off to disappear into a bush. "Six years since you're been here," she said softly, her visions of a paradise retreat crumbling like the weeds beneath the Jeep's tires.

"Damn, it can't be as bad inside as it looks outside," he said hoarsely, descending from the Jeep as if in a trance. He climbed up the porch steps which creaked beneath his weight, and Molly followed, feeling gloom fold over her like a bat's wings.

She followed Jake inside and they stood motionless as they looked around.

Cobwebs and dust filled the corners and nooks, and covered the furniture. Windows were broken out, curtains torn or pulled down; the oak floor was covered with leaves and dust and sticks.

"All the modern conveniences," Molly whispered, stunned with disappointment and weariness. "Sheets, beds..."

In a flat monotone Jake began to utter words Molly had seldom heard, and then words she had never heard. For a moment she forgot her colossal disappointment as she looked at Jake. His face was red with anger and he stood stiffly, his fists clenched, swearing steadily as he headed for the kitchen. She hurried after him and they paused just inside the entrance. The refrigerator door was open; leaves and dust filled the inside. Dust covered the counter, the table and the stove. One kitchen chair lay smashed on the floor. Jake kicked it.

"Dammit to hell!"

"Jake, we can fix it up," Molly said, feeling a deep flare of sympathy, and distressed by the anger and disappointment that showed in his face. He focused on her as if he had just remembered her. "We can fix it up," she repeated quietly. "You bought a broom and cleaning things."

"We ought to turn around and head back to Detroit! My damn glorious vacation in the Ozarks!"

"Let's get the things out of the car and clean this," she said calmly, pondering how terrible it would be to wait six years and then find ruin. "It won't take long to get a room or two in shape so we can sleep."

He squinted his eyes at her. "Who would do this?"

She shrugged. "Time, vagrants, maybe vandals... maybe a little of each."

"Damn, I can't believe it!"

"I'm going to get the broom," she said and left. Outside, thunder rumbled in the distance and she looked up between thick tree branches to see clouds racing across the sky. "Oh, no!" she mumbled, sighing with exasperation as she carried the broom and a sack of groceries inside. "The first thing to do," she said, "is to clean the kitchen and bathroom and see if you can get the water pump in working order. How do you get electricity?"

"There's a generator." He took the sack from her hand and set it on the counter. Molly began to sweep a corner of the kitchen, thinking if she didn't work hard and fast, she would scream or cry. She was bone weary and growing more aware of it every second.

Jake turned to go, but paused to look at Molly. Her back was to him and she swept as if each motion were necessary to pump air into her lungs. His gaze lowered over her tiny waist, the red shorts pulling tautly over her bottom, and her silky long legs; a corner of his mouth lifted. For a moment he conjectured what this scenario would have been like if he had come alone— how devastated he would have been. But Molly had taken it in stride and was creating order out of chaos. She was making him forget a little of his exhaustion and disappointment. And he wouldn't have guessed her reaction in a dozen tries. He had forgotten her presence at first, but when he remembered, he would have expected her to explode with fury or break down in tears—and if she had, he would have understood why. She stepped back, working furiously, a grace to her simple movements of sweeping. His smile grew as he crossed the room without a sound.

Arms closed around Molly's waist, and Jake turned her to face him. "For a gypsy who doesn't like workaholics, you dig right in."

"We can have it livable in no time," she answered stiffly, trying to keep her own emotions under control, momentarily thankful for the reassuring strength of his arms around her.

"Yeah. How much sleep do you think you've had in the past twenty-four hours?"

"Enough to last a little bit longer. You see about the generator. I heard thunder."

"You're okay, Molly," he said, staring at her solemnly, and she reacted as if he had heaped praises on her. Her heart thumped violently because he sounded sincere and grateful and his approval gave her a renewal of energy.

He turned and went out the back door while she swept. In seconds, when she heard more violent swearing, she rushed outside across the dusty screened porch and down the steps. She looked beyond him through the trees at the silvery surface of a lake only yards from the house.

"You said the lake was three hundred feet from the house," she said, stunned.

"The damned boathouse is down there in the damned lake!" he snapped, turning to look at her. "The lake used to be three hundred feet from the house—I swear it did!"

"Go see about the generator," she said, gaping at the water only twenty yards from the bottom step and listening to thunder rumble. Oaks ran far out into the water, hinting at the regular shoreline before the spring rains had come. A white heron stepped gingerly through the water, holding one slim leg up; the wind stirred ripples on the water's surface and ruffled the bird's white feathers. Another bird whistled, a high, melodic sound in the stillness, and the wind that brushed Molly's cheek was fresh and smelled of rain. The peace of the woods settled on her. The only turmoil was in the two humans running crazily around trying to clean and repair. Outside it was silent—a quiet she hadn't enjoyed for over a year, the absolute silence of nature undisturbed by civilization.

"Jake," she said softly, her eyes moving reluctantly from the lake, "it's lovely."

He paused and looked beyond her and they both stilled, watching the heron move with slow, dignified steps. A flash of silver sparkled like mercury as a fish jumped, stirring ripples in ever-widening circles. Molly sighed, momentarily forgetting her tired muscles. But when she looked at the wooden boathouse, she was reminded of their dilemma—Jake would have to swim to it if he wanted to get a boat.

She glanced at him, caught by the look of pleasure on his face; the wind teased locks of his hair and she studied his features in profile. Clearly etched was his thin, slightly crooked nose that made her wonder if he'd hurt it in a fight. His prominent cheekbones lent a rugged look to his face, his arms were muscular, and the jeans revealed well-developed legs, yet he had talked about being out of shape—maybe sports weren't as foreign to him as he'd indicated earlier. He turned, his eyes meeting hers like invisible fingers reaching out to hold her. She felt caught but was unable to look away; she recalled all too clearly his laughter, his husky, magic voice, his kisses…kisses that stopped her breath.

Wind tugged tendrils of golden-red hair across her cheek, and Jake smiled. "It is lovely, Molly," he said, his voice dropping to caress her quivering nerves, his expression silently proclaiming that it wasn't the lake or trees he had in mind. Again, she was amazed and disturbed at the current rippling between them, pulling on all her senses.

"I better go inside." With an effort she returned to the kitchen. She swept, working furiously to vent her frustration, knowing the only way they could eat would be to clean the kitchen first. She paused, pushed her hair from her face and got out a roll of paper towels to brush the dust off the counter. Suddenly she heard whoops and shouts, but this time Jake sounded happy. He came bounding in, waving his hands. "The generator works, I think. Hold your breath and pray...

She closed her eyes and did as he requested while he reached for a light switch.

"Whoopie! Electricity!" he said gleefully. He was covered with dirt, his arms and shirt and jeans smudged, and a streak ran from his cheek to his neck, yet he looked more appealing than ever, perhaps more earthy and male. Molly tried to keep from gaping at him, and made an effort to listen as he continued, "That means the water pump will work. Turn on the faucets—the water may be rusty at first. I'll see about the pilot light on the hot water tank."

She turned on the faucets and in minutes was startled as water burst out, stopped, then shot out again to run in a steady reddish brown stream that finally faded to clear water. Molly cleaned, working faster than ever, because she felt exhaustion creeping up and her stomach was complaining of hunger. She washed out the refrigerator, plugged it in and once more prayed until the motor kicked over and it hummed to life. She put the remains of the bag of ice inside along with the bottles of wine and milk and the perishables. Gradually the kitchen began to look habitable and then inviting. Jake came in to take the broom and she heard him sweeping the porch while she scrubbed the stove, working her way down to the broiler and humming as she worked.

A deep voice joined hers. Jake stood in the doorway, hip canted against the jamb while he sang softly. Having discovered he could move with a lithe, silent ease, she suspected he had been watching her for a while.

As she stood up, she commented, "I never know when you're around."

"Yes, you do, sooner or later. I was enjoying looking at the kitchen," he said, surveying only her.

"Sure, you were!" she said, her senses again buffeted by his appearance. "Jake, we logically discussed the differences between us—"

"I've forgotten them," he said, coming a step closer.

"I haven't. They're monumental...and you're covered with dirt," she said desperately.

"Huh!" He looked down at himself and shrugged. "So I am. Okay, I'm going upstairs to see about the beds and the bath," he said, drawing out the words bed and bath.

"Jake, stop flirting!"

"Who, me?" he asked with great innocence. He crossed the kitchen to her, bracing his hands on the counter on either side of her and hemming her in between his body and the countertop. "Remind me, why was it we were going to fight the attraction between us?"

"We're poles apart in personalities and lifestyles—as in ice cream and jalapeño peppers," she said. Her voice had lowered a notch and developed a breathy timbre.

"Oh, yeah," he said huskily. "And some day I'm going to get even with you for letting me dangle from that rooftop...really even, Molly."

Her heart thudded so loudly, she thought he could hear it, but fear wasn't the response his threat conjured up...a threat drawled in a deep, caressing voice as she discovered that his eyes could darken to quicksilver and change with his mood. "You're the gypsy who won't settle for commitment—you should love casual kisses. Relax and have some fun, Molly," he coaxed.

She didn't want to admit to him that what he described as casual and harmless wasn't casual and harmless to her one whit. Not under any circumstances. She couldn't recall one single male she had dated whose kisses affected her the way Jake's had. She couldn't recall such an intense attraction to anyone either, but she didn't want to tell him. He obviously didn't feel the same or he wouldn't argue so blithely about it, and the knowledge made her doubly defensive.

"Jake, you have mud on your face."

He smiled and straightened up. "Yeah. I'll have to wash. Want to bring your trusty broom along, and we'll brave the upstairs?"

"Sure," she answered quietly, worried that he might get even with her for the rooftop incident in ways he didn't realize. In the past few minutes she had wanted him to kiss her. Insanity. She knew she shouldn't want Jake's kisses. For a dozen reasons that she kept reminding herself of, she didn't want to get involved with Jake Cannon. She didn't because of their differences, because Jake viewed their attraction as casual...because her intense reaction to him frightened her.

Jake slipped his arm around her waist and together they went upstairs. Three bedrooms lined the east side of the hall, a single large bathroom and walk-in closet stood on the west. Molly braced for whatever they might find inside the rooms.

In the largest bedroom, Jake paused to stare, his hand falling from her waist. The bed was intact, covered with layers of dust and cobwebs and a red, white and blue patchwork quilt. The room seemed untouched except by time. Jake prowled around and Molly glanced at him, noting that his jaw was clamped shut, a frown creased his brow, and his hands were jammed into his pockets, making his jeans pull tautly over his slender hips. His movements were restless, his expression hurt and angry. Once more, she felt as if he had forgotten her presence, and guessed he was remembering Sheryl and their moments in the room. Suddenly Molly felt like an intruder; she hurt for Jake because he appeared to be wrestling heartaches and memories. "This will be your room," she said quietly and turned to go.

He was at her side in an instant, moving with the swift silence of a cat, his arm blocking her way.

"Don't go," he said roughly, and she looked up into smoky eyes silvered with tears.

"Jake..." She put her arms around him and held him tightly. His arms rested lightly around her waist in a reflex action, but there was no pressure.

"There are just so damned many memories," he said hoarsely. "I knew there would be, but it's still a blow when you come face to face with them," he added, as if talking to himself.

"I'm sorry."

His arms locked around her, and he held her fiercely a moment, crushing the breath from her lungs. "This room...so many hopes and dreams all gone..."

She held him, waiting, breathing deeply the smell of fresh earth from the mud smeared on his clothing, mud that now would cover her. She didn't care. Downstairs, she had used the mud as an excuse to keep him away, but it didn't really bother her. She stroked his back, feeling the long muscles, the slight curve of his spine.

Finally he turned his back to her. He waved his hands. "You can take either bedroom, the one to the right or the left.

For the first time she realized both bedrooms had connecting doors to the large central bedroom and she blurted out, "They both have doors to this room!"

He turned then, his frown vanishing as a smile emerged. "I won't slip in during the night and attack you."

Feeling ridiculous, she blushed. "I was just surprised."

He laughed. "Why don't you sweep while I throw sheets in to launder? I'll bring our things in from the car, too."

"Fine," she said, starting in a corner.

"Molly." He stood with his hands on his hips, watching her with amusement. "Start on the room you want to sleep in. You don't have to do my room. Unless—"

"Jake! I might as well start in here."

When he had stripped the bed of covers and gone downstairs, she looked into the adjoining rooms. One held twin beds, the other a double bed. Molly chose the one on the southeast corner with the twin beds and a good view of the lake.

Hunger now becoming intense, she hurried. By the time she had finished Jake's room and swept hers as well as the pink-tiled bathroom, Jake appeared from the walk-in closet with folded sheets.

"Not too fresh, but they're not dusty either."

"I won't be particular. They look fine," she assured him. Together they put sheets on first her bed, then his.

When they finished, he came around the bed to put his hands on her shoulders. "For bravery above and beyond the call of duty and cleaning like a demon, you may have the first bath."

"Thank you," she said with a smile. "The pleasure's all yours. I'll finish sweeping while you bathe first and make sure frogs don't hop out of the pipes..."

"I knew there had to be a reason," he said good-naturedly and left for the bathroom.

She heard water run, and then Jake's voice rose above the shower and filled the house, Italian words flowing in his baritone. She paused a moment, marveling at him, mulling over again what a contradiction he was—he had talent that he didn't use except in the shower or the car, and an obsession with work and money that made him wait six years between vacations though he had a very successful business. She shook her head, working to make her bedroom habitable and trying to shift her thoughts to something besides Jake Cannon. But she was unsuccessful until his singing stopped and the water stopped.

"Now it's your turn," he said quietly from the doorway. Molly's breath caught as she looked at him. He was rubbing a towel on his hair. He wore jeans, deck shoes and nothing else. His broad chest was furred with a thick mat of dark curls that narrowed in a line disappearing into his jeans. If he was out of shape, she wondered what he called *in shape*! He was muscular, but the reaction he stirred went beyond a strong, healthy, male body. She had seen beaches filled with those and never had experienced the reaction she had now. Jake's presence exuded a blatant, sexual aura that carried memories of kisses hotter than fire—an aura that was invisible, intangible, yet at the same time as devastating as a windstorm.

"There are no frogs in the shower."

"I'm glad to hear it," she said, fighting to keep her voice calm; her pulse took another lurch as he stopped toweling his hair and narrowed his eyes, focusing his gaze on her.

"I won't be long," she said, hurrying to the bathroom and closing the door behind her. She leaned against it and blew out her breath as if she'd had a narrow escape! What was there about Jake that disturbed her so deeply? He was just another man, she argued silently with herself. Stubborn, work and money conscious to the exclusion of all else in his life, casual about kisses...

But the arguments didn't diminish one iota the fun moments they had shared in the car or the vivid mental image of his bare chest, his tight jeans, the flare of curiosity in his eyes, the dark waves of damp, black hair curling over his forehead.

She bathed in a cool shower, washing away tiredness and grime, finally stepping out to blow-dry her hair and dress in blue shorts, a T-shirt and sneakers. She picked up her red skirt and hung it in the closet next to the blue blazer.

But as she lifted it, a pink plastic bag fell out of the pocket. Curious, she opened the bag to shake out a wafer that resembled a small, thin domino. Rectangular and black with markings, numbers and a copyright, it had fourteen tiny silver legs on each side. The legs were embedded in a piece of black foam. The circular window in the center revealed a tiny mirrored rectangle inside.

Frowning, Molly turned it over in her hands, then shrugged, deciding it was something of Jake's that he had dropped into her pocket by mistake. She slipped it into the pocket of her shorts and went downstairs, assailed by delicious odors of sizzling steaks.

The moment she stepped through the door, Jake glanced up to look into her eyes. Then slowly, his gaze lowered.

"Mama, mia . . . you look—" a lowering of his eyes a few more inches "—grand," he said, drawing out his compliment and letting his voice drop until the words were almost a song. And almost a touch. She drew her breath sharply, realizing too late that her action made her breasts swell against the T-shirt, and she burned as he looked at her with open admiration.

"Will you stop that, Jake! I'm clean—that's the only difference."

"No, it's not," he said softly. "I'll explain it to you after we eat," he added, the offer hinting at delicious promises of more than words.

He turned to check on the steaks, humming as he cooked. "What can I do?" she asked, but discovered he had everything done. She was also having a hunger attack of gigantic proportions.

"All we're having is green salad and thick, juicy slabs of meat. Okay?"

"Sure," she said, her mouth watering as he removed sizzling steaks and pulled them onto a platter.

"I took the dishes out of the dishwasher. You really whizzed through this kitchen like a dynamo."

"I was thinking the same about you," she said, observing the two glasses of wine, and the big bowl of crisp green lettuce mixed with fresh red tomato bits and thin slices of green pepper.

They ate on the porch, at a table Jake had washed earlier; they sat beside the screen wall where they could see the lake and enjoy a breeze. For a moment Molly thought about the circumstances and registered surprise at how contented she felt. The view was beautiful; it gave the impression that everything had to be right in the entire world because this little corner of water and trees and wildlife was so harmonious.

Jake smiled at her and leaned forward, holding up his glass of wine. "Here's to the coming week."

She touched his glass lightly and raised it to her lips to drink sweet, red wine. Jake raised his glass at the same time, watching her over the rim, feeling his pulse thump swiftly as their gazes locked and held. Molly was fun, unpredictable, but full of energy, and her kisses set him on fire. Suddenly, he was thankful he had brought her along—this week might be an interlude he needed.

His focus switched from her wide green eyes to her lips and he caught her quick intake of breath. Her instant response to his slightest glance, his mere presence, stirred him beyond belief. She was so damned sensual, yet she seemed totally unaware of it, and when it dawned on her, she seemed to try to squelch her natural inclinations, merely heightening her appeal, because it made him want to see what happened when she didn't squelch them!

"I can't eat when you look at me like that!" she said breathlessly.

"Ignore me. There's a huge steak and salad," he said, slowing his words and relishing the reaction he could get. She had to be one of the most sensuous women in bed if she reacted the rest of the time to nothing more than a glance or innuendo. Desire became a burning awareness and he wanted to forget his hungry stomach, fling aside dinner, and take Molly into his arms.

Knowing she would protest, he forced his eyes from her face, and looked down at the dark steak with rivulets of melted, golden butter running across it.

"How did you get into dancing, Molly?"

She cut a small bite of steak. "It's all I know." While she talked, he ate and listened. His frayed nerves soothed as he relaxed totally.

"My mother had a dance studio—just as I do. She had been an exotic dancer though, and did a stint on the Strip in Vegas where she was in a chorus line. Ivy and I learned to dance as soon as we could toddle around and we've been dancing ever since." Molly waved her hand in a graceful arc, her slender wrist seeming too fragile to be capable of the strength he knew she had. "I like dancing, but Ivy's beginning to dislike it and wants out. Of course—" she paused to take a sip of the sparkling red wine "—I'm not an exotic dancer. If I were, I'd feel the same as Ivy."

"An exotic dancer who... does she dance nude?"

"Well, maybe not quite," she said, wriggling with obvious discomfort.

Suddenly amused, Jake shifted in his chair as Molly talked.

"We never had any formal education after high school because there wasn't enough money, but we're both trying to get some now. I take correspondence

courses in bookkeeping and Spanish. Ivy's been going
to night classes taking accounting. We had to go to
work right after high school and we each did the only
thing we knew—dancing. I worked in a studio that
taught tap and ballet to children and saved until I could
open my own place. It doesn't take a big investment to
start. I could keep it simple. Ivy discovered she could
make three times as much money by doing exotic
dancing instead of teaching, so she did. I couldn't do
exotic dancing." Molly shivered and glanced into the
distance.

"Did you try?" he asked softly, suspecting the shiver
was brought on by something stronger than mere dis-
taste. Her green eyes widened, and she stared at him for
a fleeting second, as if she had forgotten he was the
person to whom she had been talking. The blush gave
him an answer.

"Well, yes, for only a night or two. I wasn't meant
for it."

He smiled, amused by her reaction, intrigued by the
idea of Molly attempting one night of exotic dancing.
"Anyway, Ivy wants out of it—there's no future in it
and she's really not the type for it. She attracts men
who expect her to be different than she really is." She
smiled at him. "Ivy's sweet."

He enjoyed listening to Molly's quiet talking, but at
the moment, he wasn't particularly interested in Ivy.
"That's days away. Right now I don't want to think
about people." They lapsed into silence as they finished dinner, and Jake realized the silences with Molly
were easy ones, not uncomfortable, but natural. He
turned his chair, leaning back and stretching out his
legs while the sun lowered. Birds skimmed across the
lake, and suddenly he remembered sitting there with

Sheryl while they had planned their future. Aching, touched by grief that still caught him unawares at odd moments, he pushed his chair back with a scrape and went to the kitchen to get the bottle of wine and refill their glasses.

Light spilled from the kitchen to the darkened porch when he returned. To avoid thinking about his past, he turned his thoughts to morning. He leaned forward to reach into his hip pocket and pull out a paper and pen he had picked up in the kitchen. While Molly sat, quietly sipping her wine and enjoying the view of the lake, he wrote. Finally, he raised his head to say, "Tomorrow we'll try to get the house squared away, and I'll get the boats up to dry land. I made a list of things we can do. Are you an early or late riser?"

She smiled at him, and set down her wineglass. "Both. Whichever I want to do."

"Don't you go to work at a regular time?"

"Sure. My dance classes start at ten o'clock. So some mornings I get up eight, some at nine."

"That's so damned inefficient."

"But it's fun."

He barely smiled, thinking she was as flighty as some bird on the lake.

"Well now, tomorrow we can get up at half past six. If we divide the jobs, we should get quite a bit accomplished." He wondered if she were listening to him. Her gaze was on the lake, and a bemused smile curved her mouth.

"Would you rather cook breakfast or sweep the front room and porch?" He waited and felt his temper flare. "Molly, are you listen—?"

"Look, Jake, there's an owl. Watch him fly. See over there, the tree to the right of the boat house."

"Molly." She gave him her attention with a polite smile.

"I'm trying to organize tomorrow."

Her smile widened and his patience stretched thinner. She laughed. "Jake, you can't organize tomorrow—tomorrow will just *be*!"

"I *can* organize it, and I don't know how you stay in business. Which would you rather do—cook breakfast or sweep?"

She shrugged. "I'll sweep. I'm tired of my own breakfasts and you're a marvelous cook," she said with a sigh.

"Thank you," he answered, not admitting how limited his cooking achievements were.

"Okay," he said, marking down notes as he talked, "you sweep, I cook. Next, I'll see about the broken windows and get the boats back to dry ground. While I do that you can get the laundry done—we should redo all the linens because they're dusty..."

While he talked, Molly's thoughts wandered. She watched Jake's head bent over the table while he wrote, his thick raven hair an invitation to reach across and tangle her fingers in it. His fingers were strong and well shaped; his blunt nails were clipped close, and he still wore a plain gold wedding band. She shifted, her hip scraped against the chair and she remembered the sack in her pocket. "Oh, Jake! I almost forgot. I found this—"

"Molly, are you listening to me?"

"Sure," she said, "sorry." She pulled out the pink plastic bag. "Here, I found this. You must have dropped it into my pocket by mistake."

He took the bag from her and turned it in his hand, then opened it to look inside at the chip anchored in black foam inside. "This isn't mine," he said.

"It isn't?"

"No," he answered, slipping the black foam out of the bag.

"It was in my blazer pocket. I don't know what it is."

Jake looked at the computer chip in his hand for a moment, puzzling how Molly would get a computer chip when she didn't even know what one was. He turned it and noticed the copyright mark and the blue diamond next to it. And then he felt as if the lake had suddenly risen in a tidal wave and hovered over them, ready to come crashing down.

"This was in the blue blazer you were wearing in Detroit?" he asked, hearing his voice as if it came from a distance.

Her eyes widened and she nodded. "Yes."

"Oh, Mama mia!" he exclaimed and groaned.

CHAPTER SEVEN

"YOU DIDN'T NOTICE the blue diamond on it?" he asked, already knowing the answer.

"Yes, but—Brantz Blue Diamond? What is that?"

"It's a computer chip, anchored in anti-static foam and wrapped in an anti-static bag. How close were you to Karl Brantz?"

"I ran into him."

"Oh, damn! Of all people for me to get tangled up with! You are an absolute calamity! Calamity Molly! Jane didn't know the meaning of the word!"

"Will you stop raving!"

"I'm not raving!" he snapped. "Oh, dammit! Karl Brantz must have dropped this into your pocket when you bumped him."

Molly's face paled, and Jake realized she had made a good guess about what had happened. "He didn't want those thugs to get it," she said stiffly.

"You're bright. Disastrous, but bright."

"This isn't my fault, and I wish I'd had my own mountain cabin—and if I'd known I was in for a week of back-breaking work, I might have run somewhere else! " she declared, exasperated by his attitude.

Jake didn't seem to hear. He rubbed the back of his neck. "That explains why someone has pursued us all the way from Detroit, why the keen interest in us, why the man approached you in the mall in Springfield.

This is hot, Molly, hot—as in the center of the sun! This little chip may be the reason they kidnapped Brantz.''

''Oh, no!''

''Oh, yes...and here you have it in your pocket, bringing the criminals straight to my cozy home in the hills...oh, damn, there won't be a peaceful moment.''

''I didn't do it on purpose! And *cozy* is hardly the appropriate word! And how do you know?''

''Brantz is a computer pioneer now working in AI— artificial intelligence, the latest high-tech development.''

''How do you know that?''

''I have a computer and when it breaks down I have a friend who fixes it. He's told me about AI. And it's a brand new field right now. Brantz didn't want the men to get this. Actually, the chip is hermetically sealed inside the silicon wafer. What you see inside through the little round window is the chip.''

Jake drummed his fingers on the table and she surveyed the darkening woods outside. Their peace had been suddenly shattered by the possibility of danger. ''I don't see how anyone can find us here,'' she said.

Jake barely heard her words; after a moment they registered, and he answered perfunctorily. ''We need to let the police know about this.''

She drew a sharp breath. ''If we have to go back to Detroit now it'll mean Ivy won't be safe from Willis yet—''

''No, I don't think we'll have to go back when we tell them how isolated we are, but they need to know.'' He rubbed his neck again and finally said, ''We'll tackle that problem tomorrow. In the meantime, I'll put this away,'' he said and got up to go upstairs and put it in his suit coat.

As he dropped the chip into his pocket, he glanced at the Smith and Wesson he had purchased in Springfield and hoped he wouldn't have need of it. His gaze swept the room—someone was after them and wanted the chip badly enough to kidnap a man who would attract lawmen and attention in the highest measure. Jake had no illusions about how Molly and he would be treated if they stood in the way of the men who wanted the chip.

He couldn't get over Molly carrying the computer chip in her coat. She was calamity, luscious green-eyed calamity. And he had to admit she intrigued him because she was all the things he wasn't—carefree, full of quick laughter, able to view life with a lightness he both envied and disliked. He paused, remembering her hot kisses, the instant response she had to the slightest touch, to a mere drop in his voice. He felt desire stir at the thought of her and wanted to be with her.

Downstairs, he switched off the kitchen light, moved his chair beside hers, and draped his arm across the back of her chair.

"Did you hide it?" she asked.

"I put it in my coat pocket. I don't think anyone could have followed us here so I don't think I need to hide it more elaborately."

They were silent for a time. Then she said, "The moon is over the lake. Isn't it beautiful?"

"The rain must have gone elsewhere," he said, inhaling the faintly sweet, clean scent of Molly's hair, "but it'll rain tonight. There's lightning in the distance and thunder—look at the clouds."

She tilted her head; he glanced swiftly at gray streamers rippling across the sky like banners in a parade. Then his attention turned to Molly's upturned profile, her long, slender neck, her soft red curls tumbling on her shoulders. He wanted to reach for her badly. He trailed his fingers along her arm, and moved them up to her shoulder.

She turned to look at him, her eyes so wide, her lips parted, lips sweeter than the glass of cool wine. He leaned toward her, placing his lips on hers.

She shifted her head a fraction to whisper, "One minute you call me a calamity, and the next, you want to kiss me."

His lips found hers again and parted briefly as he whispered, "You are, and I do," and then his mouth moved fully over hers, his tongue thrusting with a hot demand that she met. Sometime later Jake lifted her onto his lap and settled her against his shoulder while he kissed her until the first spray of rain sweeping through the screen struck them.

Molly raised her head. "I think we're getting rained on now."

"I don't care," he said.

She wiggled off his lap and stood up. "You're not the one getting wet!"

She picked up some dishes and ran to the kitchen. Jake gathered more dishes and followed; they cleaned the kitchen while rain fell lightly outside. When they finished, Jake reached for her, but Molly resisted. "Jake, it's late and I feel terribly vulnerable."

"Why?" He smiled and slipped his arm around her waist. "You're breaking up with Garvin, you're not interested in commitment—and this is more fun, Molly than—"

"I'm in the process of breaking an engagement—a first," she said, interrupting him hastily. "We're isolated, exhausted, thrown together for hours and hours of close contact. We barely know each other—"

"I get the picture," he said with good-natured reluctance. "And we know each other a hell of a lot more than barely." He studied her lips and felt another flurry of longing. "Shall we go up to bed?" he suggested softly, his eyes coaxing more than his words.

"You're flirting again! Yes, I want to go to my bed and you go to your bed."

"And never the twain shall meet!" he declared with laughter. "Don't sound so defensive. I'll do what you want."

She smiled at him, deciding he was as changeable as a chameleon. "Sometimes, Jake, I think there's a part of you that wants to relax and enjoy life, but another part of you won't let it."

"Baloney—I know how to relax and have fun. I have been for the past few hours," he protested, smiling. "As a matter of fact," he drawled, his voice turning to heated syrup, "if you want fun and relaxation, we can—"

"No, we can't!"

Laughing, Jake switched off lights, and they went upstairs together. Light spilled into the hall from the open bathroom but at the head of the stairs, Jake said, "I'll walk you to your room."

"It's only yards from yours!"

"Yeah, I know," he said, almost in a whisper. At the door to her room, he placed his hand against the jamb beyond her head and stood inches away. "Thanks for pitching in to help clean this place."

"Sure," she said, alternately glancing at his mouth and his eyes, wondering when he would lean down the few inches necessary to kiss her. Her pulse accelerated at the thought.

"I'll call you in the morning," he said, looking at her mouth. Her lips tingled in expectation.

"You don't need to," she answered breathlessly.

He grinned and touched the tip of her nose lightly. "You mean, you don't want me to, but if we stir around we can have the house livable sooner. Remember, you'll sweep and I'll cook."

"Uh-huh," she said, losing track of the conversation. She wanted to close her eyes, tilt her head back, and commence again what they had stopped on the porch.

"Night, Molly. Sleep tight," he added. "I've always wondered what that old saying means: 'Sleep *tight*'."

"Night," she said, drawing out the word as much as he had. He turned and walked to his room.

Molly was startled. Then she watched him as he paused, winked, and disappeared into his room.

Shaken, she realized several things at once. One—she had wanted and *expected* Jake to kiss her. She had wanted his kisses badly. Two—she was aflame with a tingling need that he had stirred. Three—she had told him to leave her alone because she was vulnerable and it would be wise. And so he had. Was that what she really wanted?

Logic said of course it was what she wanted. Her heart shouted a hundred other answers and she tried to ignore them as she cut the tags off the short blue nightgown and slipped it on with the matching cotton panties. She could hear Jake moving around in his room, singing again, softly. His voice was deep as a well, a rumbling bass that floated invisibly into the room and wrapped around her like spun sugar. She switched off the light, got on her knees in bed and looked out the window through shimmering rivulets of rain at the lake dotted by raindrops.

Then she snuggled down in bed, pulled up the sheet and listened to Jake still singing quietly. She smiled in the dark as she relaxed. Weariness from all the long hours of travel and cleaning the house invaded every limb of her body. She hovered on the brink of sleep when she heard Jake. "Night, Molly," he called. Instantly, she conjured up the image of him stretched out in bed.

"Night, Jake," she answered, now not half so sleepy as she had been before. She tried to think about the lake, the Ozarks, the computer chip...anything to keep her mind off the man in the next room.

SHE STIRRED IN THE NIGHT, momentarily disoriented, listening as thunder rumbled and rain beat in a steady patter. Lightning flashed, illuminating the room, and memory returned. One of the remembrances was the satiny spread of water just beyond the house. Once more, she rose to her knees, and leaned against the window. Her nose touched the cool glass as she peered through the water-covered pane. Lightning flashed and Molly could have sworn the lake was closer to the house. Dark shadows shifted and moved on the ground below; she frowned while she waited for the next flash. Silvery brilliance streaked over the earth, furnishing an eerie lustre to trees, turning the lake to shimmering glass, but Molly barely noticed either. Her attention was on the dark shadows...dark shadows that headed toward the house, that remained dark in the brightness of a lightning flash. She rose to rush to Jake's room, her pulse thumping with fright. Too well, she could remember plunging through the creek that poured into the Jeep. With the rain, they were trapped between the lake and the creek and both were rising. She shook her fist in the dark, anger momentarily replacing fear.

"Jake!" she whispered, entering his room.

He lay sprawled on his stomach in bed, his face turned toward her. She called louder, "Jake!"

To her consternation he didn't move a muscle. She shook him and the moment she touched his warm shoulder, all her fears evaporated like fog beneath a July sun.

He stirred and rolled over, his eyes coming open. Molly had a sudden urge to get back to her room, but then Jake focused on her and she felt trapped and held by invisible hands, mired down by eyes darkened in shadow. She knew he was fully awake and aware of her. His chest was bare, and the sheet rode low across his hips. She fought the temptation to let her eyes wander down, but she lost the battle; her gaze encompassed Jake's broad tapering chest. Then lightning flashed and his body was illuminated, indelibly stamped into her memory, muscle and bone and warm silvered flesh. Her gaze moved lower. With the sheet across his loins, his arousal was as obvious as the rain against the windows, and Molly felt as if she were standing on a burning pyre.

"Molly," he croaked hoarsely, and reached out to catch her wrist. She felt the slightest tug and then she was in bed, held in warm, strong arms, pressed against his bare flesh. The nightgown and sheet between them offered a negligible barrier.

"Jake, wait a minute," she gasped, trying to hold on to sanity, but bombarded by sensations. He rolled over and she found herself on her back, Jake's arms around her, his virile body pressing against her, his legs entwined with hers. He was nude, warm, and strong and her heart felt as if it might burst from pounding. She placed her hands against Jake's chest, fighting the urge to wind her arms around his neck, fighting overwhelming urges that made her want to cling to him, to forget logic and caution.

"Molly, oh, sweet Molly," he murmured in his deep voice, kissing bare skin above the scooped neck of her nightie.

"Jake, it's . . . raining."

He laughed softly as his lips trailed lower, pushing at the elasticized neckline. "Who cares if it rains?"

Lightning flashed as he pushed the gown away and his lips found her nipple. Molly gasped, her hips writhing with need, thrusting against him, feeling his hardness. "Jake, please!" she whispered, sensing she was losing everything she held important. Some deep instinct warned that if she succumbed to Jake Cannon, she would hand him her heart and forever after be doomed to roam the earth no longer a whole person.

She pushed harder and he paused. Swiftly, she stood up, breathing heavily, her emotions as tangled as her gown. He rolled over, placing his hands behind his head while he studied her. His voice was flat and controlled, but she detected his anger.

"Why did you come in and wake me, Molly?"

"That's what I've been trying to tell you! It's raining and the lake is rising."

He muttered an expletive, then said, "Turn your back. I'm nude."

The word was as volatile as his touch. She had known he was nude, but to have him say it conjured up an instant vision and instant recall of the press of his body against hers. She felt her heart begin to thud violently again while she turned her back to him and moved away a few feet. She heard clothes rustle and in seconds he passed her to go to the window.

"Well, hell, Molly, it's not much higher."

She stared at him, outlined against the windows, his hands on his hips, jeans low slung, his chest bare. She found herself far more conscious of Jake than of animals from the lake, and she couldn't talk. But she went to stand beside him and point out the window, wanting him to know why she had gotten him up in the middle of the night. "Jake, there are little animals coming to the house to get away from the water. Watch when there's lightning."

He stood quietly. Every nerve in her body was aware of his proximity and her lungs refused to function normally.

"Where?" he asked.

When she moved closer to the window, he stepped beside her, warmth from his body radiating against her. Lightning flashed and she pointed. "There! See, down there, something is coming to the house from the lake—are they rats or skunks or what?"

"You woke me up for that?" he asked, staring at her, feeling a hungry, fiery need and clenching his fists to keep from reaching for her. Was she a tease . . . or truly frightened of the lake rising and animals seeking shelter at the house? He knew the answer as swiftly as the question occurred, but it didn't smooth his ruffled nerves.

"They won't come get in bed with you, Molly."

"But…" she sputtered, turning to face him, "do you want the house full of furry creatures? And what about the lake rising?" she asked, suddenly feeling ridiculous.

"Scared? You?"

"I just don't want to share my room with skunks and coons and possums and turtles and snakes!"

"Want to share it with me?"

"Dammit, Jake! The lake's rising, the boats are down in the water where we can't get to them—what do we do if it keeps raining?"

"We'll get back in the Jeep," he said, far more calmly than he felt, but it wasn't the rising lake that disturbed him. Another flash of lightning revealed Molly standing little more than a foot away, her hair disheveled, her scoop-necked nightgown slipped low on one shoulder, her legs bare. He fought the impulse to step closer to her.

"And go where?" she persisted.

"There'll be high ground between here and the creek," he said, savoring his reaction to her in his bed.

"So we go down to eat breakfast tomorrow with all kinds of animals?"

"Do you have another suggestion?" he asked coolly. "If you don't, I'm going back to bed."

"You'll just lie down and go back to sleep—suppose the house gets flooded?"

"You'll wake me."

"I should've known better," she murmured and turned toward the door. Angry and aroused, he stood watching her go. A bolt of brilliant blue-white lightning flashed with a pop and crack, making Molly gasp and jump. Then a clap of thunder rattled the windows like stones in a tin can. His eyes lowered swiftly over her long, bare legs; he ached for her and realized he should have been more patient with her. He sighed and went back to bed, but it was impossible to sleep. With total recall he could conjure up the feeling of Molly in his arms, her legs against his, her softness pressed to him, the first moment he had opened his eyes and found her beside his bed. He groaned and flopped over on his side, glaring at the door.

"Furry creatures!"

FIGHTING HER WAY UP out of the depths of sleep, Molly became conscious of a rapping noise. She was too tired to open her eyes. Instead, she tried to sort out the possible sources.

"Molly! It's time to rise and shine!"

She pulled the pillow over her head and turned toward the voice. "Go away."

"Molly!"

The voice was closer and so filled with cheer she had the urge to scream, but it would have taken too much effort. "Go away!" she muttered again and turned her head, pulling the pillow down tightly over her ears.

Something tugged the pillow up. "Molly, I brought you the broom and a glass of orange juice."

"You're just doing this because I woke you in the night!" she mumbled and buried her head deeper under the pillow. Once again, a corner of the pillow was pulled from her grasp and Jake's revoltingly sunny voice said, "I'll put the orange juice here on the table."

She opened her eyes and stared into gray ones only inches away. "I don't believe you," she mumbled.

"You agreed. I cook and you sweep."

"I will in a few hours from now. Get out of my room, Jake."

"What a doll you are in the morning! I'm surprised Garvin gave you a ring."

It took too much effort to answer him. She tugged down the pillow and closed her eyes, drifting back to sleep.

"Molly!" The pillow was snatched away. "We made a deal. Get out of that bed."

She opened her eyes and glared at him, turning on her back and holding the sheet to her chin, her fists locked on it. "I'm sleepy, I'm on vacation; I didn't sign a contract with you."

"A deal's a deal. I could've dumped you out of the car on the way down here, but I didn't. You can nap this afternoon—I don't have you scheduled for anything between noon and half-past one. Here's our morning program: you sweep the downstairs while I fix breakfast. You clean the kitchen while I get the boats. You continue sweeping the house while I start repairs on the windows and screens. You fix lunch. I'll clean the kitchen and then we'll launch into the afternoon program. Now, wake up. I let you sleep while I showered and dressed, so you've had extra shut-eye time."

"You are not putting me on a schedule. That's why I live alone and went into business for myself—to do as I please. Particularly," she emphasized "in the morning!"

"Time you learned a little discipline. It makes things run smoother and increases profits."

"We're not in business here," she argued, becoming more irritated and more awake and, in spite of her annoyance, more aware of Jake's appealing presence.

"You'll learn some new habits that will revitalize your life," he said, his voice tinged with laughter.

"Revitalize my life!" she growled in a low tone of voice that would have scattered her family out of Molly's sight in seconds.

"Here's the broom. Now, don't roll over and go back to sleep."

She glared in silence, loath to make the effort to talk. But she noticed Jake in his tight jeans and T-shirt, and became conscious of her sleepy appearance and the tangle of red hair hanging over one of her eyes.

He propped the broom against the bed, leaned down to brush the lock away from her face, and smiled at her. "See you downstairs in a few minutes."

"I like to wake up in my own good time at a normal hour," she said slowly and clearly. She suspected he was holding back a grin.

"You'll thank me later. We can get worlds done." He laughed softly and left, closing the door quietly behind him.

Molly moaned and slipped lower in bed. The next thing she heard was Jake's voice. "Molly, I told you—breakfast will be ready, and I don't want it to go to waste."

She started to groan, pulling the sheet off her head as she rolled over.

Jake watched her a moment, desire a steady torment. She was disheveled, warm from sleep, and he wanted to crawl into bed with her and pull her close. His eyes roamed the sweet curve of her hip, and the long length of her legs, and then he sighed. His strong arms swept beneath her, gathering the sheet and Molly as he lifted her up.

Molly screeched and pushed against his chest, coming fully awake. "Dammit, Jake Cannon Soundmaster, put me down!" she yelled, noticing a nice scent, his warmth, his merry eyes.

Laughing, he set her on her feet in the hall. Then he leaned down to her eye level. "Are you awake now?"

She shook her fist at him. "Listen here, Mister, I didn't agree to get up at dawn and schedule my life to suit you!"

"It isn't dawn, and I need your help," he answered calmly.

"I'll be glad to give it to you at ten o'clock."

"I can't wait."

She held the sheet around her and shook her head in exasperation. "Now I'm awake!" she snapped accusingly.

"Good," he said with maddening cheer. "See you at breakfast. How long will it take before you're downstairs?"

She wanted to retort, "Two hours!" and go back to bed, but grim reality had set in. "I exercise before I eat breakfast."

"Whoops! After this I'll get you up earlier."

"How about fixing breakfast later?"

"Nope. The day's a-wasting. You can exercise later. How long before you'll be downstairs?"

"Twenty minutes."

"Good. Breakfast will be almost ready. Smell the bacon now?"

Frowning, she started for the bedroom. A long arm shot out, blocking her way, and she spun around to look up at sparkling gray eyes. He winked and leaned close. "You look adorable in the morning," he told her, with that husky voice that made her come alert in every pore. "In spite of your grizzly-bear nature," he added softly.

She wanted to glare. She was still sleepy, and it was dawn to her, but she couldn't resist smiling at him. "You are a toad—a long-legged, grey-eyed, fork-tongued toad to come pull me out of bed!"

"Sure," he said, as he touched the tip of her nose. "But you're not really angry if you're smiling."

She threw up her hands because it was impossible to resist smiling back at him. She heard his deep chuckle as she went into her room and closed the door. She glanced at the clock and yelped, turning to glower at the closed door. "I'm going to show you how to revitalize *your* life, Jake Cannon!" she mumbled as she threw on her jeans and sweatshirt.

CHAPTER EIGHT

MOLLY PAUSED in the kitchen doorway, observing Jake's T-shirt pulling across his shoulders as he reached to a top shelf. As if a silent message had been delivered he turned to look at her over his shoulder. She entered the room, embarrassed she had been caught staring at him.

"Good morning," he said with mocking amusement.

"It is now." As he laughed, she said cheerily, "Let me help." She picked up the platter of bacon and eggs to carry them to the table on the porch and returned to the kitchen to get the pot of coffee. Jake blocked her way, suddenly hemming her into a corner between the counter and himself.

She caught the trace of the nice scent she had smelled when he was holding her. He was inches away and memories of kisses, of the brief moments in his arms during the night, tugged at her senses.

"Forgive me for waking you?"

"Absolutely not! I'm not a morning person. I have great difficulty handling getting up at dawn."

He laughed. "Molly it isn't dawn. *I* got up at dawn, not you, lazybones!"

"I'll remind you about all this when it gets to be midnight tonight! Then it'll be a different story, I suspect."

"I haven't folded up early on you yet," he said.

"No, but we haven't gotten up at . . . dawn. I know it was dawn. I haven't seen the sun at that angle in years!" While she talked, he kept leaning closer and with each inch, the temperature in the kitchen seemed to jump a notch.

"Maybe we should start over," he whispered. "Good morning . . ."

"You can't—" she murmured, inhaling the inviting scent, but this time she smelled only smoke. Her eyes flew open and she pushed on his chest. "Jake, there's a fire!"

"You're not kidding!" he drawled, reaching for her.

"No, look, the toaster!"

He turned his head, straightened up and yanked the toaster cord out of the wall. He swore while he beat out the flames. "Damned old thing never did work right!"

She smiled, watching him, wanting the kiss she had just missed. She helped him carry the rest of the food to the table, and while they ate, Molly asked, "What happened to the furry creatures?"

"They were outside on the steps or under the porch, except for a coon I found on the porch. He was glad to go. You're safe."

"I don't care to share the house with them."

"You don't like pets?"

"Oh, sure, that's different. I have two cats. My neighbor will feed them while I'm gone. Cats adjust and you can move around and take them with you," she said, between bites of golden toast.

"Where have you lived?"

"I was born in Los Angeles and from there, you name it."

"You're not kidding, are you? Have you lived in Texas? Missouri? Arizona?"

"All three. At last count, I've lived in fourteen states."

He placed his fork on his plate and stared at her. "The only place I've lived is Detroit."

She shrugged. "The world is interesting."

"Yeah. How'd you settle in Detroit?"

"Mother was there and got divorced the second time and wanted me to come be with her. I did, she met a man, married, moved to Akron, and I stayed in Detroit."

"Do you go around picking up the pieces when your relatives' marriages fall apart?"

"Yes. They always need someone." She finished the last bite of crisp, thin bacon.

"And you don't need anyone, Molly?" he asked, suddenly solemn and curious.

Her breathing stopped when she saw the questioning in his eyes. "Of course, I do," she said, carefully avoiding his direct gaze. "Everyone needs other people sometimes. I just don't need them as intensely or as often." She didn't add that she didn't want to need someone either, because all her mother and sister had ever gained was disappointment and hurt.

"Have you ever been deeply in love?" he asked quietly.

She remembered the anguish in his face as he had paced his bedroom yesterday. She shook her head slowly. "I guess not like you've been."

Something changed in the depths of his eyes and she wondered whether it was satisfaction or disbelief. She felt an urgent need to change the subject of conversation to a topic other than her. "What was your life like when you were growing up?" she asked.

His voice hardened when he answered. "We were dirt poor," he said, glad the memories were diminishing. "As a little kid I did odd jobs; when I was nine I threw papers. We lived in a slum and I fought my way through school."

"Is that how you got a crook in your nose?"

He smiled and his voice eased. "Yes, it is."

"Where's your family now?"

"Dad's no longer living; Mom's in an apartment and she works in a little gift shop on a part-time basis. Thank heavens I've been able to help with her expenses."

"And your brother?"

"Ben is younger—only twenty-six. He's a teller at a bank in Ames, Iowa."

"How'd he get to Iowa?"

"On a basketball scholarship to Iowa State. Then he just stayed. I've tried to get him to come to work with me, but he says he's no salesman."

"Did he major in accounting in college?"

Jake laughed. "No—history. He wanted to be a history professor, but the only job he could find when he graduated was the teller's job, so he took it. A job's a job."

"Yeah, I know," she said. "That's why Ivy and I dance."

While Jake talked, he pulled out a paper to look at his list. He drew lines through some items, glancing at her. "I'll change the schedule. I'll help you clean the kitchen. This afternoon we'll try to go to Springfield and talk to the police."

"Why not just go to Hattersville?"

Jake shook his head. "I'd rather that word about us and the computer chip didn't go all over Hattersville."

"Look at how high the lake is—we'll never get through the creek."

"It'll go down fast with a sunny day."

"I don't know how Garvin or Ivy or Ben will get here. There really isn't a road."

"Ben's been here before. Let's hope no one else finds us. Someone wants that chip badly."

Once again her gaze swept the woods. At moments, the forest seemed inviting, and at other moments filled with sinister hiding places. "They might want it badly enough to hunt until they locate us."

"Yeah, but just hope they're still scouring Springfield for us."

She watched him write and asked, "Do you make those lists every day?"

He grinned. "Sure. That's why the Soundmaster Stores are so successful." He waved the slip of paper at her. "Organization and goals."

"Well, the mere sight of them immobilizes me. You can't see the sunrise for looking at your list."

"I see the sunrise," he said firmly, convinced she had to be a lousy businesswoman. "Don't you have goals?"

"No. Tomorrow is like the wind—who can predict it?"

"Well, hell . . . you have to have goals!"

"You keep your goals—I'll take appreciating the moment, enjoying the lake. Something you might try sometime."

After narrowing his eyes, he tossed down his pen and turned in his chair to look at the lake. Mist hovered over the water along the eastern side where the surface was still shaded by trees and the slope of the land; in the center it was bright, silvery clear in the expectancy of the new day.

Molly drew a deep breath, relishing the crisp air and speculating on whether Jake had gone from working as a child to working as an adult without ever truly learning how to play. He wasn't miserly or he wouldn't have rented the Lincoln, but he might not ever have learned how to appreciate some of the joys in life. Yet he was capable of it, because there were moments when she had glimpsed a different sort of Jake. She remembered his exuberance when he had driven through the woods and his lusty singing from an opera. She inhaled deeply, trying to get her thoughts off the dilemma of Jake Cannon.

The stillness and freshness of the countryside was breathtaking and satisfied a deep, inner need. On the surface of the lake oaks were reflected in shadowy streaks, and she was busy contemplating what lived below the still surface when Jake pushed back his chair with a scrape and broke into her reverie. "Shall we get started?" he asked.

Without waiting for her answer, he carried dishes into the kitchen. With one more wistful glance at the lake, she gathered all she could carry and went inside to help clean the kitchen. When they finished, Jake said, "I'm going to bring wood from the woodpile up to the porch so we'll have some for fires. You—"

Before he could give her a job, she interrupted him, wanting to stay outside and avoid the sweeping job she knew was on the list. "It's lovely outside. I'll help you move wood and you'll finish twice as fast."

"You can't carry wood."

Her head came up and she asked in a quiet voice, "Why can't I?"

"It's heavy—Okay, come on," he said, and made a notation on the slip of paper that caused Molly to groan inwardly. She couldn't imagine life ordered by lists, but she forced herself to bide her time and cooperate.

Jake gave her a pair of work gloves, pulled some on his hands and began to pile logs in his arms to carry to the porch. Molly knew what he'd started to say, that the wood was too heavy for her to carry... Mr. Jake Canon needed to realize that she was in good physical shape and she hadn't gotten that way by organizing her life around a list! She piled logs in her arms and jogged to the porch, passing Jake on the way. He speeded up his gait and in minutes they were working with far more speed than necessary and carrying the maximum loads in a silent, challenging competition. And in a short time, she felt satisfaction in knowing she was moving as much wood as Jake. He narrowed his eyes and observed her as she jogged to the woodpile.

Jake watched her bend over, the jeans pulling across the swell of her rounded bottom. He was hot and had to exert effort to keep up with her. He resolved he would start exercises again. He hadn't realized what the daily grind at the office had done to his muscles and it annoyed him to watch Molly. He felt a constant friction and sparks from being around her, and the kind of sparks that ignited fires and the kind of friction that made him silently challenge her and answer her challenges.

She piled on another log and smiled at him, turning toward the house, moving at a trot, and jiggling her bottom just enough to tease. He nearly stumbled over a stick because he hadn't been watching his step. She put the wood on the porch and came back, passing

Jake in seconds with another armload. Sweat beaded his forehead, and his determination grew to get back in shape. Only a few years ago carrying wood would have been a breeze instead of a chore. In minutes he put his hand on her arm. "Leave that," he ordered, and took a deep breath. "We have enough."

"Okay," she said, dumping an armload back on the pile and turning to smile at him.

"I'm really out of shape," he admitted.

"You've spent too much time studying lists," she said blithely. "I'll go sweep."

Jake wanted to give that cute derriere a swat, but he knew she was right. As soon as some of his jobs were done—exercise!

Molly hurried away, her back tingling. At the top of the steps, as she reached for the screen door, she looked over her shoulder. Jake stood frowning, hands on his hips while he watched her, and she wondered what was running through his mind.

Later, as she heard Jake hammering outside, she began to work inside, continuing to make the house habitable. Finally, she paused to survey the rustic living room with its brown vinyl sofa and chairs, and approved the choice of furniture that wouldn't be harmed by wet swimsuits or sand. The pine living room was plain, but clean and pleasant; an oval braided rug sat in the center of the oak floor. Next, she folded and put away the laundry until her watch indicated half-past eleven. Then she changed to her blue shorts and a T-shirt because the day was warming as the sun climbed high overhead.

In the living room, she pushed the furniture aside to make room to exercise. She did calisthenics, then went into aerobics, dancing to silent tunes in her head. In the midst of twirling in a circle, swinging her leg high in a kick, she stopped, startled to find Jake in the doorway watching her, a hungry look in his eyes that was impossible to misread. He was wringing wet, his shirt was off, his feet bare, his dark hair was plastered to his head and mud streaked his shoulder and arm.

"What happened to you?" she asked, trying to pull her gaze from his bare chest.

"I've brought the boats up from the boat house. The room looks nice," he said, though his eyes were glued only on her in his direct way. "What are you doing?"

"I'm exercising," she answered, amused because he knew full well what she was doing. "I told you, I have to practice if I don't want to get rusty before I go back to work."

"Rusty, huh?" he asked, his eyes conveying things that should have caused any rust to melt away. "Did you finish the front porch?"

"Nope," she said, beginning to touch her toes. "I'm exercising and enjoying the Ozarks for the next few hours. You can put that on your list."

"Molly—"

"You know if you exercised, you wouldn't get quite so winded with exertion. Want to exercise with me?" she asked, swinging her leg in a high kick.

"Look, if we'd work together, we could get the chores done and then it will be all relaxation."

She stopped a moment, putting her hands on her hips. "Jake, the vacation will be over by then. This is a big house and the jobs could go on until New Year's. I've worked hard all morning—"

"I know you have and thank you."

"You don't have to thank me, but I intend to enjoy part of the day."

He shrugged and went upstairs and Molly finished her exercises, unaware of when he came back through the room until she heard the hammer going outside again.

After her exercises, she went upstairs to change. On the landing she paused to glance at the lake out the east window of the house, and was surprised to see Jake doing push-ups down below, his tools on the grass nearby.

She laughed and observed him a moment, noticing muscles flex and bulge in his arms and legs below navy shorts. With his long legs and trim buttocks he didn't look one bit out of shape. He stood up and yanked off his shirt, then began knee bends. Molly leaned both elbows on the window to watch him.

Later, as they were finishing the lunch cleanup, Jake's head cocked to one side. "Listen..."

Molly heard the grind of a motor and drew a sharp breath. "Those men..."

"Lock the kitchen door; I'll get the front and I'm going up to get my gun."

CHAPTER NINE

MOLLY'S HEART LURCHED with fear; she locked the back door, eyeing the window in the upper half of it, and acknowledged that the door wouldn't keep out anyone who was strong and determined. She propped a chair beneath the knob and hurried to the front, looking helplessly at the long, wide windows on either side of the front door.

Jake came down without a noise, and she didn't know he was there until she turned around. She gasped in surprise.

"Sorry. I didn't mean to startle you. Don't stand in front of a window," he said tersely, moving to one side of another window, and lifting the curtain a fraction to peer out.

"Sounds like a Jeep," he said quietly.

"The creek must be down enough to cross," Molly said, her mouth dry as wool.

"Here they come," Jake said and raised the gun, releasing the safety.

Detesting the big gun in Jake's hand, and doubly aware of their isolation, Molly turned to ice.

The roar of an engine climbing the hill could be heard. Then the sound changed as the vehicle crested the hill and came down the slope to the house. "It's just one guy in a Jeep," Jake said, lowering the gun.

"You don't think it's one of them?" Molly asked, hurrying to the other side of the window to lift the curtain and peer out.

"I don't think they'd drive right up to the front door to pay us a call," Jake said dryly.

"Oh, my word!" Molly said, looking outside. "It's Garvin."

Jake swore, putting the safety on the gun. As he did, Molly went to the door and Jake followed her outside, tucking the gun into the waistband of his shorts. Curiosity plagued him; and he stared at Garvin. Surprise and consternation mixed when he beheld a man few women would want to break an engagement with. By anyone's standards the fellow was handsome. Blond, with deeply tanned skin, Garvin Yates was dressed in wheat-colored jeans and a tan T-shirt that revealed impressive shoulders and muscles. Jake felt more out of shape than ever. And Molly became more of an enigma to him. Why would she break the engagement over fear of commitment? The guy in the Jeep ought to have melted any such flimsy resistance and the diamond she had been wearing in Detroit was a large hunk of ice.

"Introduce me and I'll vanish," Jake said, watching her to see how eagerly she greeted Garvin.

"You don't need to leave. We'll go somewhere in his Jeep where we can talk."

"Hell, Molly, I'll go down and work on the boathouse. It's in bad shape from the high water."

"Fine," she said absentmindedly.

Garvin stopped and Molly went down the steps. Jake stood rooted to the spot, hating to watch, unable to go. She walked around the Jeep and Garvin stepped out. He was tall and towered over Molly. He reached for her, hugging her briefly, and they gazed solemnly at each other. She said something to him and he turned to look at Jake.

They came around the Jeep. "Garvin, this is Jake Cannon—remember Mr. Soundmaster on television? Jake, this is Garvin Yates."

Jake wished she hadn't brought up Mr. Soundmaster. He shook hands, feeling Garvin's brief, hard clasp as he looked into cold, blue eyes. The man was as handsome as Redford, and it was difficult for Jake to smile and keep his voice casual.

"Nice to meet you," he lied, wishing Garvin would vanish like a puff of smoke. "I've got a few chores down by the lake, and I know you came to see Molly."

Garvin merely nodded and returned his attention to Molly, placing his arm around her waist and pulling her closer to him.

Jake turned on his heel to put the gun away in the kitchen. He tried to stop listening to their voices, but he could hear Garvin's deep rumble, and Molly's higher voice as they came into the house and Molly offered Garvin coffee.

Jake hurried out of the house and down across the lawn, unaware he was sloshing through water until it was up to his thighs and he bogged down. He reached the boat house and climbed up on a shelf to work on a broken window, nailing a piece of plastic over it to keep out the rain until he could replace the plastic with glass.

"Garvin Yates," he muttered, pounding the hammer. He paused, staring out the door toward the house, startled to realize he was in knots over Molly's talking to Garvin. "Damn!" he muttered, knowing he shouldn't care. Molly and he didn't have anything going between them. He had his life, she had hers, and they were totally opposite. Then why was his stomach churning? He felt like pacing up and down and he wanted to run back to the house and tell Garvin Yates to get into his Jeep and go.

Jake returned to hammering until he realized he had nailed the plastic over the end of the shelf as well as the window. With a snort of disgust, he tossed the hammer down so hard it slid across the shelf, struck the wall and dropped with a plop into the water covering the floor of the boat house.

Swearing steadily, Jake climbed down and felt around until he retrieved it. He put his hands on his hips and stared at the house. He shouldn't care! Dammit, he shouldn't care, but he did.

He sloshed around the boat house, mumbling about women. "I don't care," he said aloud. "Molly Ashland doesn't mean a thing to me!" The words had a hollow ring and he knew it. He glared at the house. "Molly," he said softly, memories tugging at him, beading his brow with perspiration. For so long now he had walked around like a hollow man who had no heart, no feelings. With Molly he was beginning to feel alive again.

He shook his head, debating silently with himself. Of all women to get entangled with—a woman who would break an engagement to a man who left nothing to be desired . . .

Gloom and wariness settled on Jake. He'd better watch out or he'd really be suffering over her, he decided. She hadn't been talking idly when she'd said she wasn't ready for commitment. For someone who was so attuned to life in many ways, she was afraid to let go and take chances.

Fuming over the complexities of human beings, particularly one redheaded female human being, he sat down on a barrel just inside the doorway of the boat house, where he could watch the house. His feet were immersed in water, but Jake was oblivious of minnows swimming around him as he sat and waited and looked at his watch too many times to count.

The back door finally opened and she stepped outside.

Jake sloshed out and swam and waded back to the house, noticing that the lake had gone down a fraction since their arrival.

He couldn't tell a thing from her expression as she stood watching him walk up from the lake.

"Garvin's gone. You can come home now."

"Okay."

She smiled at him. "Thanks for letting us be alone."

"Let's go sit on the step while I dry and we can talk," he suggested.

She walked up the slope with him in silence, then sank down on a step. Jake sat on a lower one and turned to face her, propping his elbow on his upraised knee.

"It's over," she said, and he felt an enormous, overwhelming relief. But also, he was more puzzled than ever by her.

"Are you sad?"

She slanted a quick look at him and then turned away. "No. Garvin and I were really just good friends all along. We liked the same things, we had fun together. But friends—" she paused and her voice dropped "—doesn't mean lovers," she explained in such a low voice he barely heard her. Barely. He did hear, and both relief and surprise shook him.

"Isn't that kind of unusual to get an engagement ring for friendship?"

"We both thought maybe it would develop into something else," she said, looking away, and he suddenly suspected Garvin had hoped it would develop into something else.

"I'm glad," Jake said with far less emotion than he felt. He sat in silence, relishing the warm sun heating his skin after being in cold water, and still trying to puzzle out Molly and Garvin's strange relationship. Had he interpreted her statement correctly?

"Jake, Garvin said he stopped at the General Store in Hattersville and asked how to get here."

"Damn, I thought you gave him directions."

"I did, but the woods are confusing. He said the men in the store told him he was the second one to stop and ask."

"Oh, no!" Jake muttered, new worries surfacing as swiftly as the old had faded. "When did that happen?"

"They said two men were in this morning. They couldn't help the men or Garvin. The fellows in the store didn't remember you and don't know which house you're in."

"Thank heavens for that!" He squinted his eyes at her in the glare of the sun. "How'd he find us then?"

"My directions. He just wanted to double-check."

"Oh, damn, I hope no one followed him."

"I asked if he saw anyone who seemed interested in him or followed him, and he said no. He said it was hard to find this house even with directions."

"We need to get rid of the computer chip." They sat in silence for a time while Jake thought back over the morning, questions plaguing him.

"Molly," he said quietly, "Garvin Yates is as hand-some as an actor, and I take it he's successful in busi-ness. He wants you...he doesn't have any vices you've mentioned.... I don't understand how you could break off with him."

Green eyes widened, seeming to darken to the color of churning seawater. "How could I plan to marry Garvin when I react to your kisses the way I do?" she asked in a gentle voice that seemed to stop his blood pumping through his veins.

"Oh, Lord, Molly—" He moved to the step beside her and reached for her.

She scooted a few inches away. "Jake...I just told Garvin goodbye," she whispered.

He withdrew his hand, fighting the effect her words had had on him, studying her, yet trying not to stare.

"Jake, I don't want you to misunderstand me..."

He looked at her, noting the hesitation in her voice, and the pink in her cheeks, and he realized Molly Ash-land was a complicated woman. She had accused him of being complicated—he was bare-ground simple compared to her. He sat silently, suddenly feeling as if he were treading on eggshells. One wrong move and he would destroy everything.

"You and I have enormous differences" she contin-ued, "but I don't usually respond *physically* to men the way I have to you and I don't want you to think I'm always so..." Her voice trailed off as she waved her hand in the air.

"What are you trying to say?" he asked quietly, holding his breath.

Green eyes slanted a look at him, but he couldn't tell what was running through her mind. "I don't usually respond as strongly or eagerly as I have to you," she whispered and looked away quickly, the pink in her cheeks darkening.

He thought his heart would burst through his chest for the pounding and he wanted to reach out and yank Molly back into his arms, but he jammed his hands into his wet pockets and forced himself to sit still. He knew now was not the time for the wrong move on his part. He suspected Molly had opened herself up to him in a way she never had with a man.

"You're very special, Molly," he said gently, hoping he could convey some of his feelings for her without discouraging her from trusting him.

They sat wordlessly and he felt vastly better than he had for the past couple of hours. He smiled, looked at the blue sky and noticed what a nice sunny day it was. "Well, the creek must have gone down. I'm going to change clothes. Do you want to drive into Springfield with me to tell them about the computer chip? We can eat dinner there."

"Sure, but I'll have to change." He smiled, stood up, and offered his hand, pulling her to her feet while he controlled the impulse to wrap his arms around her and tell her how relieved he was.

In ten minutes, dressed in her red skirt and a clean white blouse, she came downstairs to find Jake waiting in his suit and tie and looking very handsome.

"This is all I have except jeans and shorts," Molly said, wishing she had something different to wear for him.

"You look great," he said with such intensity, she felt it wasn't a casual compliment; his words warmed her all over.

Two hours later, they were seated in the office of the Chief of Police of Springfield. He handed a phone to

Jake, who talked long distance to a detective in Detroit. Molly followed the conversation, wishing they were out of the police station and back at the house in the woods. She'd sensed disapproval from the moment the authorities had learned she and Jake had fled the scene.

Jake replaced the receiver and turned to Chief Wierman. "A detective will fly down here this afternoon and get in tonight. We're to meet him here in the morning at ten o'clock. In the meantime, I'm to leave the chip with you for safekeeping."

"You're not going back to Detroit tomorrow?"

"No. He said we'd discuss that when he gets here," Jake answered, flicking a glance at Molly. His eyes were gray, darker than usual, and when he dropped his gaze from hers swiftly, she knew there was trouble of some kind. In minutes they were ushered out. The sun sent slanting shadows across the sidewalk as they climbed into the car.

"Whoo! Am I glad to leave that little chip behind! I'd just as soon carry a million dollars in cold cash," Jake said. "The Springfield police were less than happy with us."

"I imagine the feeling is the same in Detroit. What happened? What did they tell you on the phone?"

"You're right. They're not happy with us in Detroit for leaving the scene. I reminded the Detroit detectives there must be a dozen good witnesses."

"And what did he say?"

"He sounded cynical and angry as a pinched bumblebee. I got a lecture about leaving the scene—I think a bigger lecture may come tomorrow."

"Jake, there's a policeman standing on the steps frowning at us. Can we go?"

"Gladly. Keep your eyes open for trouble. I just wish the men following us knew I'd left the computer chip at the station."

"It might not matter," she said solemnly. "You and I are first-hand witnesses. And Brantz?"

"No news there. They wouldn't tell me a thing." He smiled at her. "I asked two of Springfield's finest where the best place in town is to eat. We're on our way."

Jake drove to The Bicycle Club on Battlefield, where they sat in the solarium and ordered sizzling *fajitas*. The delicious odor of thin strips of grilled green peppers, onions and beef tempted Molly, but she was more interested in Jake than in food. As they ate, they talked about their pasts, their likes and their dislikes. Once again, Jake was relaxed and fun, far different from the hard-working, all-business type he could so easily become.

Molly set down a cup of coffee, tilting her head to study him. "I think I'd better tell you a little about Ivy. I had a picture of her in my purse, but that's gone. She has an effect on men."

Jake's brows arched a fraction. "What kind of effect?"

"Ivy's very pretty."

"I thought you said she was a quiet little thing and I wouldn't notice her being underfoot."

"I exaggerated a little. She looks sort of on the order of Loni Anderson."

Jake grinned. "Do tell." He sat back in the chair and crossed his ankles. "You two get crossways over men?"

"Never. Oh, there've been some guys I dated until they met Ivy, and then they dated Ivy, but no one I was really upset about. Ivy and I get along. Actually, she depends on me too much for me to get aggravated with her, and no man has been worth losing my sister's friendship over."

"Do tell," he said again, drawing the expression out as if he had discovered something of great significance. "Well, Ivy's looks will be lost on brother Ben. My brother is an anachronism in the modern world. He's a shy man."

"I think that's rather sweet."

"That's because you're not dating him. It's a turn-off for women who date him. I do have his picture and Jamie's." He pulled out his wallet, flipped it open and leaned over the table. "Here's Jamie when she was a day old," he said, and his voice developed the same tenderness she'd noticed when he had talked about his daughter before. He turned the picture and Molly saw a tall, slender, smiling, black-haired woman holding a baby. "That's Sheryl and Jamie," he said and his voice became gruffer.

Molly examined the picture opposite, a close-up of his wife, who had large brown eyes and beautiful, delicate features. He flipped to the next pictures. "Here's Ben with Jamie."

Molly studied the photo. Jamie looked about two and had a mop of black curls. A tall, slender brown-haired man held her hand. He looked young, almost a teen; a lock of straight brown hair tumbled over his blue eyes. He had a slender face and a long, lanky build.

"He's nice looking. How can he be good-looking and shy?"

"I've always wondered that too, but Ben is." Jake flipped the billfold closed and slipped it back into his hip pocket. "I guess we never had time to learn how to socialize when we were growing up, and then Ben didn't date much when he was in college, so he's still damned shy. He's about six feet, nine inches."

"Oh, my goodness!"

Jake grinned. "Otherwise, you might not know he's around. He's sort of bookish."

"Well, he and Ivy will have something in common there. Ivy likes bookkeeping and she likes to read and the men she attracts aren't interested in those things one whit. Except she probably won't notice anyone—she's been through an ordeal with Willis. They've only been married nine months."

"Nine months is too long if he's physically abusive," Jake said brusquely.

"I agree, but she thought she was really in love this time and she had such hopes. Then, he began to get violent. She tried to stick it out, but . . ."

"She should have packed and gone after the first time. I don't have much use for men like that."

"She's really upset this time. This is the second marriage to fail. The first marriage, the guy was alcoholic, but lots of fun when he was sober." As Jake shook his head, Molly said, "Ivy has a weakness for men."

"A weakness you don't have," Jake said with a grin.

"Not to the extent Ivy does." Molly's smile faded. "Ivy's like Cinderella, always searching for Prince Charming to solve all her problems. And she's always disappointed."

"Is that what you're afraid of, Molly? Disappointment?" he asked solemnly, startling her. Jake tried to keep his voice casual, but he watched her fingers suddenly begin to fidget with the silverware, and he guessed he had touched on a nerve with his assessment.

"Maybe so," she said stiffly. "Did Ben have as many fights growing up?"

Aware she was turning the conversation from herself, Jake gave her a level gaze; he had his own vulnerable spots he didn't like to discuss either. His voice was flat as he answered, "No, I don't think so. He's six years younger than I am and I fought for him. And then, thank heavens, when I went to college, Mom moved to a better neighborhood." He sipped his water, remembering the years he had tried to shut out of his memory. "My Dad was a dreamer, always planning big things, but he threw away any little bit of money he ever made and he wouldn't stick with any one job more than a few months at a time. He would get fired or he would become angry and quit. We had nothing. Mom never would say, but I think he gambled when he got a little cash. Anyway, it wore him down and he was an old man when I was a kid. He got pneumonia and didn't take care of himself and died," Jake said.

Molly listened, troubled by the harshness in his voice "I'm sorry."

He looked away as he said, "Soon after that I went to college on a basketball scholarship—"

"All that talk about you liking bookkeeping and me liking sports—you had an athletic scholarship!"

"Maybe I did, but I wasn't trying to hide it. It was in the past. I played a little basketball." He grinned. "Little enough to pay my way through college."

"Cheat! You wanted me to think you didn't like sports or know sports..." she accused, reassessing him and admitting that some of the differences between them were vanishing.

"Not at all. I'm just not into sports any longer. When I was in college, Mom was able to move to a small duplex, and Ben didn't have it so rough. It was still sort of poverty row, but the people were nice and it wasn't as tough an area." He turned his drinking glass slightly on the table, as if lost in thought until he said, "That's why I work hard, Molly. I don't ever want to be poor again."

"There's a difference though, between working hard and working so hard you can't enjoy life—especially if you have enough success to have a choice in the matter."

As he pushed back his chair to go, he smiled, but she knew he didn't agree with her view. They walked to the car, Jake's arm casually across her shoulders, their sides touching. She was conscious of each brush of his hip or leg because she was growing more intensely aware of him every hour they spent together.

They sang on the road going home, wind blowing through the Jeep and tangling Molly's hair. At the house they sat on the back porch and talked. As the evening grew late, Molly suspected Jake was as reluctant to part as she. His voice was a deep, steady rumble in the darkness, his hands drifted to her nape, stirring smoldering fires into flames, and finally, when he pulled her onto his lap, she wrapped her arms around his neck swiftly and returned his kisses with eagerness. The moment came when she knew she had to stop or neither of them would be able to. She scooted away, and stood up.

"I'd better go in now."

He stood too, dropping his hands on her waist. "Molly—" he drew her name out in a tone that played over her like a stormy wind, but she put her hands on his wrists and held him away.

"We'd better say good-night. I know what I can handle and what I can't. I'm afraid I can't cope with my emotions, Jake, if we continue. And I just told Garvin goodbye today. I don't want to get out of one entanglement and right into another."

"Ah, Molly. I don't want to let you go," he said, surprised at how intensely he didn't want her to leave. His own emotions seemed to be undergoing another upheaval.

"And I don't want to let you go," she said solemnly, "and that frightens me. Give me time to think."

Jake stared at her, recognizing that she was different from the women he knew, and becoming convinced that she was deeply afraid of commitment. He didn't want a lasting commitment either, but he didn't want to push Molly. If a woman was in his arms or in his bed, he wanted her there because she wanted to be there...not because he had overcome her arguments. And he knew now Molly was not one for casual relationships.

Together they walked upstairs. Molly couldn't breathe for wanting him, yet she was the one who had stopped their kisses downstairs and she knew she didn't dare start them until she had her own feelings more under control. And how difficult it was to heed wisdom!

"Night, gypsy," he whispered.

She smiled. "Night, Jake. Today's been fun."

"Yeah," he said and something flickered in the depths of his eyes.

"Jake, is everything all right?"

He met her gaze and smiled. "Sure, it's great. The house still needs a thousand repairs, thugs are after us, the police are unhappy with us, you have me tied in knots..." He threw up his hands. "Life's marvelous."

She smiled. "Look on the bright side. The house is livable and nice. The thugs can't find us. The police have the chip."

"And my knots?" he drawled, coming back to lean a hand on either side of her.

"They match mine," she whispered, losing her smile.

He leaned closer and she tilted her head up, unable to resist. "One kiss, gypsy... I promise."

She slipped her arms around his neck, clinging to him while she made the most of one kiss...one kiss that lingered and deepened until both of them had lost their breath. Jake stepped away abruptly.

"Night, Molly." he said and was gone swiftly, hurrying to his room and closing the door.

Molly drifted into her room and gathered her bathroom things, suddenly remembering what she had intended all evening to tell Jake and had forgotten. She stopped beside the connecting door. "Jake?"

"Yeah?" His voice came through the door.

"Don't wake me up in the morning."

"Night, Molly."

She frowned. "I mean it! Don't wake me."

"I heard you. Didn't you enjoy the morning after you were up?"

"No!"

"Tell the truth," he accused.

"Later, I didn't enjoy it until later. I'm going to shower. You want in the bathroom now?"

"No thanks. Go ahead," he said.

After her shower, once she was back in her room, she heard Jake's voice rise in song from his room. She smiled and placed a chair beneath the doorknob on the adjoining wall. Then she pushed the bedside table against the closed hall door and brushed the dust off her hands, satisfied Jake wouldn't disturb her morning sleep.

He was singing softly when she climbed into bed and turned out the light. After a few moments she joined him, and both of them sang until she stopped. Smiling, she turned over to stare at his door and listen to his deep voice. Drowsiness began to take away all thoughts until she heard his deep voice say, "Night, gypsy."

"Night, Jake."

"IT'S THAT TIME," called a deep, cajoling voice.

Molly felt as if she were fighting her way through a river of cotton. Hands shook her. "C'mon, gypsy. Time to get up and tackle today's chores. And I've already put bacon on, so you have to get up."

Molly detected an annoying buzz in her ears; the words barely registered. "Go away," she mumbled.

Laughter and another hard shake. "Molly! It's getting late!"

This time she stirred and realized several things at once. It was dawn; Jake was in her room; he was sitting beside her on the bed. "How'd you get in here?"

Grinning, Jake answered, "Just knocked and pushed. Did you think that table would keep me out?"

"I prayed it would! Get out of here and let me sleep!" She covered her head with the sheet, but her awareness of Jake's thigh touching hers, was making her come awake in every inch of her being.

"Molly!" The sheet was yanked down from her face, she was hauled into his arms, and he kissed her throat, tickling her at the same time.

She squealed. "Jake!"

He laughed and held her. "Seems like I remember someone telling me all's fair in a crisis—and getting you awake in the morning is a crisis!"

"Will you go away!" she begged, embarrassed to have him see her with her hair falling over her eyes, no makeup on, and her gown tangled around her.

He smiled and stood up. "Don't go back to sleep. Breakfast will be waiting."

She did shake her fist at him and he laughed, leaving the room.

In seconds the door opened. Molly thought she heard a sound and opened her eyes in time to see Jake bending down to scoop her up.

"You seem," he said, pulling her against his chest and ignoring her protests and shoves, "to get awake when you get on your feet. So..." He carried her to the hall and set her on her feet. "Now, good morning."

She glared at him, clutching the sheet to her chin. "I declare war, Jake Cannon!"

"I'm shaking in my boots. See you at breakfast," he chirped, one gray eye closing in a wink that brought her fully awake. It was a gesture that made her feel special and she would have smiled if she hadn't been so groggy and annoyed. Humming a tune, he bounded downstairs and she went in to dress in red shorts and a red T-shirt.

As she walked down the stairs, turning at the landing and smelling the aroma of hot coffee, she met Jake starting up. He paused, his eyes lighting with pleasure as he gave her a slow, all-encompassing look.

"I thought maybe you had gone back to sleep," he said.

She came down to the step above him, where her eyes were on a level with his. He stretched out his hand to touch the banister, blocking her way as he smiled at her. "I seem to remember something about a declaration of war," he said in a rolling, deep voice that held more heat than the coffee. "Truce?" he asked.

"No. I declared war," she said, her voice dropping to a breathless alto. "It's war, Mr. Jake Cannon. You've woken me up two mornings at dawn and you'll have to pay the consequences!"

"So when's the first shot going to be fired?" he asked, a sexual taunt in his voice.

She tried to match it with a tease in her own. "I'll warn you, but you brought it on yourself—just remember!"

"You know the only thing I can remember?" he asked in a gravelly voice, his eyes giving her a broad hint.

"What?" she said, her gaze dropping to his mouth, to lips that could feel like warm velvet, and then scalding flames. She didn't hear if he answered. His arms wrapped around her, and he kissed her awake, fully awake, causing her nerves to quiver with longing when he finally released her.

"The kitchen may have burned down," he whispered.

"It might have been worth it," she said in a daze.

"You're not helping me to get back to my cooking."

"Mmm . . ."

Suddenly, he scooped her into his arms and carried her to the kitchen, smiling at her. "Maybe this is the way I should wake you up."

She smiled. "That's a bad habit you're going to have to break!"

"What? Kissing you?" he teased, setting her on her feet as he moved away.

"No! Waking me at dawn."

He winked at her and they both went to work getting breakfast on the table. They ate on the porch. It was just as beautiful a morning as the previous one, and Jake was just as annoyingly oblivious to it; he whipped out his ever-present list to go over the tasks of the morning, including their drive to Springfield to meet the Detroit detective.

Molly complied with Jake's assignments, cleaning the third bedroom and then changing for the drive into Springfield.

They each spent time alone with Detective Wellston, who wanted to know all the details and descriptions they could give him. On the way home, they stopped to get groceries.

When they returned to the house it was early afternoon and once more Jake produced his lists, reading the tasks aloud before going to change. Molly changed back to her shorts and T-shirt to sweep the front porch. Finally, she decided the house was sufficiently in shape for them to stop work and enjoy the vacation. She did her exercises and calisthenics, then went upstairs to shower. Once again, when she looked out the window, she saw Jake down below, dressed in his blue shorts and T-shirt, doing exercises.

Watching him, she smiled. "All right, Mr. Cannon—we're at war and you'd better get ready for the first shot," she declared softly. "I'm aiming at your list."

Still smiling, she went to her room to shower, wash her hair and change into her new, bright blue swimsuit. She let her hair tumble free and stepped into sneakers, throwing a towel carelessly over her shoulders. She applied some mascara, a faint bit of blush and some cologne and stood back to look at herself. Satisfied, she went downstairs and followed the sound of hammer blows until she heard Jake.

CHAPTER TEN

JAKE WAS OUTSIDE, standing on a ladder, his shoulders beaded with perspiration as he pounded screen wire back in place near the top of the porch.

"Jake, where's your list?" she asked loudly above the hammering.

Biting on the two nails between his teeth, he spoke out of the corner of his mouth. "Just a minute!"

As he pounded a nail into place, she asked again, "Where's your list?"

He took the last nail out of his mouth while he answered and hammered it into the wood. "In my shirt pocket down there somewhere. I'll be right dow—"

He had finished driving the nails and had looked down over his shoulder while he was talking. His words ended abruptly when he saw Molly straighten up and remove a paper from the pocket of the shirt she had in her hand. A part of his mind registered her action. The rest of his brain had gone blank and turned all functions over to his eyes and blood.

Molly was wearing a swimsuit that would fit into his hip pocket and leave room for his handkerchief. The pattern in the shimmering fabric was like Swiss cheese; the suit came complete with holes in interesting places. The warm day became tropical, and he knew he was staring, but damned if he could stop!

He took in every detail, her smooth, rosy skin, the full soft breasts and tiny waist, the flare of her hips and shapely dancer's legs. Her silky red hair fell in curling flames over her bare shoulders, and her sensuous lips were parted in a smile that made him feel as if he would melt and slide off the ladder. He couldn't move or talk or think. All he could do was look and look and look.

If he'd had the strength and sense to look into her green eyes, he might have seen what was coming, but he didn't until too late. Her voice was throaty and teasing and his heart underwent another jolt when she said, "Jake, you know I told you this morning we're at war."

"Yeah," he managed to croak. "I surrender!" He came down one step on the ladder as she moved a bit closer. His blood heated to a froth and he ran his hand over his brow.

"I told you I'd warn you when I was about to fire the first shot."

"Yeah," he said, only half hearing what she was saying.

"Here's your warning," she trilled in a come-hither voice and enticed him to come down another step. She pulled out a match, struck it with her thumbnail and held the bright flame to the piece of paper.

He didn't really give a damn about the paper, so at the moment, he missed the significance of what she was doing. The paper burned until she dropped it. They watched it blacken and curl till the flames went out on the grass. "There goes your list."

"Yeah," he said, finally getting his feet on the ground, but he felt as stunned and dizzy as he had on the ladder. "You look great, Molly."

"Thank you," she answered, her green eyes sparkling. "I think you just received a direct hit and don't know it!"

"I think you're right."

"You got me up at dawn and we worked like Trojans this morning. Ditto yesterday." Her simple words shouldn't have sounded like a sexy invitation, but they did. "Now, Jake, we're going to do the afternoon...*my* way," she announced, the last two words tantalizing, conjuring up erotic fantasies. "I'm going to show you how to relax and enjoy life. Toss the hammer down."

He did without a qualm.

"Come on," she coaxed, taking his hand.

With his imagination beginning to charge into full swing, he laced his fingers through hers. He felt a flicker of disappointment when they headed for the water instead of the house. They stopped beside the long, flat-bottomed boat and Molly sat down inside. "Want to push off? We'll go for a ride on the lake."

"Sure," he said and in minutes they were on the water and both rowing. Gradually, the hot sun and the pull on his muscles as he rowed began to cause his mind to function. He breathed deeply, watching Molly enjoy the lake and the creatures they spotted and marvel at the little fingers of water that ran beneath tall, cool trees. She looked gorgeous, and it was impossible for him to keep his mind on trees and water, but he couldn't get close to her while they were rowing, and finally he began to think of the tasks at the house that waited. "Shall we go back now? I want to finish that screen before nightfall."

"How about a swim first?"

"The water's cold."

"You swam when you got the boats out of the boat house."

"Yeah, and it was cold."

"Too cold to swim?"

"Nope, but not the most enjoyable temperature. And whether you want to hear about it or not, there are jobs waiting."

"Jake, I don't want to hear about jobs, your list, or the chores waiting. You woke me up this morning to work—I'll repeat myself—this afternoon it's my turn." She stood up, balanced with as much ease as a tight-rope walker while she stepped over a seat, and moved closer to sit down facing him, her knees touching his. She smiled a smile that took his breath and addled his mind again. Dimly, he was aware when her hands moved. She reached out, took the oars out of the oar-locks and heaved them into the lake.

"Hey!" Jake came out of his euphoria as the oars splashed and bobbed yards from the boat.

She smiled at him like a playful kitten and suddenly, he sensed a silent challenge from her.

"All right, Molly," he drawled and saw something flicker in the depths of her eyes. In a swift movement he stood up and scooped her into his arms.

"Jake!" she yelped, and flung her arms around his neck just as he started to pitch her into the water.

"Hey!" he bellowed when she caused him to lose his balance. For a moment he tried to regain it, making the boat wobble crazily, and then they went over, splashing into cold water.

He gasped, thrashed, felt her push and slip away. He grabbed an ankle, but she wiggled away from him. He bobbed to the surface, but she was yards away.

"I'll get you!" he threatened. She flung herself over and began to swim away from him with long, swift strokes.

Jake stretched out, his arms slicing into the water in a fierce determination that this time Molly wouldn't outdo him. In seconds he caught her and yanked her back to duck her.

She splashed water over his face and they wrestled while she giggled. Jake tried to get a grip on her slender writhing body; their legs tangled and his hand closed on her narrow waist as he fought to duck her and she struggled to prevent him from doing so.

His arm tightened around her waist and he pulled her against him, holding her tightly and looking down into laughing green eyes. His breath stopped. She was soft, almost bare, and fighting him playfully; each twist and wriggle inflamed his desire. The game had changed for him, and he watched her to see when she would become aware of the change.

She pushed, her hands slipping over his chest. Then she slanted him a look and her eyes narrowed. Her smile vanished, and he saw a langourous transformation come over her features. Her lips parted, she sucked in her breath, and held it for heartbeats. His arm tightened again around her. Her breasts pressed with enticingly soft fullness.

"Hi, gypsy," he murmured huskily.

She tilted her head back, her eyes half closing in the way she had when she wanted to be kissed. She twined one arm around his neck and wrapped the other across his shoulders while they treaded water, her fingers slipping up the back of his neck to the back of his head.

"Jake," she whispered, pushing lightly on the back of his head.

Jake needed no push, but when she did that, he thought his heart would burst. He leaned forward; the water was cold, but her breath was sweet and hot as golden fire.

Tongues touched, demanded more, sought and discovered. Jake's hands followed her curves, feeling the sleekness of her swimsuit, searching for the thin strap that he tugged over her shoulder. His hand found her breast; his thumb flicked the hardened peak. Her back arched, her hips writhed, hearing her moan; he became so hard he thought he would burst with need of her.

"We're going to drown..." she murmured as they bobbed in the water and Jake tried to keep them afloat.

Finally she pushed against his chest and when he relaxed his hold, she swam away from him a few yards. She treaded water as they stared at each other, both breathing raggedly.

"You scare me sometimes," she whispered, pulling her swimsuit into place.

"Why?" he asked, aching for her, amazed that even though she was yards away, her red hair plastered to her head, and her body a shimmering reflection under the water, she could still set his blood boiling.

"Because I can't control my reaction to you," she said in a small voice, suddenly struck with the idea that her views of commitment might be undergoing a change.

"Oh, damn, Molly. You would tell me that when we have part of the lake between us."

"I think we'd better swim—it's safer."

Without waiting for his answer, she disappeared below the water, then surfaced several feet farther away as her arms moved in a steady rhythm away from him.

Jake retrieved the oars, dropped them into the boat and then went after Molly. She kept a distance between them and he didn't try to chase her down and catch her as before.

Almost an hour later Jake climbed into the boat. Then he helped Molly up and together they rowed back.

"I'm turning to ice," he said as they hauled the boat up onto land.

"Come over here in the sunshine," she called, running ahead of him to a treeless patch of grass sloping away from the house.

He stopped to watch her, feeling a tightness in his loins as he observed her long legs stretched out in a run and her bottom jiggling just enough to be inviting. She stepped up on the porch and in seconds she had turned on the small portable radio. Through the music was turned low, it carried well in the stillness, and Molly moved back to the lawn to dance, her rosy body a flickering flame in the sunlight. She motioned to him. "Come on!"

"I can't dance like you can."

"I'll show you how. Come here." She swirled and kicked gracefully, moving in time to the music, wanting Jake to join her, wanting more…and puzzling over what it was about this man that appealed to her so overwhelmingly.

"I'm going up to change."

She turned, her arms outspread as she spun across the lawn to block his path. She knew she was flirting with danger—Jake was a threat to her peace of mind—but in a breathless voice she said, "If you'd dance in the sunshine, you'd warm up."

The corner of Jake's mouth lifted in a crooked smile as he said dryly, "I'm warming plenty. You're the sun dancer, Molly." He added, "You go right ahead," his maleness hard and throbbing with desire as he watched her weave sinuously in front of him.

The music changed to a low piece, a familiar old love song, and Molly's movements became languid. Her auburn hair swung out as she turned, carrying its own fires. Her hips moved in time to the steady beat, her body fluid motion. She reached out, her fingers catching his as she tugged so lightly, and then he was swaying with her until he couldn't stand watching and not touching her. He reached out, pulling her into his arms and wanting to kiss her until she fainted. He forgot his resolve not to push her into a relationship; he forgot everything but his need for her. She was a sun dancer, flickering gold and fire, elusive, magical, someone who had brought something exciting and special into his life, into an emptiness he had lived with too long now. Logic spun out of mind as her tongue darted into his mouth, seeking, tormenting.

Her skin had dried and was warm from the sun; his hands caressed it while desire flared like a sunburst inside him, taking his breath, stopping his pulse, making him throb with longing. He scooped her into his arms and knelt on the grass, stretching out and pulling her down.

Her legs straightened until she was lying over him, her softness pressing against him while his hands explored curves and flesh. Molly sighed with pleasure, lost in a giddy spiral.

"You gypsy sun dancer, you've turned my life inside out!"

"Oh, no, I haven't..." Her protest was lost in a gasp as he kissed her throat, his hand stroking silken thighs.

Molly's heart pounded in hammer blows and the roaring in her ears drowned all sounds as she clung to Jake, forgetting wisdom, caution, fear—Jake was worth risking her emotions for, she decided. He was intelligent, fun; he stirred her as no one else ever had. Absolutely no one...

Jake rolled her over. There was so little clothing between them, but he wanted it gone. He kissed her hard while his hands tugged the slim straps off her shoulders. In seconds her suit was flung aside, and she lay beside him, golden, heartstoppingly beautiful, bare for his eyes.

"Lord, Molly," he whispered, cupping her breast, her softness filling his hand as his thumb moved slowly, feathering lightly over the throbbing nipple. She moaned, shifting closer to him, wanting him with a desperation she wouldn't have thought possible.

Jake wanted to look and touch for the next hundred years. He trailed his fingers down her flat stomach to her thighs and she writhed, stroking him and then tugging at his shorts.

He stood up and peeled them away, looking down at Molly as her thick lashes rose and a burning green-eyed gaze flicked over him like a searing flame. She was beautiful beyond all his imaginings, golden, rosy, soft...

He was beside her again, his hands seeking, touching, trying to please her, trying to seduce, to make her melt as he was, inch by inch.

"Molly, gypsy...my sun dancer," he whispered, caressing her, trailing kisses from her throat down over soft flesh, down to pink, thrusting nipples that begged to be kissed, to be loved. His fingers moved between her thighs, fondling her, touching secret places, trying to excite her as she excited him. Her hands moved like dancing sun rays on his body, touching and stroking, until he could stand it no longer.

"Molly, I need you...I really need you," he whispered, and he meant it through every fiber of his being.

He moved above her, pausing a moment while she looked at him, her eyes sleepy lidded. Green cat eyes, sun-bright skin, hips rising to seek and seek...

He lowered himself, his throbbing maleness feeling resistance momentarily. Her brows flew together in a frown, white teeth biting her lip, and he realized Molly hadn't been with a man for a long time.

"Molly," he said, gasping, unable to stop...

She tugged at him. "Jake, please," she whispered, the words barely audible. Yet they reached his ears, his heart, and his soul...

"Gypsy," he whispered, wanting suddenly to take her and at the same time wanting to give...and give...

Jake filled her slowly and Molly felt impaled, wanting him in a way she had never wanted a man. He moved so slowly that she couldn't bear it. Her hips shifted, ecstasy rippled through her and she moved again and again. And then she was caught in a whirlwind of sensation. Her hips moved; Jake filled her, hot and fast. Faster and she was caught...lost in a giddy spiral of tension and need...

"Ahh, Jake!" she cried and clung to him.

"You gypsy, sun dancer," he whispered in her ear. "My Molly...oh, love..."

Molly felt as if she had disintegrated into a billion flaming sparks. She clung to Jake, feeling his muscles clench.

Crying out, she wrapped her arms and long, slender legs tightly around Jake, moving her hips as he thrust deeply, until rapture flamed like the sun coming over the horizon, lighting the world.

He shuddered, calling her name again, coming down with a weight that she wanted to hold forever.

Eternity... he rolled on his side and held her close, fitting her against his shoulders. "Molly—"

She put her finger on his lips. "Don't talk. Don't say words you don't mean; nothing, nothing," she whispered, clinging to him and refusing to think about consequences or problems. Yet she sensed she had made more of a commitment in the past hour than ever before. Fleetingly, she wondered if she would suffer heartache because of it; she mused about Jake's feelings, too, yet was determined to avoid empty promises given in a moment of passion.

He rained kisses on her shoulder and throat, then sank down with a sigh, holding her tightly against him. He wanted to tell her many things, but she had sounded desperate when she had stopped him with a finger on his lips and her urgent, "Don't talk . . ." He lay quietly stroking her, desperate to stay that way and not loosen his grip; he was fearful she would slip out of his life as swiftly as she had come into it. He had pushed her too far, too soon, and it scared him to think of her telling him goodbye as she had Garvin. Not yet . . .

He needed to sort through his feelings. He kissed her shoulder, trying to make the moment lighter by commenting, "You're right, this is better than hammering nails."

Molly laughed softly, her breath fanning on Jake's chest as she moved her hand to tangle the soft curly hair on his chest between her fingers. She had lost

control in a way that frightened her. She wanted Jake
wildly.

Jake stroked her head. "Molly, why did you come
downstairs and get me while I was working?"

"We work in the morning—that's enough. We vacation in the afternoon. You need to learn how to play,
Jake."

"You can show me," he murmured, his voice lowering, slithering over her nerves like a sparkling sun-
beam. He rolled her over. "We have another day before
people start arriving."

"Don't start planning."

He grinned. "Yes, ma'am! Absolutely not! Plans go
to the winds. Tomorrow is the wind, unpredictable as
you." He chuckled, lowering his head to kiss her
stomach. He made her laugh and draw up her knees,
and she turned to bite his shoulder playfully.

"Hey!" he exclaimed. She pushed him down, her
green cat eyes sparkling as she looked at him. "For
someone who keeps talking about being out of shape,
I think you're very in shape," she said, trailing her
fingers over his stomach.

"Thank you. If you don't want to complicate your
life, you should stop that," he said quietly.

"Sure," she answered. "But I'm not scared of complications," she added lightly, surprised at herself. She
wasn't scared of becoming involved with Jake as she
had been with other men because she was finding in
Jake companionship and fun. She leaned down to
brush his flesh with kisses that made him gasp and put
his arms around her. Molly continued to trail her lips
over his stomach and thighs, and then ran her hand
over his sharp hipbone until he pushed her down and
leaned over her.

"Gypsy, you make me feel drugged, on fire."

She wound her arms around his neck as his hand sought and found her breast to fondle. Then he placed his mouth over hers and the magic commenced between them again.

The lazy, sensual afternoon became cooler. Blue shadows slanted over the lawn before they got up and moved inside, and it was dark before they went down to eat a dinner that was never finished. Molly felt lost in intimate discoveries, lost to an insatiable appetite, but she refused to look too deeply. Instead, she seized the moments and their fires, and Jake's lovemaking grew more passionate instead of less, his caresses tantalized more; they increased need instead of diminishing it.

When dawn crept through the windows of Jake's room, he rolled on his side to look at the woman sleeping beside him.

He was amazed she was there. He wanted to touch her, yet he wanted to study her. Desire stirred as his gaze drifted over her pale skin, the soft, red curls framing her face and spilling over her shoulders, her breasts rising and falling as she breathed deeply and steadily. She was a sorceress, blinding him to everything except sensation; she took his breath away with her beauty. And deep down he felt a twinge of sadness and worry. Molly was a golden sun dancer, light, elusive, impossible to hold. He pushed the thoughts of tomorrow aside, tried to follow her lead and forget the future.

And with her lying against him, it was easy to do. He recalled the past hours and his blood seemed to slow, to heat with lethargy. Molly was even more sensuous than he'd suspected. She was meant for love and bed.

He ached with wanting her; yet, at the same time, he knew he might not ever have another moment when he could watch her sleep. But soon he couldn't bear letting another second tick past without touching her. His hand drifted over her shoulder, down her arm, over her hip.

She stirred and smiled, her arm slipping around his waist, and he felt his heart slam against his ribs.

He leaned down to kiss the fullness of her breast. Then he caressed her, rubbing the tips of his fingers slowly, lightly back and forth over the velvet bud, and watching Molly to see when the sensation would cause her to stir.

She moaned softly and moved her hips in a slow, sensuous stirring that seared his nerves.

He knew how hard it was to wake her, yet his light strokes were causing a sleepy reaction. His fingers drifted down where her thighs were pressed close together. As lightly as a breath, he stroked her silken legs. Molly moaned softly again and rolled on her back, opening her legs, allowing his hand to touch freely.

His fingers worked while he watched her. Molly's hips shifted, a movement that was erotic. Her lips parted and he leaned closer, letting his fingers press the damp warmth between her thighs.

Her eyes opened drowsily, focusing on him. "Morning, gypsy," he whispered and leaned across the last bit of space separating them to kiss her.

She wrapped her arms around his neck, returning his kiss instantly, and Jake crushed her to him, an arm around her waist, while he kissed her and kissed her.

"IS IT DAWN AGAIN?" she murmured later as she lay against his chest.

"It might have been when you woke up. It's late in the day now."

Her fingers played over his chest. "This morning I forgive you for waking me."

He chuckled, the laughter a deep rumble in her ear, and she smiled, slipping her arms around his waist to hug him and feeling a contentment she wouldn't have guessed possible.

It was nearly noon when they finished breakfast. There was no talk of lists or jobs or tomorrow. Jake found the water skis and put the motor on the boat. They walked through the woods, they lay in the sunlight, letting their bodies warm and dry from a swim, and then later they ran to the lake to cool from making love in the sunshine.

They ate on the lake in the boat and sang as they rowed back. They turned on the portable radio and danced on the porch, continuing to sway when the news came on and the music stopped. Finally Jake carried Molly to bed, but not until nearly dawn did they fall into an exhausted sleep.

BEN WAS THE FIRST to arrive. The sound of a car reached them long before the vehicle came into sight. Jake was lying in bed, his hands propped behind his head, watching Molly dress when they heard the noise. She stood in the center of the room, fastening shorts around her waist. A white blouse lay over the back of the chair beside her.

He threw back the sheet, his eyes meeting Molly's solemnly, and she knew he was thinking the same thing she was. Their special time together was over.

Nude, so virile and handsome she couldn't help staring, Jake crossed the room to her to take her in his arms. "Here comes civilization. Our interlude is over."

"I know," she said, trying to stop the thoughts and emotions beginning to torment her. To her amazement, she didn't want an intrusion. Her fear of commitment was melting away, ice beneath a tropic sun in the warmth of Jake's attention. Realization of the changes Jake was causing to her attitudes didn't alarm her—yet was she being as foolish as Ivy?

He wrapped his arms around her to kiss her passionately and Molly returned his kiss eagerly. Then she pushed on his arms. "Jake, someone's here."

She moved away, picking up her things as he quickly pulled on his jeans. At the door to her room she paused to look at him. "I'm glad you let me come along with you," she said.

"Yeah," he answered solemnly. "I feel like I'm back up there, hanging nine stories above the pavement."

Puzzled, she narrowed her eyes, trying to decide what he was trying to tell her, when someone pounded on the front door.

"Jake?"

"I'll go down," he said. Molly combed her hair and was a few steps behind Jake when he opened the door and extended his hand. "Ben! Holy geez! What happened to you?"

CHAPTER ELEVEN

MOLLY COULDN'T SEE BEN for the open door, but she heard his deep voice answer, "This place is damned hard to find! I got stuck in the mud and then some woman came over the hill and crashed into me. Look at my car."

"Holy geez!" Jake said.

Molly stepped to Jake's side and he looked down. "Molly, this is my brother, Ben. Ben, meet Molly Ashland. I told you about her on the phone."

Looking up at a tall man who bore only a slight resemblance to Jake, Molly extended her hand. Ben was splattered with mud, covered with it to his knees. Smudges darkened his face and hands and he shrugged, showing Molly the mud on his fingers instead of taking her hand.

"Let's have a look at your car," Jake said, opening the screen door.

"You have to go around it to see all the damage, but the back fender and driver's side are what she hit hardest. The front fender is from a little fender bender in Ames this winter. She was in a red compact and she said she didn't know how to drive a standard shift. She wasn't kidding."

"Where did this happen?"

"On a dirt road coming here," he said, as all three of them walked around the car. Molly looked at a battered, ten-year-old four-door blue sedan covered in mud. The windshield was spattered with big splotches. Jake paused, pointing at the windshield. "How in hell did you do that?"

Ben shrugged. "She went around me and bogged down in the mud and her wheels threw it over my car. Actually, she's back there waiting for me. I told her I'd get you and a tow rope and we'd get her out of the mud.

"What's her name?" Jake asked.

"I don't know. She seemed really upset."

"Does she have insurance?"

"I don't know that either. I didn't want to worry her."

"You didn't *what*?"

Molly began to realize who the woman in the car might be. "Ben, what's she look like?"

Ben turned around, his voice changing, his eyes glazing over. "An angel. She's the most beautiful woman I've ever seen in my life."

Molly watched Jake's eyes widening in shock. "Ivy's here," she said.

"I'll be damned," Jake said. "Well, let's go see. I'll get a rope. You want to wash first?"

Ben shook his head. "I don't think there's any use in it. Her car's sunk in pretty deep."

They climbed into the Jeep with Ben and drove toward Hattersville. They forded the creek and topped a hill. Below where the road dipped at the lowest point, they spotted a car and a woman sitting inside. She saw them, stepped out, and waved her arms to flag them down.

Surprise jolted Jake as he beheld a tall, leggy woman with a Dolly Parton bust. She wore skin-tight hot pink tights and a knit shirt; her platinum hair fell to her waist. He glanced at Molly. "You said a quiet little thing...I wouldn't know she was around."

"I exaggerated a mite."

"My, my," he clucked. "Little sister Ivy who likes to read."

"She really does."

"That's your sister?" Ben asked from the back.

"Yes," Jake answered with amusement. "I think this is your lucky week, Ben. She's going to stay with us."

"She is?" Ben murmured, sounding dazed, and Jake laughed as they slowed.

"Molly!" Ivy screeched, hurting Jake's ears as she took another step toward them in heels that Jake would have guessed to be six inches high.

He sat and watched as Molly waded through the mud to hug her sister. Ben climbed out and stood in the road while Ivy looked around. She was an absolute knockout; Jake pitied Ben for a moment. Ivy had wide blue eyes, flawless skin and eyelashes inches long that couldn't have been real. Golden earrings dangled to her shoulders and the knit shirt plunged in front, revealing cleavage that would stop traffic. Ivy's waist was narrow, her hips slim, her legs shapely. Jake didn't see one splatter of mud on her anywhere, except on her feet, and she'd just done that. For a moment he wondered how Molly could have spent a lifetime in Ivy's shadow and remained so loyally attached to her sister, but as he looked at the two of them together, it was Molly who made his pulse skip a beat.

Resigned to mud and work, Jake hitched the looped rope over his shoulder, climbed out and walked through the mud to the car.

"Ivy, this is Jake Cannon. You already know his brother Ben. Jake, this is my sister, Ivy Bronski."

"Oh, thank you for the help!" Ivy said to Jake and Ben, and then she turned to Molly. "I'm so glad to see you," she said and burst into tears, throwing her arms around her sister's neck. After a moment, she stepped back. "I rented this car in Springfield, and when I came over the hill, I couldn't stop and ran into Ben's car..." She broke off in fresh sobs.

"Now don't cry," Ben soothed worriedly, waving his hands in the air. "My old car has lots of dents." Molly glanced at Jake to see him shake his head. Then he turned his back to hitch the rope to his bumper.

"I'm so sorry I hit your car," Ivy said, looking up at Ben. "I don't have a handkerchief. Molly, do you?"

"No—I didn't bring anything with—"

"Here's my handkerchief," Ben said.

"Oh, thank you!" Ivy exclaimed, moving closer to Ben. Molly looked up at him and sighed. "You cheer Ivy up. I'll help Jake."

Molly and Jake soon had the rope knotted to both bumpers and in minutes they pulled the car free. Ben drove Ivy's car, and Jake drove the other as they headed home.

"Ivy has insurance," Molly said. "She's sorry about Ben's car. It didn't hurt her rental car."

"He doesn't seem worried. Matter of fact, I don't think he'd care if Ivy crumpled the whole thing into a scrap heap. Is she your older sister?"

Molly smiled. "No—Ivy's twenty-four, five years younger than I am."

"You look like the baby of the family."

"When you put it that way, I don't know whether to say thank you or not." After a moment she said, "Ben's nice. He doesn't seem so shy."

Jake shrugged. "Maybe he's outgrowing it. I'm not sure your sister's giving him a chance to be shy."

Molly laughed. "You'll like Ivy when you get to know her."

Jake's eyes left the road for a moment. "Do you always try to talk men into liking Ivy? It seems sort of... redundant."

She laughed and placed her hand on his thigh, making Jake momentarily forget the road, Ivy, or Ben. "Ah, Molly—"

"Jake!"

He straightened the car and they slid through squishy mud.

"When you have a chance, ask Ivy if she noticed anyone following her as she drove along the dirt road from Hattersville."

"I'll ask, but Ivy's so accustomed to men staring, she wouldn't have given it a thought."

"Yeah, well, if they'd known who to look for, a marching band would have been more inconspicuous. I just hope no one followed Ben or Ivy."

"They couldn't have!"

"Your sister doesn't look like the type to enjoy the isolation of a house in the woods."

"You've got the wrong impression of Ivy, just like every other man she meets."

"Molly, she's a knockout, dressed to attract the maximum attention," he said dryly, watching the deep ruts ahead. "I'd say she's asking for certain reactions. She shouldn't go into shock when men ignore her mind. It sort of pales to insignificance."

"You're right," Molly agreed solemnly, but Ivy's building a reputation as an exotic dancer and she says it's necessary to look that way."

"Then she might as well accept the consequences. Her mind isn't what she's drawing attention to, hon." He reached across the seat to give Molly's shoulder a squeeze. "And you better brace up for my in-laws' reaction when they discover Ivy's profession. The only way to describe them is 'old-fashioned'."

"They won't approve?"

"They're nice," he said easily. "They'll probably approve of Ivy and be shocked to their toes about her career. They raised two girls who were quiet and nice. My in-laws were older when Sheryl came along and then Ginger was born four years later."

"When do you think they'll get here?"

"I look for them around dinnertime tonight. We'll have a houseful. Molly, I'll tell Jamie about the robbery, but I'll keep it simple. I'm going to caution her about strangers, but I don't want to frighten her and tell her someone is after us."

"Sure. I'll leave all that up to you."

"I may not mention it to the Devons if I don't get an opportunity away from Jamie."

"That's your business, Jake. I won't say anything."

At the house, everyone hosed the mud off their feet and Ben and Ivy listened to Jake and Molly tell about the robbery. They unloaded Ben's and Ivy's things and wrestled with a momentary dilemma about where each would sleep. Ben agreed on the sofa; Molly and Ivy said they would share a room, leaving the third room for Jake's in-laws. Jamie would sleep on a cot in Jake's room.

While Ben and Jake hosed mud off the cars, Molly and Ivy put lunch on the table. Ivy poured two cups of steaming black coffee and handed one to Molly. "I can set the table. This is nice."

"Does Willis know you've left Dallas?"

"I told him I was going. He didn't want me to leave, but now he knows it's over. We talked on the phone once after I moved out. You know, I really am over Willis. He was mean and vindictive and I was always upset trying to please him."

"Ivy, be more careful about men in the future."

"I will! Believe me, I will!" Suddenly she began to cry and Molly set down a plate of sandwiches to pat Ivy's shoulder.

"I'm sorry, Ivy."

"I'm just so dumb when it comes to men. Drew was always hitting the bottle and Willis was mean as sin, and no one I've dated has ever understood me!"

Molly thought about her conversation with Jake. "Ivy, maybe you should try changing yourself a little."

"Big blue eyes peered at Molly over Ben's handkerchief. "What do you mean, change?"

Molly shrugged, waving her hand in the air. "Try projecting a different image, a little more subdued."

"Ivy gave a dry laugh. "You mean my hair and makeup. I know I attract the wrong men, but it helps with my job. If I looked mousy, I wouldn't get top billing."

"I suppose that's right," Molly said, realizing the choice was Ivy's and that Ivy knew what helped her job. She paused at the counter and looked out the kitchen window at Ben helping Jake carry boards from the boat house. Jake had pulled off his shirt and wore jeans and sneakers. Sunlight splashed over his shoulders, and she noticed his skin was becoming darker each day. For a moment she was lost in memories; Ivy's voice faded out of hearing and consciousness as she recalled being in Jake's arms in his bed.

Lunch was quiet and slightly strained, and Molly couldn't understand why. As they passed cold-meat sandwiches and drank glasses of iced tea, Ben seemed preoccupied and shy; Ivy seemed subdued for once.

"What kind of work do you do?" Ivy asked Jake politely.

"I sell stereos and stereo equipment, radios, that sort of thing."

"He has the Soundmaster Stores in Detroit," Molly added.

"Oh, how nice!" Ivy said, turning to Ben. "And what do you do, Ben?"

Ben's face flushed, becoming almost as rosy as his red cotton shirt. "I'm a teller in a bank."

Ivy laughed. "That's nice. You sound as if you rob banks for a living instead of working in one."

"Yeah," he said glumly, his blue eyes full of worry as he glanced at Jake. "I made another mistake the other day and they warned me this is my last chance. The money I handle has to balance from now on—forever!"

"You didn't balance again?" Jake asked.

"No, I couldn't account for two thousand dollars."

Jake choked and Ivy dropped her fork and in unison both of them spoke. "You lost two thousand dollars?" Ivy asked while Jake exclaimed, "Two thousand!"

Ben's face flushed an even deeper red, and though Molly was stunned over the magnitude of mismanagement, she felt sorry for him because he looked so miserable.

"Yeah, we had a one-day special with higher interest rates on a twelve-month certificate of deposit, and we were swamped with customers until my drawers were full and I threw the money in a pile in a corner by my feet."

Jake groaned. "You lost it?"

"Well, I finally found it, but I had shuffled the two thousand into a stack of papers and we couldn't go home until I found it. The other tellers stayed to help me and we were there until eleven Thursday night."

"Geez, I'm sorry," Jake said, frowning and looking concerned.

Ben looked miserable as he stared out the window. "I tried again to put in my application at the University, but they're facing budget cuts and they said there's no hope. They wouldn't even take the application."

"Yeah, well, I'm sorry about that too," Jake said.

Ben smiled, glancing at the others. "What do you do, Molly?" he asked.

"I have a dance studio. I teach little girls tap and ballet."

"Gee, that's interesting and nice," Ben said and turned to Ivy. "What work do you do?"

"I'm an exotic dancer. My business name is Luscious LaRue."

Ben's eyes widened. He looked as if his bite of sandwich had gone down the wrong way as he stared at Ivy. "Do you live in Detroit?"

"Nope, but I'm moving there when we leave here. I just got a divorce," she said and sniffed.

"I'm sorry!" Ben said, and Molly wished lunch were over and all the embarrassing questions done.

"Why don't we take the boats out after lunch?"
Jake suggested and everyone agreed immediately. The
conversation changed to talk about the lake.

All four cleaned and Ben and Jake were already
outside when Ivy and Molly came down the steps.
Standing in the sunshine by the boats, Jake and Ben
both turned at the same time. Molly was so accustomed to men staring at Ivy that she fully expected Jake
to demonstrate the usual reaction, but he gave Ivy a
cursory glance and his eyes shifted to Molly. One corner of his mouth lifted crookedly, reminding Molly of
the moments they had been alone and how he had
peeled away her bathing suit. Unaware she was giving
him a lingering perusal that matched his own for her,
she felt her flesh heat from his attention. She wanted
to walk into his arms and turn her mouth up for his
kiss. "I'm ready," she said, realizing it came out
breathlessly and full of double entendre.

"So am I," Jake said huskily, so softly she didn't
think anyone else could have heard him.

Ben nicely broke the tension between them when he
fell over the canoe, causing it to slam into the flat-
bottomed boat. He stood up, blushing while he stared
at Ivy in her black bikini.

"Are you all right?" she asked.

"Yeah," Ben answered with a happy grin. Jake
rolled his eyes.

In a sunny part of the lake, they swam. Jake raced
Molly between the canoe and the boat, after he won,
he paused, clinging to the far side of the boat out of
sight of Ivy and Ben as Molly came around beside him.

"You win!" she cried.

"Yeah, come give me my prize," he demanded, reaching to pull her to him and kiss her. His body seemed warm in spite of the cold water.

Molly wound her arms around his neck eagerly. She felt his legs tangle with hers, and his swift stirring of desire. He held the side of the boat, neck-deep in water, while he tugged a shoulder strap off Molly's shoulder, his fingers seeking the softness of her breast. She moaned and pulled away, her lashes rising slowly as she stared at him. She wanted him so badly, she hurt. "Jake, we're not alone."

"I know," he said gruffly, pulling her suit in place, his hand lingering, drifting down and down.

"Jake..."

He groaned and swam away from her. "Okay, Molly! We better race back...let me work off my frustration!"

She laughed, silently agreeing wholeheartedly. "Thank you for taking in Ivy."

"Sure. I think Ben's gone into a trance. All he can do is stare at her."

She laughed. "She has that effect on men. I don't know how you're so immune."

He swam to her, coming within inches, but not touching her. "I've been immunized," he drawled in his furry voice, "absolutely blinded by soft red hair and big green eyes. There's only one woman who puts me in a trance."

She smiled and drew her fingers over his shoulder and down to his waist. "You're never in a trance. You know exactly what you do to me."

"And I want to do all I can right now," he said slowly, each word a burning caress on tingling, hungry flesh.

"We better get back," she said, her heart thudding in reaction. Swimming a few feet from him, she turned and said, "It's nice Ben's here. I like your brother."

"Thanks. Wait until you meet Jamie. She's my pride and joy," he said, his voice growing tender. "I hope you two like each other, but then I can't imagine anyone not liking either Jamie or you."

"Aren't you nice! I remember when you were up on a roof and didn't feel that way."

He grinned and shrugged. "I didn't know how charming you could be then."

Laughing, she splashed water on him and flung herself away when he gave chase.

That evening, while dinner cooked, they sat on the porch facing the lake. Jake had grown quiet and Molly suspected he was listening for a car. He was the first to hear the motor and they all went to the front to watch a gray Ford, now spattered with mud, roll to a halt. Molly glimpsed a white-haired couple and a child with her face at the window. The moment the car stopped, she opened the door, smiling as she stepped out and called, "Daddy!"

Jake crossed to her in long strides to scoop her up in his arms. He held her tightly, his eyes squeezed shut while she hugged him, and Molly felt a tightness in her throat when she saw how badly Jake must have missed his daughter.

Jamie was a beautiful child; she had Jake's gray eyes, thick black lashes and black hair that was done in long ringlets, parted in the center and clipped away from her face by yellow barrettes. She wore a pale yellow dress and sandals. Her smile was like her father's.

Ben introduced Ivy and Molly to Fred and Lena Devon. Molly nodded, murmuring a greeting to the short, smiling couple.

Jake set Jamie down, and held her hand. "Jamie, this is Miss Ashland and Mrs. Bronski."

As soon as the introductions were over, Jake led them to the back porch. "I'm barbecuing a brisket, and then I'll show you around."

"This is a hell of a place to find," Fred said. "We got lost twice."

"Sorry. When you leave in the morning, I'll lead you back to Hattersville," Jake offered.

"I'd appreciate that. Hate to get you up early."

"I get up early," Jake said, winking at Molly. When they sat down, Jake took orders for drinks. Jamie sat on a chair between Mr. and Mrs. Devon where Molly couldn't talk to her easily, but as the adults chatted, Molly glanced occasionally at Jamie and realized the child was very self-possessed. Almost unnaturally quiet and mannerly, she sat as still as the adults, holding a raggedy brown bear under her arm. Once her big gray eyes met Molly's and Molly smiled. Jamie smiled back and looked away, turning to watch Jake as he mixed drinks in the kitchen.

As soon as he had served everyone a drink and handed Jamie a small glass of lemonade, he said, "Why don't I show Jamie around right now?" He asked her, "Are you tired of sitting?"

Jamie needed no urging and scooted off the chair to slip her hand into Jake's. Casually, he glanced at Molly. "Why don't you come with us?"

"You two go ahead," she said softly, as Fred Devon resumed telling Ben and Ivy about the trip to Missouri.

"Come with us," Jake urged and Molly looked at Jamie to see if the child seemed to care that a stranger was intruding on time with her father. But Jamie was waiting, smiling at Molly, so Molly went outside with them, and Jake and she strolled with Jamie between them.

"Molly, you didn't meet Alfred."

Jamie held up the brown bear. Hair was worn off the ears and stomach, spots darkened its coat, and stuffing protruded from one toe.

"How do you do, Alfred," Molly said solemnly, and Jamie nodded, then turned to Jake. "Daddy, his toe needs sewing."

"Ah, so it does! If anyone has a needle and thread, we'll fix Alfred tonight."

"My sandals are going to get muddy," Jamie said.

Jake knelt, turning his back to her. "How about piggyback?"

Eagerly, she put her arms around his neck. Alfred flopped against Jake's shoulder as he locked his arms around Jamie's thin legs and stood up easily. They made their way down the slope. "See, there are the boats. I'll take you out on the lake tomorrow. There's the boat house."

"Can we walk in the woods?"

"Sure, we can."

Jake talked easily, learning about Jamie's friends and school, and while they talked, Molly felt a twist of sadness. Jake obviously loved Jamie with all his heart, and he was just as obviously a good father. He was interested in Jamie, able to communicate with her, and it made Molly ache to think how it must hurt him to part with her. Something she couldn't do, she realized. She had never known poverty as Jake had, and if she had, perhaps she could understand better why he didn't chuck his career and move to be with Jamie.

"I'd better see about the brisket," Jake said, starting toward the house. "I wouldn't want to burn up dinner."

Jamie tightened her arms around his neck and leaned forward to kiss his jaw. "I love you, Daddy," she said softly.

He stopped and swung her around into his arms, hugging her tightly. "I love you," he answered hoarsely, kissing her cheek. He set her on her feet and took her hand.

After dinner they sat on the back porch again. Molly wondered if Jamie had a regular bedtime and Jake was letting her stay up since it was a special occasion, or if the child stayed up every night. The hour grew late and the Devons went up to bed, but Jamie didn't seem sleepy. She sat quietly on Jake's lap, listening to the adults while she played with Alfred and tied bows around his neck. During dinner Molly had agreed to read a bedtime story to the little girl, but Molly presumed the child had forgotten.

When they all went inside, Ben stopped in the living room, where he would sleep. "There are more blankets in the linen closet upstairs, if you need some," Jake said.

"No, I'll be fine," Ben said, beginning to unfold a sheet. Ivy paused beside the end table and picked up a book, reading aloud the title: "*Waterloo and Other Napoleonic Battles.* Is this yours?" she asked Ben.

"Yeah. I'm about halfway through."

"You like history!" Ivy asked, her voice rising in eagerness.

"I majored in history," he said, as Jake, Jamie and Molly continued upstairs. "I wanted to be a history professor, but I couldn't get a job in that field."

Molly heard Ivy's high voice clearly say, "No kidding! I love to read history books. I have a book you can read, *Early Memoirs of Napoleon*, if you're interested in French history."

Jake hoisted Jamie to his shoulder. As she laughed with delight, he said to Molly, "You weren't kidding, were you? Ivy really reads history!"

"Yes, she does. She likes bookkeeping, history and dancing—in that order."

"I'll be damned. And none of the ex-husbands did?"

"Hardly."

"Duck your head, sugar," Jake said at his door, lowering his voice so they wouldn't disturb the Devons.

"I'm going to Miss Ashland's room," Jamie whispered quickly, "Because she's going to read a story to me from *The Wind in the Willows*."

"I can read to you, and Molly can go to bed."

"I'd love to read to her, Jake," Molly said. "I haven't read that book in years."

"And then when Miss Ashland gets through, you can read another part to me," Jamie said to Jake, and he laughed, jiggling her.

"Working everyone for a story, aren't you! Come get your pj's," he said, swinging her down to the floor. "I'll start the bathwater."

"I can do it, Daddy. I do it all the time now."

"Oh," he said gruffly, realizing Jamie had grown and he had missed watching her change. It hurt badly. He wanted to pull her up and hold her and never send her away from him again, but the asthma attacks had been terrible and frightening and he wanted her where she would be well. He watched her as she went into the bedroom to get her pajamas.

Molly smiled and went on to her room, and his attention shifted, watching the slight sway of her hips as she walked away from him.

In a few minutes, after the water had stopped running in the bathroom and he knew Jamie was in the tub, he rapped lightly on the connecting door to Molly's room.

When she called to come in, Jake opened the door, smiling at her and looking around swiftly. "Can you come here a minute?"

CHAPTER TWELVE

SHE DROPPED THE NIGHTGOWN she was holding and walked into his room. He closed the door behind her and turned to lean against it. Then he pulled her into his arms and fit her against his length.

"We have a minute alone. Ivy's downstairs, Jamie's bathing."

"Just a minute," she said, her green eyes darkening.

"You've been great with Jamie."

"She's a beautiful child."

"I think so too." He lowered his voice, wanting to get a reaction from her. "Do you know how long I've had to wait?"

She looked up at him breathlessly. "Almost seven hours and fourteen minutes," she answered.

He smiled, but his grin faded swiftly as desire burned. "How I want you!" he whispered, pulling her to him, cupping her buttocks to thrust her hips against his. He leaned down to kiss her hungrily. Molly returned his kisses eagerly, her hips shifting against him, her hands seeking, drifting down his sides, feeling the warm tight denim on his thighs.

Her senses were caught in a swiftly churning eddy that drew her deeper and deeper. She wanted to be in Jake's bed, to feel his warm flesh against her, to have his mouth and his hands explore, to touch and kiss him.

"Oh, Jake!" She twisted her mouth from his. "This isn't reality. We're out of the real world, away from everything. It's dangerous," she murmured, her voice fading as he kissed her throat.

Jake bent his head down, his lips trailing lower. He wanted to make her lose control. He wanted to peel away the shirt and shorts. The vision of the lacy underthings beneath them set him afire. Molly was a golden flame whose scalding kisses drew him closer and closer . . . but what pulled him was more than physical. The depth of the attraction frightened him when he faced it because he didn't want to end up a man who had had two great loves in his life and lost them both.

She moved away. "Jamie will be here in a few minutes and Ivy will come upstairs."

"I want to be alone with you again," he said roughly, tangling his fingers in her hair, his eyes silvery with longing.

Molly felt as if she might melt. It was so difficult, knowing they had no privacy. Their time alone was over, but she didn't want it to end. "I should go," she whispered and he finally stepped away from the door. She stood on tiptoe, brushing his lips with hers, wanting him more than she had ever wanted anyone, wanting him for more reasons than she cared to explore.

In her room once the door was closed between them, she changed to her nightgown and pulled on the cotton robe. She turned down her twin bed, waited until she heard a knock, and then called, "Come in."

Jamie opened the door and stood shyly in the doorway, a book and Alfred tucked under her arm.

"Ready for a story?" Molly asked, realizing again how beautiful Jamie was. She could have been modeling the pale pink dimity gown and robe she wore. The darker pink rosebuds on the outfit matched the pink slippers on her feet and for a fleeting second Molly wondered if Jamie had ever had a smudge of dirt on her in her life. Jamie seemed a lot like her daddy— drifting through life without really knowing how to enjoy it. She smiled at Jamie and told her *"The Wind in the Willows* used to be one of my favorites."

Beyond Jamie stood Jake, bare-chested, wearing jeans and holding a box in his hands. He was watching Molly through the open door between them. Tearing her gaze from Jake, Molly patted the bed. "Come up here."

Smelling of lilac powder and soap, Jamie climbed up to sit beside her. Molly tried to avoid looking at Jake, who continued to watch them as Jamie opened the book to a dog-eared page. "I like this," she said, pointing a slender, dainty finger, and Molly began to read.

It was thirty minutes later when Jake rapped on the door. When he opened it, he stood there in brand new pajamas, creased from the package. Molly suspected he had bought them for Jamie's arrival. "Hey, Miss Night Owl. It's getting late."

Jamie closed the book and looked up at Molly. "Thank you."

"You're welcome," Molly said, brushing a lock of hair away from Jamie's cheek. "We'll read some more tomorrow."

"Okay." Jamie scooted out of bed and crossed the room to Jake, who picked her up in his arms.

"It's your turn now to read, Daddy. And you said you'd sing to me."

"If I sing now, I might wake up Gran and Granpa."

"You can whisper it."

"Night, Molly," Jake said, looking at her for long moments and winking.

"Night," she answered, barely able to get breath enough to answer. He turned and closed the door and his voice became a soft, deep rumble as he sang an old lullabye to Jamie. Molly smiled, snuggling down in bed and longing for Jake, refusing to think about the days ahead and what would happen when they left the Ozarks.

The hall door opened and Ivy came in, carrying a book in her hand. "Been waiting for me?" she asked.

"No. I've been reading to Jamie. She's gone to bed now."

"Will I keep you awake if I read? It calms my nerves."

"No. I can turn over and go to sleep."

Ivy dropped the book on the bed and began shedding clothes as she walked around the room. "I'm going to shower and do my hair. This is a nice family, Molly. I do appreciate Jake letting me come stay."

"His good nature wouldn't let him refuse," Molly said dryly, as she picked up the book and read: "Darwin *Travels in Patagonia*. I'll take *The Wind in the Willows*," Molly said.

"My book? It looks interesting. I'm so relieved to get away from Willis. Thank you for coming down."

"Well, I didn't quite get to Dallas."

"You know what I mean. I needed you and you came. Here you are with me, and I'm away from Willis forever. I can start all over."

Molly smiled, hoping Ivy had learned something from her experience. "Next time, Ivy, try to get to know the man first," she said, her words carrying a hollow echo as she reminded herself she should learn to heed her own advice.

"Yeah, I will." Ivy cocked her head to one side. "Do you hear someone singing?"

"It's Jake singing to Jamie."

"It's foreign."

"He sings Italian opera."

Ivy's mouth dropped open. "No kidding! Real opera?"

"Absolutely," she said, watching Ivy cross the room and put her ear to the door and listen.

After a moment she moved away. "No, kidding! He really does. Italian opera, and Ben knows history. They're interesting men, you know? You find interesting men. I find jerks."

Molly laughed. "Night, Ivy."

The next morning Molly felt a hand shake her shoulder. She opened her eyes to see Jake with his finger on his lips. He leaned over her ear to whisper. "Shh, you'll wake Ivy. I need you."

On the last words she opened her eyes again. He looked at her solemnly and nodded his head in the direction of his room. Then he stood up and tiptoed out without looking back. Molly began to come awake and wondered if something had happened, if some danger threatened. She slipped out of bed, forgetting her robe as she moved sleepily across the floor, and stepped into Jake's room.

He smiled, picked her up and carried her to bed. "The Devons are gone, Ben and Jamie are out picking dandelions or something on that order, the door is

locked, and I want you," he said, rolling on the bed
with her. She wrapped her arms around his neck as delighted and eager about the moment of privacy as he.

AN HOUR LATER when she went down to breakfast,
Jake was cooking and singing something in a foreign
language, but she didn't recognize what. She winked at
Jamie as she entered the room, her glance sweeping
over Jake frying bacon and Ben pouring orange juice.
Jake was dressed in green shorts, white socks and a
white T-shirt, his hair damp from a shower, his back to
Molly so she could savor the sight of the curls on his
nape as he turned the bacon.

She turned her attention to Jamie, noted her outfit,
and became all the more convinced that Jamie had
never been allowed to get a smudge of dust or dirt on
her. She sat with her curls combed neatly, pink barrettes in her hair, a crisp pink blouse with ruffles on the
sleeves and collar and matching pink cotton shorts.

"Morning," Molly said softly.

"Hi, Miss Ashland," Jamie answered solemnly.
Jake turned instantly; Ben said hello and went back to
pouring juice. Jake smiled, a radiant smile that made
appealing creases in his cheeks, that made Molly want
to cross the kitchen and kiss him. Instead, she asked,
"What can I do to help?"

"Come turn the bacon," Jake said, giving her a hug
around the waist as he handed the fork to her and
moved away to get eggs from the refrigerator. "What
time does Ivy get up?"

"She's used to working until three in the morning
and sleeping until noon. You won't see her for a
while."

Ben looked surprised, but Jake said cheerily, "Drowsiness runs in the family."

Molly shook the fork playfully at him and he grinned. Then she turned her attention to the bacon. After they had eaten and Ben was settled on the porch with a book, Molly surveyed Jamie's pink outfit and white sandals. "Jamie, it may be damp and muddy walking through the woods today. Do you want to wear jeans and sneakers?"

"I don't have any."

Jake glanced at Molly over Jamie's head. "Lena doesn't buy jeans. Molly's clothes will wash."

"Her legs will get scratched."

"I'll put on my knee socks," she said and picked up Alfred to go upstairs.

"She doesn't own a pair of jeans?"

"The world won't end," Jake said.

"Can I get her a pair the next time we're in Hattersville at the general store?"

"Sure," he said. "She used to wear them. Jamie likes you and Ivy."

"I'm glad."

"She's serious this morning. I think it's because she misses Lena and Fred. It's one more upheaval in her life," he said regretfully.

Molly glanced at him thoughtfully. "She's sweet, Jake, and so beautiful."

"Takes after you know who!" he said and grinned. He crossed the room to hug Molly. "How I'd like another hour alone," he whispered, his eyes telling her more than his words.

"She's rather mature for her age," Molly said, returning to the subject of his daughter. "It's sort of like being with an adult when I'm with her."

Jake's smile vanished. "A lot of things probably contribute to her being that way—she's an only child. She lost her mother because of a terminal illness. She's lived with adults always, and this year she's moved to a new place and the people closest to her are her grandparents. I love Lena and Fred, but they're solemn, old-fashioned people in many ways. Very friendly, but particular."

"Has she always been so quiet and docile?"

His eyes darkened to slate gray, and Molly realized her question had disturbed him. "No, not quite like she is now."

"Maybe she'll relax and become a little more outgoing while she's with you."

"I don't know." He ran his fingers through his hair. "Now she misses her grandparents. There are so many little things about her that have changed. She's grown so much since we were last together." As he talked, Jake's voice took on an edge of pain. It was as obvious as the sun shining on the lawn how much his daughter meant to him. "Oh, Lord, I miss her!" he said suddenly.

Molly tightened her arm around his waist, feeling him stiffen and take a deep breath.

"Jake, why don't you start over in Arizona? You have money saved, don't you?"

He turned. His face looked ashen, his eyes a flat gray. "Molly, I used to go to bed hungry every damned night. I'd be beaten up from fights, my clothes were crummy, we were poor—so damned poor! When I think about chucking it all to go south and be with her, then I remember about her medical bills and what I can give her if I stay in Detroit. Oh, Lord!" He ground out the last words and jerked away from her to stand in front of the window.

Molly waited, knowing he was trying to get a grip on his emotions. Then she slipped her arms around his waist from behind, pressing against his back. "Jake, you're not doomed to that life again if you start over."

"I'd be taking a chance!" he protested. He turned and looked at her. "I can't risk security on chance."

"You're scared to take a chance," she said softly, musing about how big an emotional risk she had already taken with Jake.

"I'm ready for a walk," Jamie said, interrupting them. Jake went outside with his daughter, but Molly trailed behind a moment, watching him walk down the slope of land. She wished circumstances were different for him.

AFTER THEIR WALK Jake and Ben went down to salvage what they could from the water-soaked floor of the boat house. Ivy lay in the sunshine, and Molly and Jamie sat down at the water's edge. "Want to build a sand castle?" Molly asked Jamie.

"I don't know how. I might get dirty."

"You just build. You and your clothes will wash. Come on," Molly urged, extending her hand.

"I better not." Jamie gave a shake of her head.

Molly felt mildly frustrated. It seemed as important to try to break through Jamie's seriousness as it had been to part Jake from his everlasting list of jobs. "Will you come watch me?"

Nodding, Jamie moved to the grassy slope where the land became sand and mud. Molly sat down with her feet trailing at the water's edge. As brownish-green waves washed up, they curled over her toes, then receded swiftly, only to return again in seconds.

"See?" Molly said, pinching a bit of salt and mud to shape it into a rectangle. "We'll start here and make a wall. This will be a castle for—what do you want? A prince? A princess?"

"A princess," Jamie answered, watching Molly intently.

"We could use a stone walk at the front door. Do you want to hand me some pebbles?"

Clutching Alfred, Jamie moved barefoot off the grass and wandered along the water's edge to gather small stones. Sunlight sparkled on the lake's surface; farther from shore the water was blue, reflecting a cloudless sky. Jamie handed the pebbles to Molly, who asked, "Where shall we put the front door of the castle?"

"Right here," Jamie suggested, pointing her finger.

Molly began to push the pebbles into the earth. "Can you get a few more?" she asked.

Jamie did. Then, as she watched, Molly said, "Can you put down about six more?"

"Sure. That's neat," Jamie said. "I think I'd call it a mud castle instead of sand. Alfred won't want to do this. He doesn't like mud," she said earnestly, moving the bear to a dry grassy spot several feet away before returning to get the stones and add to the pebbly walk.

They talked and laughed as they worked. Molly wasn't aware of Jake's or Ben's approach until they were beside her. "That's a super castle," Ben said enthusiastically, squatting down to look at it.

"Good thing the lake is nearby," Jake said cheerfully to Jamie.

She giggled and motioned to him. "Come help us."

"No, thanks," he said dryly. "I think we'd better get a pair of jeans soon."

Jamie tilted her head, regarding him with a puzzled stare. "Why?"

He laughed, looking at Molly. "Jeans wash better than pink play clothes."

Jamie still seemed puzzled, but she shifted her attention back to the castle. "Alfred doesn't want to help because he's too big to live in this."

"Well, maybe I should take Alfred up to the porch for a glass of lemonade with me," Jake said.

Jamie grinned. "He'd like that."

"Maybe, if someone's nice to us, Alfred and I will bring lemonade out for everyone."

Jamie laughed and held up her hands. "Come here Daddy. I'll be nice and give you a hug!"

He laughed and winked at Molly. "The mud castle was a fine idea," he said, and his praise made Molly feel as if the sun had just brightened. Jake snatched up Alfred and headed for the house in long strides, but Ben sat down to join them.

"What'cha doing?" Ivy asked, sitting up and squinting at them. Molly wondered if Ivy's sudden interest had developed because of Ben. "Ooh! A mud house!" Ivy exclaimed eagerly, coming to join them.

Ben turned toward her. "Let's you and I start another part over here; then maybe we can join the two."

"Sure enough!" Ivy said enthusiastically. "I was reading for a time. That book of yours is interesting. All the Indian tribes Darwin found in Patagonia are gone now?"

"Yeah," Ben said, piling up a mound of wet mud. "They died out—there are a few descendants, but none of the tribes still exist."

"You wonder how they got there in the first place—it's sort of the end of the world."

Molly listened to their conversation, unfamiliar with their subject, but amazed that Ivy had found someone with whom she could discuss her reading. And Ben seemed to have lost most of his shyness. But then Molly had never seen a man remain shy around Ivy.

She watched Jamie work. Her curls were tangled; mud was smudged on her hands, arms, and cheek. The top of her tongue flicked in the corner of her mouth.

"Jamie, would you like your hair put up in a ponytail so it won't be so hot?"

"Yes, ma'am." Jamie nodded without looking up from the wall she was building.

"We'll do it after we wash up."

Molly worked, putting a tower on one part of the castle. Jamie touched her arm. "I like you, Miss Ashland."

Molly felt a tug on her heart. "I like you too, Jamie. Why don't you just call me Molly?" she suggested.

Jamie smiled shyly and went back to work.

Later, Ben, Jamie and Jake went inside to get bits of foil and material to use for decoration. While they were gone, Molly paused and watched Ivy working as diligently as Jamie had. Ivy even held her tongue in the corner of her mouth just as Jamie had.

"It's nice you and Ben like the same books."

Ivy looked up, a bemused expression on her face. "Isn't he a marvel?" she asked in a breathless voice. Molly felt as if someone had delivered a blow to her midriff.

"Oh, no! Ivy, don't get interested in another man so soon!" She didn't add that with Ben, Ivy might be interested in a hopeless case.

Ivy frowned, her tone changing to one of resignation. "I know you're right. He'll go home to Iowa soon and I'll go to Detroit, but he's so nice, Molly. He knows history and he loves it like I do. He doesn't like his job at all. I've been urging him to try again to get a teaching job."

"You have?" Molly asked in surprise, remembering that in the past, men in Ivy's life had been too aggressive to take career suggestions from her. Nor would Ivy have offered any, because she became a clinging, adoring female around them, to the point that Molly had been uncomfortable being in their company. "What did he say?"

"He gives up without even trying. He's been hoping to get on the staff at Iowa State. I told him if he started teaching in a high school and maybe got some experience first, he might get a job in a college later."

Molly stared at Ivy, realizing there was a new and unique development in Ivy's life. "That sounds like a good idea," Molly said.

Ivy sighed. "To tell the truth, I don't think he knows I'm a woman half the time. The other half, I'm too much woman. He's the first man I've met who doesn't like my looks a lot."

She sounded so sad at the last comment that Molly had to hold back a smile. "As long as he likes you as a person, that's more important, Ivy. The other guys in your past have all liked your looks."

Ivy paused and looked at Molly intently. "You remember telling me if I wanted a man to notice me for something besides my looks, I should change my looks?''

Molly nodded. "Yes, but I might have given you bad advice. You said your looks are important in your career."

"My career embarrasses Ben," she announced glumly, and Molly had a sinking feeling. The Cannon men might turn out to be disasters for the Ashland women.

"He's nice about it," Ivy added, "but I know he doesn't like it. He thinks I should pursue my accounting, but I don't have the heart to tell him how much more I can earn dancing."

"You can't dance forever."

"No, I'm saving my money and taking accounting, and the way I figure, in another eight years I'll have an accounting degree just from night courses and I can quit dancing then. But in the meantime..." She sounded so wistful—as uncharacteristic of Ivy as acute shyness would be—that Molly paused to look at her. Ivy sat frowning, looking down at herself. "I want Ben to notice me and to like what he sees."

"I don't think you have to worry about that," Molly said dryly, smoothing a mound of mud.

"I don't know. I get the feeling I sort of overwhelm him and he can't see beyond my dancing and my appearance."

"He seems to enjoy being with you."

"Not enough to kiss me!"

"You want him to kiss you?"

To Molly's amazement, Ivy blushed. "Yes, I do. Here he comes. Jake and Jamie are with him. I don't want the time here to end," Ivy said, watching Ben. Molly studied Jake walking beside his brother and her heart constricted. She didn't want the time in Missouri to end either. Could she see herself settling down with Jake, she wondered.

Shorter than Ben, heavier in the shoulders, Jake strode bare-chested, his skin tan, his shorts revealing his muscular legs sprinkled with short dark hairs. Sunlight gave a sheen to their skins as both men sauntered across the lawn, and Molly felt her pulse jump just watching Jake. Gray eyes focused on her and she could feel a pull; the others faded momentarily and all she was aware of was Jake. He listened as Ben talked, but his gaze never left Molly's, and she knew she had handed her heart over as swiftly as Ivy often had.

With a carefree abandon she hadn't shown before, Jamie danced around them, finally causing Jake to pull his eyes from Molly's. He scooped Jamie up, giggling and she got muddy handprints on his chest. As he waded into the lake to wash them off, Jamie squealed and playfully tried to wriggle away. Molly enjoyed watching them, but was saddened once more by their situation.

All of them sat in the mud and finished two three-foot-high connecting castles with tiny flags fluttering from the battlements and shiny foil in the windows. Ben took pictures of the castles and the builders, complete with mud smudged from head to toe. Then they waded into the lake for a swim.

During the afternoon, Jake and Molly were left alone when the others drove to Hattersville to get groceries. Jake had suggested it would be safer if he and Molly remained out of sight at the cabin as much as possible. The moment the car turned out of view and the sounds of the motor faded, Jake reached for Molly, and turned her to face him. "Do you know how badly

I want to kiss you?" he drawled in a syrupy baritone that poured heat over her.

She walked into his arms, hugging him, her pulse racing in eagerness. "About half as much as I want to kiss you."

"Impossible! I want you in my arms when you're out there in your sexy swimsuit, when you're at the stove cooking, when you're piled up in bed reading a kid's story...oh, Molly!" His tone changed, and the last word came out almost a groan. He leaned down to kiss her, she marveled that each time, his kisses were more exciting than before. She knew in her heart that she loved Jake, but she wouldn't acknowledge it because it frightened her. It had happened too swiftly; something might change when they went home. The differences between them were going unresolved in the frictionless vacuum of the vacation in the Ozarks, but she worried about everything being as good when they got home. She wanted what she had with Jake to last. She realized he had caused her to rethink some of her values and face her fears.

Together they went inside, drifting toward the stairs while entwined in each other's arms. Finally they made love on the braided rug in front of the hearth, because they didn't get around to going up the stairs.

Later, she lay in Jake's arms, running her fingers through his thick, wavy hair. "What a nice family you have! Ben, Jamie...they're wonderful."

"Thank you. I think so too. And I like Ivy. You were right—she's no trouble. As a matter of fact, Jamie's had a whale of a time with her."

"They're chums."

"And you..." He rolled her over so that he was leaning above her as he smoothed damp tendrils of hair away from her face. "You're wonderful to Jamie; you seem truly interested in her. She's coming out of her shell a little, thanks partly to you."

Molly was barely aware of what he was saying. She traced her finger over the crooked bump in his slender nose, across hard cheekbones, and down to his jaw. "You're handsome."

"Thank you, sweetie. I seem to remember, as I hung by my fingers high in the air, promising to get revenge," he reminded her.

"Should I try to run now?"

His arms tightened around her waist and his leg slipped across hers, pinning her down. "Too late. I'm going to get revenge," he whispered, "until you yell help...." He kissed her throat, his lips moving down over her collarbone and lower to the soft, eager flesh. "Kiss you and kiss you and do—" his mouth found a trembling peak "—this to you—" his tongue and teeth tormented sweetly "—until you cry help; until you feel like you're hanging in the air with nothing solid to save you...."

She wound her fingers in his hair, tugging his mouth up to hers. "You're not doing anything to help your cause the next time you hang from the side of a building. I'll know to wait and let you—" Her words stopped as his mouth took them, changing the playful moment to one of intense need. Desire escalated heatedly until finally Jake rolled on his back, pulling Molly on top of him. "Come here," he said hoarsely, his hands seeking, driving her to abandon as both moved to a rhythm of pleasure, trying to satisfy a desperate longing.

THEY DRESSED IN SWIMSUITS and cooled off in the lake when they knew it was time for the others to return. Molly wanted more time alone with Jake. She wanted to talk, to touch Jake every moment, to be touched by him, and she suspected he had the same compulsion. He draped his arm over her shoulder as they went up to meet the car and help carry in the groceries. Ben handed Jake two sacks, one with something long and flat inside. "Here's the package you wanted."

"Good. Thanks," he said, thrusting the smaller sack under his arm. "Molly, come here. Let me show you this," he said while Ivy and Jamie unloaded the groceries. In the living room, he turned to hand the sack to Molly. "This is yours."

Startled, she looked at the sack, then at Jake. She took it and pulled out a Scrabble game. Smiling at him, she said, "You remembered I said I liked Scrabble! Thank you!" Stepping close, she hugged him. She was happier that he had remembered than she was interested in the game. "That's great."

Jamie appeared in the door. "Did Daddy give you his present?"

"Yes, he did."

"And this one is for you," Jake said, winking at Jamie as he held out the smaller sack. "I told Ben what I wanted him to get."

"Thank you," Jamie said, taking it and carefully opening it. She smiled and pulled out a small stuffed lion. "Thank you, Daddy," she said, hugging the lion.

"Hey, when do I get a hug?" Jake asked, hunkering down.

Jamie put her arms around his neck and he stood up, holding her close. "Thank you," Jamie said. "I'll name him . . . Louie."

"Louie Lion. Fine. We'd better help with the groceries. Jake held Jamie with one arm and draped the other over Molly's shoulders as they returned to the kitchen.

After lunch Ivy disappeared upstairs while Molly exercised. The men cleaned the kitchen and Jamie went out to build some more on the mud castles.

Molly was alone in the living room when Ivy came down and Molly almost dropped the clean laundry she was holding. "Ivy!" she gasped, staring at her sister. Ivy wore no makeup; the thick, false lashes were gone, her hair was cut to shoulder length, and the ends curled under slightly. As Molly gaped in amazement at Ivy's simple cotton shirt and shorts, she realized Ivy must be falling madly in love with Ben to go to such an extreme for him. In the past Ivy wouldn't have set her foot out the door without makeup.

"You look . . . nice," Molly said.

"Huh. I look like . . . Miss Ordinary Nobody, but I want Ben to notice my mind," she said stubbornly.

"I think he will in due time," Molly said, speculating how long Ivy would go through this phase of her life.

"What do you think he'll say?" Ivy asked.

Molly heard the back door slam and voices. "You'll know in seconds because here they come.

She clutched the laundry tighter and started toward the stairs as the others came inside. Molly saw Jake's brows arch and his eyes widen. Ben glanced at her and went to dig into a box at one end of the sofa. "Ivy, here's that book we were talking about in the car."

Shrugging at Ivy, whose mouth had dropped open, Molly picked up the rest of the laundry, and hurried upstairs. Jake and Jamie came up behind her.

"We're going to swim. Want to go with us?" Jamie asked.

"Sure," Molly answered. "I'll be ready in a few minutes."

Jamie ran into the bathroom to change clothes and closed the door. When Molly looked at Jake, his mouth was curved in amusement. He asked, "What brought about the transformation?"

"Ivy? She wants Ben to notice her mind," Molly said, shaking her head. "Poor Ivy—Ben didn't notice anything. He's more interested in his books."

"He noticed. Ben doesn't show what he feels, but he doesn't miss much that goes on."

"Like his brother."

"I show my feelings. Come here and I'll show you some now," he said, sweeping her into his room and closing the door.

"Jake, we're not alone."

"Jamie thinks I'm changing clothes and she'll go downstairs by the lake to wait for us. Ivy and Ben are reading, no doubt." While he talked, he took the laundry from Molly's arms and placed it on the floor.

"Hey, that's clean laundry. I—"

He kissed her, ending conversation, crushing her to him and bending her over until she flung her arms around his neck and clung to him. Her body curved to fit against his while he kissed her hard. He finally swung her up and released her. "I'd rather go to bed than swim," he said gruffly.

"We don't have a choice." She looked into solemn, silver eyes and wondered what was going through his mind. Neither of them had ever declared love...she suspected Jake never would because he wasn't in love with her. Molly was still afraid to make a declaration, but the fear was vanishing swiftly. He smiled, but his smile had a touch of sadness and regret that made her curiosity grow about what he was thinking. He scooped up the laundry and tucked it beneath his arm. "I'll put this away."

"No, you won't," she said, taking it from him. "It's mine and Ivy's."

Jake tugged a lock of hair gently. "Your hair is like silk," he said, but his gaze was on her mouth and she doubted he was contemplating her hair. They heard a door bang and Jamie called. "I beat you, Daddy. I'll be downstairs."

"Okay, Jamie," he called back and Molly moved away, going to her room and closing the door.

THE NEXT TWO DAYS PASSED in lazy swims and late lunches. All of them piled into boats and rowed, singing until nearby birds flapped out of the trees and flew away. They water-skied and walked in the woods, and Molly felt as if she had stepped into a dream world without cares or responsibilities or a future. Jake was more relaxed; his lists had disappeared. Ben had lost his shyness and Ivy continued to appear with a schoolgirl scrubbed freshness that Molly had yet to see Ben acknowledge. Molly dreaded Sunday; she couldn't envision how meeting Jake would affect her life when she returned to work in Detroit.

On Wednesday afternoon while the others fished, Molly and Jamie decided to take a walk. Molly stopped in the kitchen to get a ball of twine and two dozen small strips while Jamie watched. "I want to mark our path. Your daddy can walk in the woods and know the way home, but I'm afraid I might get us lost, so we'll mark our trail. Want some?"

"Yes, ma'am," Jamie said, taking a dozen little strips. As soon as they were out of sight of the house, Molly was careful to mark their path, and made sure Jamie draped the twine on bushes and trees as she went along. It became cool and shady; a soft, damp mat of leaves on the ground surrounded the dense trees. They were silent, pausing to watch a ground squirrel, stopping while Jamie pocketed a rock and picked wild-flowers.

They moved without noise and Molly relished the stillness. She decided Jamie enjoyed it as well. On a ridge overlooking the silver lake, Molly saw the canoe paddle past with Jake. Jake. Just the thought of him made her pulse quicken, but she had to face the fact that their days in Missouri were numbered. Maybe there was a future for them, because their differences seemed to have evaporated—even to the point that she was beginning to appreciate opera, she thought with a smile. She breathed deeply, inhaling the fresh forest air as they changed direction, moving away from the lake and deeper into the woods.

A bird's melodic call made her stop and look around. She caught Jamie's sleeve and both of them scanned branches for sight of the bird. Jamie pointed silently as another call came. Following the direction Jamie had indicated, Molly saw a bright yellow bird high on the gnarled branch of an oak. She stood immobile until the tiny bird flew away and silence once more descended. Molly was about to take a step and proceed with her walk when she heard sticks break and leaves crunch in the unmistakable sounds of something moving nearby. Something larger than a squirrel.

Panic froze Molly, turning her to ice. She instantly imagined some kind of large animal and wondered what kind of beasts were native to the Ozarks.

Seeing Jamie's eyes widen in question, she reached to take the child's arm. Molly placed her finger on her lips for silence, and Jamie nodded. But Molly realized she had no way to protect herself or Jamie, and if she screamed, she was too far from the lake for Jake to hear or find her.

The sounds were growing louder and her pulse drummed in her ears heavily. She tried to gather her wits and hear what direction the noise came from. Deciding it was somewhere ahead and to her right, she surveyed the trees, and chose one she could climb if it became necessary. Pulling Jamie down beside her, she knelt behind some bushes, ready to spring as she watched through the underbrush. Her heart slammed against her ribs when she spotted the source of the noise.

CHAPTER THIRTEEN

THROUGH THE THICK TREES and branches, a man was clearly outlined. He seemed to be picking his way carefully, and Molly realized he might pass by without noticing her. She held her breath, revising her initial impression of a hungry animal to that of a man. He could be a fisherman or a woodsman or a tourist, someone enjoying the woods just as she had been. She peered through the shade to study him and suffered another jolt when she glimpsed his profile. It was the man who had approached her in the mall in Springfield!

A new fear overwhelmed her—Jamie! She had to protect Jake's daughter. She glanced down at the child, who sat as still as a rock.

The man moved closer, his gaze sweeping the area ahead of him. Molly, her fingers icy, dared not breathe. Then the man veered away from her to the north, moving steadily, looking to the right and left, his back to Molly. He stopped again, looking around before moving ahead cautiously. She waited, her thoughts racing; she felt terribly alone and wanted to get up and run back to Jake.

She waited until the man was out of sight and hearing, and then she studied her watch until another three minutes had passed. Frightened to wait any longer in case he doubled back, she nodded to Jamie and began to retrace her way, picking up the bits of string as swiftly as possible, yet trying to keep quiet. She paused every few minutes to listen for anyone, but all was silent except for the song of birds.

Her heart thudded with fear. She wanted only to get safely back to Jake and to get Jamie back to him. When she saw the house, she curbed the urge to break into a run.

A new problem arose. How could she get word of danger to Jake when both boats were gone and he was on the lake fishing? "I want to talk to your father. He needs to know about that man," she said to Jamie as they walked to the water's edge.

"Is he a bad man?"

"Yes, I'm afraid he is. He had something to do with the robbery. You stay with me," Molly said, scanning the still surface of the lake but seeing no sign of the boats. "We need to get your daddy home. Let's walk along the shore," Molly suggested, praying she wouldn't lead Jamie into an encounter with the man. But she couldn't just hide in the house and do nothing but wait.

They wound close to the water, sliding in the mud in spots, wading where it was shallow, then moving to dry ground as they rounded first one bend and then another.

"Molly, there he is!" Jamie said excitedly. "Should we call to him?"

"No. Just wave your arms." They both waved but Molly became increasingly frustrated as Jake sat quietly fishing, watching the water, a broad-brimmed straw hat pulled low over his eyes. He pulled out his line and cast again, flicking his wrist and sending the hook far from the boat. It landed with a plop, and just as Molly was beginning to decide they might have to call to him, he looked around.

He waved in return.

"Keep waving at him," Molly said, trying to motion to him to row to shore.

He stared at them a moment, then began to reel in his line.

"You can stop. He's coming."

"How do you know?"

"I'm sure he is. He's just getting in his fishing line." They watched as he paddled to them, the canoe slicing silently through the water. Molly turned to inspect the thick, dark woods that had become menacing. The canoe slid to the bank and Jake's smile faded as he looked at Molly's face. "What's wrong?"

"The man who came up to me in the mall in Springfield is there in the woods walking around as if he's looking for something."

"Oh, damn! Get in. We'll paddle out and get Ben and Ivy and go home."

As Molly helped Jamie into the canoe, she asked, "Would you rather I go back to the house now so it won't be empty? Nothing's locked."

"Get in. You're not going up there alone."

She stepped in, trying to keep her balance as the canoe wobbled. Jake steadied it by poking a paddle into the soft mud, and when they were seated, he pushed off. The canoe slipped through the water and rounded a curve; all of them were quiet. In seconds, Molly spotted Ivy and Ben basking in the sunshine in the flat-bottomed boat. As Jake paddled up beside them, they lowered their fishing poles.

"Ben, Molly saw one of the men who's connected to the robbery in Detroit."

"Are you going to get the police?"

"First we need to get back to the house. I don't think you should turn on the motor. Why don't you row back? It won't take long and it won't attract as much attention. Follow me, okay? We'll hide the boats near the house."

While he talked, Jamie looked up and Molly smiled at her reassuringly. She hoped the child wasn't frightened. Jamie squeezed Alfred in her arms and smiled in return.

As they glided silently across the lake, Molly felt exposed to any prying eyes that might be observing from the woods. Someone could easily be watching them without their knowing it. Tension mounted when Jake pushed the canoe close to shore and waded in to tug it up on land. Ben followed, and Jake reached into his jeans' pocket to withdraw the car keys and give them to his brother. "You stay here. If everything's okay at the house, I'll whistle. If not, get everyone to the Jeep and out of here. If you have to, get in the boat and use the motor. Go where there are people and get help. Just be careful."

"You can't go up there alone," Molly said to Jake.

"No need for more than one of us to run into the thugs."

"They don't know me," Ben said. "Why don't I go?"

"No," Jake said flatly and Ben shrugged, turning away. Molly guessed it was an old pattern from childhood—Ben yielding to whatever Jake thought best. Jake winked at Jamie and squeezed her shoulder, then turned toward the house.

Molly, uncomfortable with the thought of his walking into danger, wanted desperately to pull him back as he strode away. Taking Jamie's hand, she suggested, "Let's get into the other boat. If we have to leave, we'll be ready."

When Jamie complied, Molly paused, and said to Ben, "I've always hated to wait. Jake may need some help. I'm going to follow him. I'll be careful."

"I don't think you should," Ben said.

"Neither do I," Ivy said. "Don't go!"

"I'll be careful. I'll just stay back and watch."

She turned away to avoid further arguments. Jake was nowhere in sight, but she moved silently and in seconds came into view of the house. Jake shouldn't have had time to be inside, but there wasn't any sign of him outside. She stayed within the shelter of the trees, but tried to get closer to the house, moving around so that her view was of the back and west side.

And then a man with a gun in his hand came out of the house and moved across the porch, and Molly froze.

He sidled carefully along the porch around the house. Then, through the screen she recognized his walk and the slight movements of his broad shoulders with each step. Jake! She let out the breath she'd been holding as she realized that he must have gone in through the front and had been checking the porch to be sure it was safe. In seconds he was out of sight. Then he reappeared as he made a full circle to the back again. He stepped to the door and whistled a bird call. Molly hurried across the lawn.

"That was damned fast!" he said as he held open the door.

"I followed you."

"You don't take directions well, do you, gypsy?" he whispered, running his finger along her cheek.

"I was worried about you."

"Everything looks all right here. This house is hard to find, but they'll find us."

His words chilled Molly and she shivered involuntarily. "What'll we do?"

"Get out of here as quickly as possible."

"Now?"

His gray eyes became flat and hard. "I don't want to stay one second longer than necessary. I don't want danger around Jamie. Here they come."

As the others entered the house, Jake approached them to drop his hand on Jamie's shoulder and take Ivy's arm. "Why don't you two take Alfred up and begin to pack. We'll leave here tonight to drive home to Detroit." He winked at Ivy and her eyes widened. Then she seemed to guess what Jake wanted.

"Sure. We'll put Alfred's coat on him to travel. How's that?"

"Fine," Jamie said agreeably, following Ivy. Molly couldn't tell if Jamie had forgotten the danger or was merely trying to please her father.

As soon as they were out of earshot, Jake pulled out a chair for Molly and hooked his toe around another to pull it close to hers and sat down, his elbows resting on his knees.

"We need to get out of here. Ben, I'm sorry to cut your vacation short, but I don't think you should take a chance on staying here. I know we can't."

"That's fine," Ben said. "I understand."

"I'll be glad if you want to come back to Detroit with me."

Ben nodded, and Jake continued, "They haven't found the house yet, or they would have been in here waiting for us. It's only a matter of time, though, until they do find it. They'll probably try to get in tonight when they think we're asleep. They don't know Molly has spotted one of them searching the woods for us.''

"So what should we do?" Ben asked.

"We'll eat, pack, get the house ready to shut down and as soon as it's dark, slip out.''

"Suppose they see us putting luggage in the cars and try to stop us?" Molly asked.

"I think we might have to leave a few things behind. What I figure we should do is get whatever we can carry in one trip. Walk out and get in the cars and drive off fast. Thank heavens the roads are dry now. We'll stay together until we get to the Springfield police and talk to them. I have to alert the Detroit police if we leave the Ozarks.''

"I hope Brantz is back safely by now," Molly said.

"I doubt that he is," Jake said dryly, or I don't think they'd be combing the woods for us. Anyway, Molly and Jamie can go with me. You and Ivy will each have to drive a car.''

"Sure," Ben said.

"Between now and then, everyone should stay at the house. You can move around on the porch so we look normal, but don't leave here.''

"You'll have to get the boats back," Molly said.

"I can do that," Ben said. "They won't know me.''

"Okay. Put the boats in the boat house and drop the padlock on the door, because we won't be using them again," Jake said grimly, his gray eyes fixing on Molly. To her, his words signified the end of their special time. Was that the thought she was reading in his eyes, too?

"I've locked up the front, but it would only take seconds to get it open. You go see about the boats. I'll stay here. Molly, you can pack."

"I'll help Jamie, too," she said, feeling a constriction that overrode fear as she stood up and left the porch.

Upstairs, she paused in the doorway. "We're going to pack now," she said to Ivy. Molly watched Jamie concentrating on Alfred. After a moment she asked, "Want some more help with packing?"

"Yes, ma'am," Jamie said, pulling a green coat on Alfred and fastening the buttons beneath the bear's jaw.

"Alfred looks ready to travel," Molly commented, her gaze drifting over the room; over Jake's bed, where she had lain in his arms, over his suitcases, one with a pair of jeans spilling out.... She loved him and everything that belonged to him. The suitcase was special, the jeans were special—all his belongings lost their ordinariness because of his ownership.

"Molly, are bad men after Daddy?"

"Did your daddy tell you about seeing a robbery in Detroit?"

"Yes."

"The man we saw in the woods is one of the robbers, we think," Molly said calmly, trying to put the situation in as simple a light as possible. "He wants something that he thinks your daddy has, but actually the police have it, so we're going back to Detroit, where it will be safer," she explained, wishing she were as confident about their safety as she'd tried to sound.

She began to help Jamie, but realized the child needed little help. She was neat and careful as she folded her clothes and placed them in the suitcase.

"Will you carry Alfred?"

"Yes. He doesn't have his hat on yet."

"Want me to put it on or fold something for you?"

"If you'll fold my blouse, I'll put Alfred's hat on. Alfred goes almost everywhere I go," she said as she fussed, her dainty fingers twisting the straw hat on the bear's head. "Daddy gave Alfred to me when I was a little girl."

"How little?" Molly asked, amused.

"My third birthday. I love Alfred!" She picked up the bear and hugged it. "Sometimes I miss Daddy and I hug Alfred and pretend its Daddy with me instead of Alfred."

Molly felt a pang for Jamie and ran her hand over the child's curls.

"Would you put my hair in a ponytail?"

"Sure," Molly said and stood up to get the brush. But she stopped, momentarily startled. Jake was standing in the doorway, such a look of anguish on his face that for an instant, Molly thought something terrible had happened. Then she realized Jake had heard Jamie talking about missing him and she understood how painful the child's words must have been to him.

His gaze shifted to meet hers and he drew a deep breath, a shuttered look hardening his features.

As he entered the room, he said, "I thought I would pack. How's Jamie doing?"

"Molly's going to fix my hair," Jamie announced, sitting cross-legged on the foot of the bed.

While Molly brushed, Jake put his suitcase on his bed. "Did you explain to Jamie why we're going?"

"Yes."

He smiled at Jamie and winked. "We'll be home tomorrow night and you'll be in your own bed."

Jamie wriggled with pleasure. "Alfred wants to go home. Can Molly come see my room?"

"She sure can," Jake said with a smile. Jake paused as he passed the window and Molly realized he was scanning the woods and lake for signs of danger.

She parted Jamie's soft, black hair, brushing carefully so she wouldn't pull, smoothing the hair and slipping a rubber band over it to hold it. As she brushed, Molly glanced up. Jake wore an intense, solemn look as he watched her, making her breath catch when she tried to guess what was on his mind. He winked at her and she smiled, but felt a tug on the hair in her hand as Jamie looked up expectantly to see why Molly had stopped. Molly returned her attention to Jamie, but she continued to speculate about Jake's thoughts, and for the first time, she acknowledged that a serious commitment to Jake would include taking on responsibility for Jamie. As she brushed Jamie's raven hair, she reflected on the situation.

They ate on the back porch and afterward, Ben and Ivy tried to teach Jamie Scrabble while Jake and Molly walked around to the front to sit. Jake propped his feet on the porch rail, and draped his arm around Molly's shoulders.

"Jake, when we go—why don't I ride in the back seat with Jamie?"

"That's a good idea," he said.

"Do you think they'll try to stop us when we leave?"

He waited a long time before he answered, running his fingers over his knee where his jeans had gotten snagged. "I don't know. They may not have found the house yet, but if that guy in the woods was so close hours ago, I don't see how they could avoid finding us."

"How'll they know we're the right people?"

"They'll know. They'll have high-powered binoculars. You and I have been on the porch enough this afternoon. I'll be glad to leave here."

"I won't," she said softly and his head turned.

She noticed the change in his features as the harshness left them. He removed his arm from her shoulders and took her wrist to pull her toward him. "Sit on my lap," he urged.

She moved, draping her hands on his shoulders as he smiled at her. "I didn't mean—" he began.

"I know what you meant," she said. "You'll be relieved to get us all out of danger."

"Yes, but what we've found—it's special, Molly."

She leaned down, closing her eyes as her lips touched his. When his arms tightened, crushing her to his chest, she held him, wishing she didn't ever have to stop. Thoughts and worries evaporated as they kissed. Finally, she pulled herself together, then stood and moved away, smoothing her hair.

"I'm going up to finish packing."

Jake didn't say a word but as he watched her go, he felt a sense of loss. He was beginning to want more and more of Molly, and he would soon face a time when there would be less and less. He knew her well enough now in every way to understand that she was afraid of a lasting commitment. From all she had indicated, she was deeply attracted to him, but there had never been a declaration of love on her part any more than there had been on his. His pulse beat faster as he thought about her, remembering moments shared, remembering moments she had been with Jamie.

He shifted in his chair, and ran his fingers through his hair distractedly. He thought he was in love with

Molly, but they had only known each other a short
time, and under unusual circumstances. He was cautious enough to want to wait until he got back to Detroit to see what developed when their lives became
routine, because there were fathomless differences between them. Yet with each day spent in her company,
the importance of their differences was diminishing;
they were even working some of them out. He was
more into exercise again, thanks to her, and he felt
much better and more relaxed.

"Jake!" Molly stood inside the front door. "While
I was packing, I saw two men moving in the trees near
the boat house.

"Damn." He stood up and walked into the house.
"It's almost nightfall, but with binoculars they can see
what Ben and Ivy and Jamie are doing. Is the light on
in your room?"

"Not yet."

"Are you through packing?"

"Yes. You know how little I brought. It's in the
sacks from the department store."

Jake looked down at the pile of luggage and sacks
ready by the front door. "I think we're all ready to go.
Will you go upstairs and watch while I see about the
others?"

"Sure."

Jake went through the house, feeling a cold prickle
of fear. It terrified him to have Jamie around when
someone was after them; he wanted to climb into the
Jeep and get going. He felt responsible for all of them
and kept glancing at his watch, calculating how soon
they could go.

Finally he switched on the kitchen light, knowing he
would be silhouetted in the doorway and wanting

whoever was watching to think things were normal. He made a show of observing the Scrabble game and casually turned the portable radio on to music. Then he knelt down by Jamie. "How's the game?" he asked.

"Uncle Ben's winning," Jamie said.

"Bedtime for you before long," Jake said. He lowered his voice to whisper. "Someone might be watching. Keep the radio on, the lights off. Stop the game now or you'll have to turn on the porch lights. I'll take Jamie inside, supposedly to bed. Ivy, you come in ten minutes after Jamie." She nodded, and then he added, "Will you go into the kitchen now and get a drink, so when you get up again later it won't stir undue attention?"

As she left, Jake turned to Ben. "Wait a few minutes after Ivy leaves and then you come inside. Okay?"

Ben nodded and asked, "Want me to lock the kitchen door when I come through?"

Jake debated. "I think they'll break in anyway. They might hear you lock it. Just leave it open. Our lives are more important than the house."

"Okay."

"We'll each pick up what we can carry, go right out to the cars and leave fast. If we get separated, we'll meet at the police station in Springfield. The first chance we get, I'll stop at a pay phone and call the police to alert them about the men being in the area, but I don't think it'll be safe to stop in Hattersville."

"Okay," Ben said. Jamie watched Jake solemnly. He squeezed her shoulder and smiled. To his relief, she smiled in return and didn't appear frightened.

As Ivy returned and sat down to help put away the game, Jake picked Jamie up in his arms. "Off with you, now," he said, kissing her cheek.

She wrapped her arm around his neck and they went inside. Then he switched off the kitchen light and walked quickly through the dusky living room. At the foot of the stairs, he stood in the glow from the hall light upstairs. "Molly!"

In seconds she appeared at the top.

"Leave some lights on up there. Are you ready?"

"Yes," she said and came downstairs. "It's pretty dark outside now."

"I know," Jake said, switching off the upstairs hall light and throwing the living room into darkness.

"I can't see!" Jamie said.

"Our eyes will get used to the dark in a minute," Jake answered soothingly and sat down on the sofa, pulling Jamie onto his lap. "Molly?"

His voice was deep and resonant, and she moved cautiously toward him until she bumped into his knees. His fingers closed around her wrist and he pulled her down beside him, cuddling her close. His solid bulk was reassuring, and his air of calm confidence helped the tense situation. "As soon as my eyes adjust, I'm going to move to the window," he said softly.

He squeezed her hand. Though she was anxious to leave, the last minutes at the house held memories of the most exciting time in her life. She loved Jake— whatever the consequences.

In seconds he stood. Molly's eyes had adjusted enough to see Jake pick up the pistol and approach the window. A few minutes later Ivy joined them, and finally Ben.

"Okay, here we go," Jake said, picking up Jamie's suitcase and sacks with his things. Molly gathered hers and followed. They crossed the porch quietly, and crept quickly to the cars. Doors slammed, motors revved to life and they were on their way, headlights slicing sharply through the high weeds and trees.

Suddenly, a man stepped from the trees with a gun raised.

CHAPTER FOURTEEN

"GET DOWN!" Jake ordered, but Molly had already flung herself over Jamie. Jake fired a split-second after they heard the first shot. The Jeep careened wildly as Jake fired again and drove toward the man, who jumped out of the way. Jake roared past him, and Ivy and Ben followed.

The Jeep bounced and swept over high weeds, then scraped a tree with a metallic sound. "You can get up now," Jake said, his voice tight with anger.

They flew through the woods, Jake slowing when the gap widened too much between the Jeep and Ivy's car. Finally they reached the dirt road, and soon they were racing into Hattersville. The tiny town had gone to bed for the night. Jake slowed to observe the speed limit, then stepped on the gas pedal, and sped through the darkness.

Tense and quiet, Molly rode in the back, her arm around Jamie. She could see the angry set of Jake's profile in the lights from the dash, and the tightness of his grip on the steering wheel. But they were on their way to safety—on their way home.

When they reached the four-lane highway, Molly still couldn't relax. Too clearly, she remembered the man stepping out and aiming at them. She dearly wanted to see the Springfield police, and she couldn't help but wonder what dangers they would face in Detroit.

"I hope Brantz is safely home and they've caught the men involved," she said.

"Yeah," Jake said tersely.

"How could one computer chip be worth so much risk?"

"You're talking about the latest in high-tech development—money, Molly. Big money."

"I suppose, but I wouldn't think it would be of use to individuals."

"They could sell to the highest bidder—in this country or out of it. Or they could have been hired by unscrupulous competitors. There are numerous possibilities."

Molly shivered. "I'll be glad when life returns to normal," she said, aware Jake was still exceeding the speed limit.

He glanced in the rearview mirror. "Damn, where's a patrolman? I'm going over the speed limit and there's no one around."

"You want one?"

"I sure as hell do. We could get an escort to Springfield. Those thugs can't be far behind us."

Molly hadn't wanted to think about anyone in pursuit, and it was useless to watch out the back because Ivy and Ben were behind them. She looked down at Jamie, busy smoothing Alfred's coat. Then she glanced at Jake, and suspected Jamie felt little fear in the security of Jake's presence. She felt better herself, remembering how she had followed him away from the kidnapping in those first few moments.

And now, how glad she was that she had! Whatever heartache lay ahead, she would never regret having known Jake. He glanced in the rearview mirror, his gaze mometarily meeting hers. He winked. "Okay?" he asked softly.

"Yes. I was wondering how I could ever have used the word 'mulish'." She didn't add, *to describe you*, but she didn't have to. He smiled and winked again before his attention returned to the road.

Jake signaled, indicating he would turn into a gas station. "Watch for Ivy and Ben; I'm going to call the Springfield police. The keys are in the ignition. Motion Ivy and Ben to go ahead because we can catch up. Do you two want to go with Ben?"

"Can I ride with you, Daddy?"

"I'd rather wait for you, too" Molly said: "I think it's better to be with you."

"Okay. I like having you two with me." Jake stopped in the station parking lot, sprinted to the phone and dropped quarters in the slot.

Molly leaned out, waving to Ivy and Ben to go ahead, and in seconds Jake dashed back to the Jeep. He stepped on the gas pedal and whipped onto the highway. "What I'd give for the Lincoln right now."

"They have to be in something like the Jeep to get around in the woods."

"Yeah, but they could have kept a car like the Lincoln in Hattersville."

His statement sent a chill through Molly and she twisted in the seat. The highway and surrounding area appeared totally black and she decided no one was behind them. Then headlights topped a rise and Molly calculated. She figured there was a long distance still between them and the vehicle behind.

She turned in the seat to see Jamie. Then, a few minutes later, she glanced back again and the lights seemed much closer. She straightened, telling herself it could be tourists, the police, a businessman, a truck. She caught Jake's solemn glance in the rearview mirror as he reached up to adjust it.

"The police will meet us soon and we'll have an escort. I gave them a description of Ben's and Ivy's cars."

"Thank goodness! You don't know how soon?"

"No. The dispatcher put the call through to Detective Burns, and he said he'd alert a car to lead us in." Jake kept looking in the rearview mirror, and Molly kept twisting in her seat. Each glance confirmed that the car was gaining on them. She heard the Jeep's motor roar and clutched the sides as it gained speed.

Molly felt Jamie slump against her. "She's asleep," she said softly.

"Good. I don't want her frightened."

Molly smoothed Jamie's hair.

"Molly, the car behind us is really traveling. As it gets alongside us, get down."

The words were chilling, the grim tone conveying Jake's worries. Once more she turned to look and saw that the car was narrowing the gap between them swiftly now.

"Holy Hannibal!" Jake declared. "There's the patrol car!" He leaned on the Jeep's horn.

"Where?"

"Going the opposite direction, but if he notices us—" His words broke off as sirens began to blare and the patrol car skidded, swung in a curve and bounced across the grassy median to pull up alongside the Jeep. The patrolman fell into line behind Jake, the siren still cutting above the roar of motors, the red lights blinking.

"At last!" Jake said, slowing a fraction. "We can relax a little." He blinked his lights at Ivy in the car ahead of him. Then he ran his fingers through his hair. Molly put her head back against the seat, holding Jamie against her. Jake glanced over his shoulder quickly at them. "She's still asleep?"

"Yes," Molly said, feeling the tenseness drain out of her shoulders. "What a relief to have the highway patrol here!"

"Right. The car following behind us is dropping back."

"Should you stop and talk to the police?"

"I suppose." He honked, signaled, and slowed. In seconds the four cars stopped and Jake walked back to talk to the patrolman. She waited, exhausted, until Jake climbed behind the wheel and motioned to Ivy and Ben to go on again.

"The car pulled to one side of the highway and its lights went off," Jake said, keeping his voice low. "The patrolman said he'd put out the word about them, but he's staying with us. I'm willing to bet they're across the median and heading back toward Hattersville right now."

"I'm too tired to look back and see."

"I'll wake you in Springfield. I don't know how you can fall asleep with sirens going."

"Easy," she mumbled.

"Molly, I'm getting us tickets and we're all flying home. I don't want to hear any arguments about it."

"I can't argue now. I don't have ten cents."

Jake chuckled, and then his voice became furry. "I can't wait to be alone with you again."

His words stirred her to awareness, and her eyes opened wide. She stretched out her hand, careful to avoid disturbing Jamie, and brushed her fingertips across Jake's neck. Just the warmth of his flesh stirred a flock of memories. He turned swiftly and winked at her. Then his attention shifted back to the road.

"What'll Ben do with his car?" Molly asked, her mind returning to the proposed flight to Detroit.

"We'll find some place to leave it in Springfield, and then I'll get him a ticket to fly back here and pick it up. He can drive home from Missouri to Iowa; it'll be closer from Springfield to Ames than from Detroit to Ames."

Molly nodded and then began to doze, her arms locked around Jamie and Alfred.

In a short time they arrived in Springfield and talked with the Springfield detectives. The officers agreed to turn in the rental car for Ivy and allowed Ben to leave his car at the station until he flew back to pick it up.

At the Springfield airport, they waited in a private office until it was time for their flight. Jake paced the room, stopping beside Ben to talk in a low voice to him. "I've talked to a detective, Sergeant Wellston, who'll meet us at the airport. I haven't told Molly yet, but we're going to be put under police protection. They've arranged to take us to a hotel."

"What about Jamie?"

"I discussed it with Detective Wellston and we agreed it would be better for her if she went to stay with you and Mom. They don't think there's any danger to Mom because there are so many Cannons in Detroit that they don't expect anyone to try and hunt down relatives I might have. I called Mom and of course, she's delighted to have Jamie, but I'll feel better if you're with them."

"Sure. I won't let Jamie out of my sight."

"Good. I have to break the news to Molly that we'll be hidden away. Ivy shouldn't stay at Molly's either. She'll have to find her own place. I told Mom about her and she said she has a friend in the neighborhood who might rent Ivy a room temporarily."

"Good." Ben thumped Jake's shoulder. "Don't worry about Jamie. I promise, Mom and I'll take good care of her."

"Thanks. I want to tell Jamie."

Jake picked Jamie up and held her on his lap, talking softly to her to tell her the arrangements. Then he settled Jamie down on a sofa near Ivy, who was talking to Ben. Briefly, Jake glanced at them. He noticed they were holding hands. If his brother was finally in love, the match with Ivy was even more remarkable than Jake's relationship with Molly. Ben and Ivy were eons apart, yet Ben had seemed more relaxed and happy during the time in the Ozarks than Jake had seen him in a long time.

Jake liked Ivy. He'd gradually adjusted his first impression of her. She was a knockout, but she was also all Molly had claimed, warm-hearted, cheerful, and intelligent. If Ben loved her, it was fine with Jake. He had his own concerns over Molly with her damned fear of commitment. He watched her as she sat across from him, her head back in the chair, eyes closed, her thick lashes shadowing her cheeks. How he longed to kiss her awake—to have her put her arms around him. He drew a sharp breath, dismissing his reflections and trying to bring his thoughts back to the problems at hand.

They all slept on the flight back to Detroit. Then, in the Detroit Metropolitan Airport they were met by two detectives, and Ben made arrangements to rent a car.

Molly hugged Jamie goodbye, and then turned away, leaving Jake alone with his daughter.

He was solemn as he and Molly climbed into an unmarked dark green car and were driven away. Headlights reflected on the wide, four-lane highway, illuminating the roadside. Lighted billboards shed a glow and Molly could see the trees had greened and foliage had grown up along the roadside in the short time since they had left Detroit.

She knew Jake hated to part with Jamie again. And Molly could understand why. Besides being his daughter, Jamie was an easy child to have around. Very easy. Molly knew she was growing more attached to Jamie every day.

Detective Wellston was a stocky, sandy-haired man who looked as if he should have been a professional wrestler. He talked in a gravelly voice that was as deep as Jake's, but it didn't have the same effect on Molly at all.

"We have a safe house, an apartment where we usually can put someone, but we already have a witness stashed there, so we've taken connecting suites on the top floor of a hotel and rooms on either sides of the suites. You'll have some privacy, but we don't have the whole floor, so we'd rather keep someone in one of the suites with you most of the time. We'd like to go to the station first, though, and let you look at mug shots. We had appointments scheduled for both of you to talk to our artist, so he can do a composite drawing, but he's sick today, so the appointment will have to be postponed until he's okay."

"Fine," Jake said, lacing his fingers through Molly's.

"Can I get my purse back?" Molly asked. "Do you have it?"

"Yep, and we have your credit cards. We picked your purse up at the scene. From what you've told us, you don't have much to give us on their appearances, Mr. Cannon. Is that right?"

"Yes. I was in the center of the action for a few minutes, but too much was going on, and I was trying to protect Miss Ashland and myself."

"We've had contact with them and demands for the computer chip and ransom money, but the night we were going to make the exchange, something went awry, and the plan was scuttled. We'll hear again."

"So Brantz is alive?"

"We think so. They're after the computer chip you had in your possession."

"And you'll give it to them?"

"In exchange for Brantz—yes."

"Have any of the witnesses identified the men?"

"We don't have very clear descriptions. Mr. Arlington wears bifocals, Mrs. Thompson wasn't wearing her glasses. Mr. Byerly doesn't remember anyone, Miss Jenkins has given us the same description for every man she claims to have seen on the premises," Sgt. Wellston said flatly. Jake wanted to groan. It meant they needed his and Molly's testimony badly.

"Do you have any idea who's involved?" Jake asked.

"Frankly, no. This job was carefully planned," he admitted, and became silent. Jake figured that was all they would learn on the subject.

At the station, after looking at books with a multitude of pictures, Molly couldn't find any that looked like the men she remembered. She gave the detectives careful descriptions and went over the crime again. Finally she and Jake were dismissed and on their way to the hotel.

As they passed the front of a hotel called The French Quarter, Molly glimpsed black decorative grill work, green shutters, balconies, and a fan transom window over the front door. They were driven to a side entrance and whisked upstairs on a service elevator.

In the suite, Jake talked to the policemen while Molly walked through his suite to hers. The rooms, overlooking the Detroit River were decorated in muted colors; Jake's was gray and white with maroon accents. Hers was beige and white with forest green drapes and pillows. They were comfortable—elegant after the Ozark house—and Molly was relieved to be out of danger. An officer had carried her sacks of clothing to the bedroom for her; she stepped into a large room with an oversized bed, pale curtains and drapes, a desk, and an armchair.

"Molly?"

She returned to the living room to see Jake approaching from his suite. He smiled as he crossed the room and held out his arms. "We're alone."

She walked into his embrace, feeling as if she were at last coming home. Her mouth rose eagerly to meet his as his hands drifted down her back, holding and caressing her.

"It's been too damned long," he murmured, kissing her neck.

"Jake," she whispered with her eyes closed. Then she wound her fingers through his soft hair which had grown longer during the trip to Missouri, and asked, "What about the police?"

He raised his head, his gaze taking in her features in a slow, lingering glance.

"I've had a little talk with those guys. We're *alone* for tonight."

Molly clung to him, weariness and fear melting as her needs changed.

THE NEXT DAY, they spent long hours on the phone to Jamie and Ivy. They talked with Sergeant Wellston and met Kettering and Price, the morning shift of detectives. Most of the time they spent to themselves, and Molly realized they hadn't come home to a real world, but to another situation where problems were shut away, conflicts diminished and no decisions had to be made. But every hour spent with Jake was heavenly!

Late in the afternoon, he knocked lightly on the connecting door. He closed it behind him after entering her suite and told her, "Barnes and Johnson are cooperative detectives. Actually, all of them have been great. They're going to have dinner sent up and eat in my place. You and I are going to have dinner sent up and eat in here—just the two of us. All alone, no interruptions, no police to guard us..." As he continued his list, his voice slipped lower and lower, playing over her nerves, holding promises that excited and beguiled her.

He ran his fingers over her collar, twisting her silken red curls. "I'm going to shower, change, and I'll be back for the evening."

"Jake," she said, thinking of the hours to come. "I'm tired of jeans and shorts. I know there are shops downstairs...I still don't have my purse or money."

He smiled. "I've already thought about that. They won't let us go shopping, but I described to Detective

Barnes what I wanted, and he said he'd see if he could get it. He should be back shortly. I'll bring the dress to you."

She tightened her arms around his neck, smiling at him. "You know, you're really not mulish at all!" she exclaimed, convinced it was a massive understatement. He was considerate, intelligent . . . so sexy.

His arms tightened around her in return. "I want to win your gratitude, m'dear," he drawled mockingly.

Molly ground her hips against him playfully. "You have my . . . gratitude . . . my . . . kisses . . . my . . . body," she murmured, moving sensually against him. Suddenly, the fun was gone, replaced by urgency.

Jake drew a ragged breath, his smile vanishing. "Molly . . ." he said hoarsely, hugging her until her breath stopped. And then he leaned over her to kiss her passionately.

When he released her and moved away he asked, "See you in about . . . how long?"

"I'm fast," she said, drawing out the word so it held a double meaning.

He reached out, catching her shoulder and pulling her close again. "You won't get dinner with answers like that," he commented. Though his smile was teasing, his eyes seemed solemn and hungry. After a pause, he asked, "How fast?"

She pushed on his chest. "You hurry now. I'll explain 'fast' to you when you come back."

He winked. "I'm going to call Jamie so I'll be back in an hour. But if I don't get out of here right now—I won't be gone at all," he said quickly and left, closing the door behind him. Her heart skipped beats in eager anticipation of the hours ahead. They still could put off real life and real problems, shut away high in the hotel, and for the moment she was glad.

She luxuriated in a hot tub. Then she washed and dried her hair, and emerged wrapped in a towel to find a sack on her bed.

Rustling tissue paper fell to the floor as Molly removed the green silk dress. The skirt fell in a shimmering fold on the bed. It was a simple design, beautiful, and Molly prayed it would fit. She peeked at the tag, amazed that Jake had guessed the right size. She pulled on white lace panties and bra and her stockings, then stepped into the green silk.

The plain, straight-lined sheath was sleeveless, with a deep vee neckline. She fastened the narrow belt, and turned in front of mirrors that lined one wall of the bedroom. The dress fit perfectly; she loved it, and relished the softness of the cool silk against her skin.

When Jake knocked, she was seated in one of the white chairs. "Come in," she said, watching as he stepped inside, she hoped he liked her in the dress, because she liked what she saw: his white dress shirt, his dark slacks, and his navy tie. Looking at him, her breath escaped in a rush. She wanted to run across the room and fling herself into his arms, but instead, she stood up and strolled, feeling on edge as Jake studied her in the dress. His assessment lingered like a caress, drifting so slowly down over her breasts, then her waist and her legs.

"Jake!" she began, sighing.

He caught her hands, holding her away so he could continue to look at her. Jake felt his heart thud against his ribs. She was emerald and flame. She took his breath and made his pulse race like a hurricane wind. He wanted her badly, permanently. He had intended to be careful and logical and wait to see how he felt after knowing her longer, but he had decided he couldn't wait.

To save his soul he couldn't remember any disturbing differences between them. They had become nothing in his eyes. He had changed because of Molly, and some of his views of life had changed. He knew Jamie would love her, too—a factor just as important to him as his feelings. He wanted to crush Molly in his arms, but he made himself wait and look, relishing the sight of her, a sight that excited him in a way he thought he would never experience again in his life.

Finally, he wrapped his arms around her, his mouth covering hers passionately as he kissed her, trying to stir her. But her touch was setting him on fire.

"Molly, I've ordered dinner," he whispered. "It'll be here any minute."

"That's nice," she murmured, kissing his throat, and he doubted she had understood a word he had said.

"The policemen will bring it in here."

"That's nice."

"Let's have a drink while we wait. I have a bottle of wine."

"That's nice," she murmured, continuing to kiss him.

He smiled and held her away. Her eyes widened. "Do you know one thing I've said to you?" he asked, wanting her back in his arms, amused at her befuddled expression, aching to peel away the green dress and kiss her all over.

"I don't know. You said something about... something," she said, shrugging while she ran her fingers over his shoulders.

He laughed softly, moving away from her to open the wine. "Molly, stay ten feet away from me until we have dinner in here."

"Is that what you told me?"

"Yeah," he said, studying her and feeling a swift, heated arousal. He wanted her, but he knew they were going to have an interruption any minute now. He poured some chilled white wine and handed her a glass.

"Here's to us," he said.

She watched him over the rim of her glass, her green cat eyes dancing. When she touched her glass to his, her fingers brushed his. But she watched him steadily, then raised the glass to drink without taking her gaze from his. She was sensual, sometimes unconsciously, and sometimes, he suspected, because she wanted to be. Either way, she took his breath. The temperature in the room seemed at inferno levels and he knew he should move away, yet he couldn't. He couldn't stop looking into green eyes that coaxed and flirted.

"Molly!"

"What?" she whispered.

He took her arm, walked to the window, and pushed aside the curtain to open a glass door to a wide balcony. It had a waist-high wall with ornate wrought iron grill work above it and more grill work running to the roof. Pots of flowers decorated the enclosure, and there were chairs and a table where they could eat outside. While Molly walked around the small area, Jake leaned against the inside wall.

"You're getting over your vertigo?" she asked him.

"Hell, no. I feel queasy. That's why I'm standing on this side of the balcony instead of over there enjoying the view."

She smiled and came back to stand by him. He reached into his pocket to withdraw a package. "This is for you. It's all I could get while we're locked away up here."

Startled, Molly took a small box from Jake's hand and opened it. In the soft glow of light from the open doors, she saw the diamond pendant sparkle. "Oh, Jake, it's lovely!" she exclaimed and started to take it from the box.

Warm, tanned fingers closed over hers, and he set down his wineglass. "It's a substitute for a diamond ring. Will you marry me?" he asked, feeling as if his heart had stopped. He waited, but heard only the sigh of the wind.

CHAPTER FIFTEEN

MOLLY COULDN'T GET HER BREATH; shock broke over her in waves. Never once had she expected a proposal from Jake at this stage. She had assumed they would date after they returned to their routine lives and see if time would help to bridge their differences.

She stared at the diamond winking in the light, too stunned to think or say anything. She looked up at him, but his gray eyes were unreadable. She wanted to cry yes, but too many years of carefully avoiding entanglements made her hesitate. The swiftness of her attraction to Jake—beyond reason from the first day—the knowledge of their differences, his addiction to work and her casual approach—all these factors still needed to be considered. She wanted Jake as part of her life, but was she prepared to rush into marriage? And into motherhood?

She drew a deep breath and looked up at him. "I don't think we should . . . make a lasting promise until we're back in a regular routine. We're in a dream world—we don't know if we'll adjust to each other when life's normal."

He smiled at her, running his fingers over her shoulder. Now it was her turn to wonder if he had heard a word she had said.

"Molly, I know what I want. I'm sure. You're wonderful with Jamie," he said softly.

Startled, she frowned. Was he proposing because she might make a good mother for Jamie? "Jake," she said gently, closing the box and leaving the pendant inside, "I love Jamie, but I can't marry for that reason."

He smiled and tilted her chin up, his voice touched with amusement. "I didn't ask you because Jamie needs a mother." He became solemn as he added, "I wouldn't ask you, though, if you two didn't get along."

"Wait," she suggested, sensing to the depth of her being that he really did want a mother for Jamie, "and see how you feel a month from now. This has been a whirlwind—something my mother or Ivy would do."

"I love you, Molly," he said firmly, silvery depths in his eyes holding her captive.

"That's the first time you've told me."

"I was waiting, and now I'm sure."

She waved her hand helplessly, torn between what her heart had been telling her for days now—but it was only *days*—and the years of caution that her mind was adhering to. "What about your efficiency, your working constantly—your lists?"

"You made me get rid of my lists, learn how to dance in the sun…" While he talked, his voice slipped down to the huskiness that made her knees jelly, that played over her senses like his hands. "You're a golden sun dancer, Molly, and you've made me see there is something more important than work in life." He leaned forward to kiss her; Jake wanted to kiss her into saying yes to him. He tried to convey all his hungry need and love for her through the warmth of his lips. Finally, he released her, and put his hand over hers on top of the box.

"Molly, I don't want an iffy engagement like you had with Garvin. When you wear the pendant or my ring, I want it to be something you want as badly as I do."

She felt as if something were tearing her insides in two. "Jake, all these years—this is exactly what I've opposed in Ivy and Mom—this rushing into marriage."

"Yet, you told me you've never rushed into intimacy with a man before—never even knew it with Garvin."

"That's right," she whispered. "I know what I feel now, but I've spent all my adult life and part of my childhood opposing a brief, casual—"

"Never casual," he corrected softly.

"Ivy and Mom have been hurt over and over. I don't want that."

"Okay, when we return to normal, I'll give you a diamond." he said, taking the box from her fingers and dropping it on a table. He kissed her again and she felt regret, agony, desire all tear at her until every emotion was lost, borne away like the wind, and Jake's scalding kisses became the world.

Finally he released her, and she stood breathing deeply, a breeze tugging at tendrils of her hair while she stared at him, her emotions churning. A noise from inside broke into her thoughts and she said, "Jake, I think I hear someone knocking."

"Ah, dinner." As she followed him, one of the detectives appeared from Jake's suite to answer the door and wheel a cart into Molly's room. He closed the door on the hotel employee without Molly or Jake even seeing him. Detective Barnes smiled. "There's your dinner. Anything else?"

"No, thanks."

"We'll be close," he said and left.

The moment the door closed, Jake set his wineglass down on a table and took Molly's from her fingers. He pulled her into his arms, moving toward the bedroom as he began to shower kisses on her. "Dinner... can wait," he whispered and tightened his arms around her.

THE NEXT DAY Molly dialed the phone, smiling up at a Sgt. Kettering, who was standing nearby, watching her. His dark eyes met hers and then he moved across the room to sit down in front of the television. He changed channels several times as she listened to rings. Then Ivy answered.

"Ivy?" Molly asked. Ivy was settled in a room in the house of Mrs. Blair, a friend of Jake's mother, and she had started teaching at the studio in Molly's place.

"Molly, I was going to call you. We can't find the patterns for the bumblebee costumes. And Mr. Wilkens wants ninety dollars more than you paid last year to rent the Maple Auditorium for the recital."

Molly discussed the problems with Ivy, and then her sister announced, "I've been offered a nighttime job."

"I thought you were going to wait until I'm back at the studio. Do you want to work day and night?"

"I can use the money." Ivy sighed. "I just don't know what to do. It's dancing in a club, and Ben opposes it."

"Well, he doesn't have any say in what you do."

"I know. I'm trying to take your advice and use my head and be cautious and logical, but I think I'm in love with Ben."

Molly wanted to groan aloud. But she wondered what Ivy would say if Molly admitted she couldn't take her own advice! "You don't know Ben much better than I know Jake," she said, talking more to herself than to Ivy.

"He's wonderful to me. He's so considerate, and we read the same books. I don't want to tell him I can get this job, because he doesn't think I should dance in clubs. He thinks I should get a bookkeeping job, but you know what kind of money I can earn as a dancer."

"You'll have to decide for yourself. You're running my studio now and making money. Why don't you wait a week and then make a decision? Ben will go back to Iowa this weekend, and then you'll have time to think everything over."

"I know," Ivy said, her voice filled with sadness. "I don't want him to go."

"His home and job are there."

Ivy sighed, then asked, "How are you doing? Okay?"

"Yes. It's not boring yet, and with you taking care of the business, I'm still on vacation."

"Shut away with Jake. Are you in love with him?"

"I might be."

"Really?" Ivy squealed so loudly, Molly had to hold the phone away from her ear.

"I don't know!"

Ivy giggled. "I wonder if he realizes how particular you are about men! I told him in Missouri that you really are—that you aren't like me at all."

"Thanks," Molly said dryly, but she admitted to herself that she had acted exactly like Ivy where Jake was concerned. Maybe it was a congenital defect in all the Ashland females.

"I gotta run. You be careful and give Jake a hello. Ben and Jamie are fine and Mrs. Cannon is really sweet and nice. Jamie misses Jake a lot, but she's okay. I'm teaching Jamie some cute dance steps. Bye.''

Molly replaced the receiver. When she glanced over to find Sgt. Kettering watching her, he slouched lower in the chair and looked back at the television. Then she went into the bedroom and closed the door.

She walked to the dresser and picked up the box with the pendant to look at it again. Jake had told her repeatedly that he loved her but she felt dazed. She was still fighting the part of her that wanted to say yes and forget practicality. They were in more of a dream world now than they had been in the Ozarks, she kept reminding herself. Molly was beguiled by hours in Jake's arms, yet she knew they were living in a bubble that could burst at any moment and thrust them back into a real world. What they had found together was special, but was it lasting? Her heart was already committed and had been since the afternoon of love in the sun. Yet every time she was on the verge of telling Jake, caution made her wait. And there was Jamie to consider....

She turned the pendant in her fingers. ''I love you,'' she whispered, closing her eyes.

A knock on the door interrupted her thoughts. She turned to see Detective Nash.

He grinned. ''Hi, Miss Ashland. I'm on duty now and it's almost lunch time. Want to order?''

''Sure,'' she said, putting the pendant back in the box and slipping it into the drawer.

ON SATURDAY Sgt. Wellston called her and made arrangements for her to meet with the artist that afternoon to give descriptions of the criminals. During the morning they had taken Jake to the station so he could have a session with the artist, and while he was gone the phone rang. Molly picked it up, expecting Jamie or Ivy, the only people other than the police who knew the correct room number. Instead she heard a raspy male voice. "Molly Ashland?"

"Yes? Who is this?" she asked, sure it must be a policeman.

"Are you alone?" Startled, she stared at the phone. She looked around for one of the detectives who seemed to be ever present during the day, but no one was in sight.

"Yes. Who is this?"

"Don't give a description of the men you saw. We have your sister, Ivy. If you want to see her again, forget everything you know." The phone clicked.

CHAPTER SIXTEEN

FEELING AS IF she had turned to ice, Molly stared at the phone in horror. She replaced the receiver and started for the door to get one of the policemen.

Suddenly she stopped and looked back at the phone. Frowning, she stared at it a second, then ran to her bedroom, closed the door and dialed Ivy's number.

The phone rang. It rang again and again and Molly held her breath, fear rising in her, hysteria threatening. Then the ringing stopped and Ivy said hello.

"Ivy!" Molly felt dizzy with relief.

"I was just leaving. I'd already locked the door."

"Listen to me. Has anything unusual happened?"

"Unusual? No. Your friend Walter called, and I was just on my way to meet him."

"Walter?"

"Yeah, you know. He said you told him all about me and Ben and Jake. He has the part to your car you wanted and he asked me if I could meet him and I'm going to be real late if I keep talking because I'm supposed to be there in two more minutes. This phone—"

"Ivy, listen!" Molly glanced at the door, her mind racing over what had just happened.

"I'm listening, but I'm going to be late."

"I don't know a Walter."

"You don't? I don't—"

"Listen to me!" Molly ordered. "Someone set you up. They want to get you and stop me from giving the police artist a good description of the criminals."

"Oh, lordy, Molly!"

"Get out of there and get to a motel and call me later. Register under another name. Stay away from Ben and Jamie so you don't involve them, and let me think. I don't know how anyone could have gotten your number to call you. If they knew where you were—did he ask where you live?"

"He offered to bring them over, but I said I was leaving. That's when we decided to meet."

"Did you tell him where you live?"

"No. He wanted to know. Oh, lordy!"

"Then the only thing they know is your phone number." Molly's icy fear returned. Only the policemen would know to talk to Ivy about Ben and Jake and Jamie. Detectives from each shift could have seen her dial Ivy's number. Police. She looked at the door, realizing what danger she was in. And what danger Jake might be in.

"Molly?"

"Yes. I'm thinking. Get to a motel and call me, but be careful. When you're safe in a room, call Ben and warn him. Ivy—" she lowered her voice to a whisper "—tell him it had to be a policeman who got your number. No one else could."

"A policeman? Lordy, Molly, you're scaring me!"

"Hurry and get out of there! And be careful!"

Molly replaced the receiver, her mind working feverishly. Jake was at the station giving his description of the one man he remembered, but he wasn't too clear about the fellow, and he'd said there was no other description he felt confident giving.

She paced the room, trying to think what to do. Someone—or maybe more than one—on the police force assigned to guard them was involved with the kidnappers. The implications made Molly's head ache. Could she trust Sergeant Wellston if she called him?

She rubbed her forehead, trying to go back over conversations. Coming in from the airport, he'd told them they'd tried to make an exchange for Brantz and it had failed. Had it failed because someone in the department had warned the criminals not to make the exchange?

Sergeant Wellston should be safe. She crossed the room to the phone and picked up the receiver to call, then hesitated. If he weren't safe—what jeopardy would she put Jake in? Uncertain whom she could trust, she lowered the receiver.

Who had watched her call Ivy? She tried to think back. Sergeant Wellston knew Ivy's number, but not where she was staying. She thought Detective Baker had seen her call Ivy. Detective Kettering had been in the room when she had called Ivy, too.

She prayed Jake had been more careful—yet there hadn't been any reason to be suspicious of the men who guarded them.

She stared at the door. Fear and the acknowledgement of her vulnerable position tugged at Molly. She needed to try to decide which one of the detectives she could trust. She sat down on the bed, thinking about each one, eliminating every one, remembering some moment each had done something suspicious. Time was ticking past, adding to her dilemma. When Ivy didn't meet "Walter," and he tried to call her, he'd soon realize something had happened.

Molly paced the room. She felt in danger and she had to warn Jake.

A knock on the door made her jump. "I'm coming," she called, trying to inject cheer into her voice.

She opened the door. Detective Kettering held a tray of steaming food.

"Here's lunch," he said, his dark eyes impassive.

"Thank you. I have a headache. I think I'll eat in my room," she said stiffly, now suspicious of everyone.

"Fine," he said and carried it inside to a small table beside the bed.

"If you want anything, just call."

"Thanks."

He left and closed the door and Molly inspected the bowl of clam chowder, a green salad, crackers and a small pot of coffee. Kettering would have had a chance to have dropped something into the food.

Telling herself she was being too jumpy, she sat down, staring at the tray. But her appetite was gone. The food had been good up till now, she told herself. But someone could have been waiting until now for the chance to slip something into her food in order to eliminate the threat of Miss Molly Ashland.

She couldn't eat. She stood up and paced the room, trying to think what to do. They wanted to stop her before she made it to the station this afternoon. Again she went to the phone and picked up the receiver to call the station, but if she told the wrong person, Jake's life as well as hers would be in jeopardy because the guilty person couldn't take a chance.

She replaced the receiver and walked out on the balcony to stare at the street below. Restless, she went back inside and moved to the windows on the east, overlooking the side of the hotel. A black-haired cook wearing jeans with a long white apron tied over them came from the kitchen to empty a drum of trash. When he turned to return to the kitchen, Molly saw his face. A scar ran across his cheeks and the bridge of his nose. And she remembered exactly the last moment she had looked at that same face on the lawn of the Brantz Building!

Panic seized her; she felt surrounded by men who wanted to destroy her. She couldn't reveal his identity to the policemen on duty because they might be in cahoots with him.

Fright kept her icy as she walked around the room, frantically trying to formulate a plan. She had to get out of the room; she felt as if she were a sitting target. But she couldn't leave the hotel because she had to warn Jake.

Her eyes narrowed and she walked out on the balcony again to look below. It would be possible to climb down. The wrought iron decorative grill work ran from the ground floor to the roof. She leaned over to look up at the roof, her mind churning.

Once more she debated about taking a chance on Sergeant Wellston. Finally, she decided to try to hide until Jake was back and she could talk it over with him. She went inside, changing to pumps and her skirt, blouse and blazer. She threw the food away in the bathroom and carried the empty tray through the suites to Kettering and Johnson.

Johnson stood up and took the tray. "I'll have this sent down to the kitchen with ours.

She smiled. "Is Jake back yet?"

"Nope. How's your headache?"

"Better. I'll be in my room."

She left, closing the door as she returned to her suite. There, she changed clothes again fast, pulling on jeans, sneakers and a T-shirt. She folded her blazer, blouse and skirt, and hid them along with one pump between the mattress and springs. They would hunt for her, but not for clothing. She put the pendant in her pocket, took one pump with her and went outside.

She looked around and noted a taxi unloading passengers below. She waited until no one was around there, and dropped the red pump over the balcony. She watched to see if anyone came to retrieve it.

No one seemed to notice. She looked up, scanned the buildings across the way, took a deep breath and began to climb up the grill work. She made it easily and swiftly to the roof and climbed over to look around and decide her next move.

Should she go downstairs and try to find a place to hide, or stay on the roof? It was a big hotel with a wide roof, and she remembered being on another roof with Jake less than two weeks—an eternity ago. She remembered the helicopter too. As she walked around, passing vents and air conditioners, she spotted a pile of lumber beneath a black tarp. After tugging on some boards, she managed to pull a few out, so that she could crawl under them and be out of sight.

She sat down to wait until she thought Jake would be back, and mulled over every time detectives had been in the room when she had called Ivy. After an hour, she walked to the edge and cautiously peered over.

By now, Jake should be back. She climbed back over the edge of the roof, descended the grill work swiftly, and landed on the balcony leading to Jake's bedroom.

She felt vulnerable once again as she tried the door and opened it. The room was empty, so she stepped inside, pausing to listen to men's voices.

To her relief, Jake was in the other room talking with policemen. She stood listening and praying Jake would get up and come into the bedroom. And finally, some twenty minutes later—he did. He had his coat off, his tie loosened and the top button of his shirt unfastened. His hair was tousled from running his fingers through it and he looked so adorable, Molly momentarily forgot what was on her mind.

He stopped, his jaw dropping when he saw her. She put her fingers on her lips for silence and motioned frantically to him to come closer.

She went into the bathroom and when Jake followed, she closed the door and turned on the fan and the water. "Where the hell have you been?" he snapped, his face flushing with anger. "Do you know—"

"I've been on the roof."

"Holy geez! Do—"

"Will you stop raving and listen!"

"I thought those guys got you!" he exclaimed, and suddenly Molly realized how anxious he had been over her.

"Oh, Jake! I'm sorry! You've been worried!"

"Damn right—" he started to answer, but she threw her arms around his neck and kissed him until she felt the stiffness and anger go out of him. And then he crushed her tightly to him and began a passionate kiss.

But abruptly, he leaned away, and his eyes narrowed. "On the *roof*?"

"Yes. Listen, I got a call from a man this morning telling me they had Ivy, and if I wanted to see her again, I wasn't to give an accurate description to the police artist. I panicked and started to run and get one of the policemen. Then I called Ivy just to see—she answered the phone. She had been delayed and was on her way out again and had the door closed when I called. She said she was going to meet my friend Walter. I don't have a friend Walter. I told her what had happened and to go to a motel and call later and give me her number. After I talked to her, I thought it over and it seems to me that if they had known her address, they would have gone and taken her by force. So all they had was her phone number. The only way a stranger could get Ivy's phone number would be if one of the policemen who've been with me watched me dial."

"Oh, damn," Jake said, beginning to run his fingers through his hair again.

"I had to warn you. They wanted to keep me from talking with the artist because I can give the best descriptions. I started to call and tell all this to Sergeant Wellston, but I didn't know if I could trust him."

Jake had listened quietly. Now Molly waited in silence while he thought over what she had said. "I think we should call him," he said.

"Also, while I was pacing around my room, I saw a guy in an apron come out of the kitchen to dump some trash. When he turned around I recognized him as one of the kidnappers."

"Dammit! It figures though, that if one of them is on the police force, then every move we make has been known to them. He's probably here waiting to get a chance at us."

"I've been thinking about who watched me call. I can't say every time, but I remember two times. Kettering and Nash. And Jake, there may be more than one of them on the police force. You don't know about Sergeant Wellston."

"No, but we have to take a chance somewhere and he's higher up the line. Also, Molly, he's had chances to eliminate us if he'd wanted to. Let's call him."

"Okay," she said, feeling suddenly better.

"Let's go to your bedroom so no one will hear us."

Quietly, she moved ahead of Jake to her bedroom, where Jake held Molly against him while he called Sergeant Wellston and told him all that had happened. When he replaced the receiver, he turned to kiss her briefly. "He said to sit tight and act normal. He'll be here right away. I'll go back and talk to them so they don't come looking for me. No one will bother you in here." He squinted his eyes at her. "The roof, Molly? You have a penchant for rooftops?"

"It was the only place I could find to hide and it's easy to get up there."

"Yeah, I can imagine how easy," he said gruffly. "You'll risk your life shinnying up ladders and over beams, but you won't risk your heart on a guy who loves you."

Shocked, Molly drew a sharp breath. Before she could answer, he touched her jaw lightly with his knuckles. "I'm going to get double revenge now—you worried the hell out of me. They found one of your red pumps on the sidewalk."

"I threw it over there so they'd think I'd climbed down instead of up. I'm sorry I worried you," she said, wiggling closer against him. "It never occurred to me you'd think someone had taken me out from under the nose of all those men."

Jake's hands slipped down over her and he patted her bulky pocket, raising his brows questioningly.

She withdrew the box with the pendant. "I didn't want to go off and leave it."

He looked at her solemnly, winked, then turned to go.

She watched him, thinking about what he had said to her. Then she set the box on the dresser and moved around the room restlessly, finally drifting to sit down on the edge of the bed. The door to the balcony still stood open.

Minutes passed while she waited. She glanced at the closed bedroom door and stiffened. The knob was slowly turning.

CHAPTER SEVENTEEN

EXPECTING JAKE, Molly stood up. Instead, Sergeant Kettering moved silently into the room. For a split second they looked at each other. Then Molly saw him reach for his gun.

She screamed and sprinted through the open door of the balcony.

"Jake!" she screamed again, climbing up the grill work with speed born from terror. "Jake!"

She looked down to see Kettering coming after her, gun drawn, anger burning in his features.

She flung herself over the edge of the roof and ran for the door to the stairs inside.

The blast of the gun shattered the silence. Molly lunged for the door, flung it open and ran down the stairs, half-sliding on the railing. She pushed open the door on the floor below, and raced toward the suite of rooms. "Jake!"

A detective came into the hallway and Jake stepped out behind him. Molly flung herself into Jake's arms as Sergeant Wellston and another detective emerged from the elevator.

"Sergeant Kettering. He's...on the roof," she gasped, feeling as if she would never get enough breath back into her lungs. Jake's arms were a haven, locking around her. He led her back to his bedroom, kicked the door closed behind them and held her tightly, stroking her hair.

"I'm torn between holding you and going after that guy myself. "I'd like to shove him off the roof."

"He has a gun. Stay here and hold me."

"Molly, I've asked this before, but I have to again—is your life always like this?"

"It never was until I met you," she declared. Her breathing had become more regular, but she was beginning to shake all over in reaction. "He shot at me! I was shot at!"

"Try and forget. They'll have him now."

In a few minutes she had calmed down and Jake said, "We'd better go into the other room. I'm sure Wellston will want to talk to you." He paused. "Molly, I put your pendant in my pocket."

She stared at him, uncertain of his meaning—had he put it away for safekeeping or had he changed his mind after her hesitation?

But then she had little time for worrying about it and no time to discuss it with him. Within the hour Molly, with Jake beside her, sat watching a police lineup. With no difficulty, she picked out the man she had seen in Missouri. Kettering confessed. Molly and Jake were escorted back to the hotel and by mid-morning the next day, Sergeant Wellston appeared to tell them that, with Kettering's confession and information, they had been able to set up a trap and catch the others involved. Brantz was home and safe.

Sergeant Wellston leaned forward, giving them a rare smile. "Brantz wants to thank both of you. His secretary will call and make arrangements for you to have lunch with him."

"Thank heavens he's all right," Molly said, enormously relieved the whole matter was over.

"Yes, and thanks to you he has the computer chip in his possession. We're sorry about Kettering. He hasn't been with us long. He had been offered a large amount of money to work with them. That happens." He stood up. "My men will take you home. Brantz can identify everyone involved, so we probably won't need your testimony at all," he said to Jake. Turning to Molly, he added, "And we'll only need yours about Kettering."

"What about the men who followed us to Springfield?"

"Brantz identified them also. They came back to Detroit shortly after you did. They moved around freely and let Brantz see them—they probably didn't plan to return him alive."

Molly closed her eyes, thankful again it was over. When she opened them, Sergeant Wellston offered his hand. "Thank you both for your cooperation."

In a brief time they were on their way home, each in separate squad cars. Jake had said he would call but suddenly Molly felt bereft. She had been with him steadily since the crime. Life without his constant companionship would seem empty, yet she was still plagued by fears of rushing into marriage.

Ivy returned to the room she had rented from Mrs. Blair, telling Molly she would find her own place and just move one more time, so Molly was alone. The first Monday night she returned after work, the small apartment seemed incredibly empty.

She fed the two brindle cats and jumped when the phone rang. She ran to answer it, and her heart leaped when she heard Jake's deep voice.

"Are you as lonesome as I am?"

"Yes!"

"That's good. Put on your green dress and let me take you and Jamie out to dinner."

"I'd love it!" she said, wanting to hang on to the phone, to listen to Jake's voice. She had missed him terribly. Though she'd hoped she would be able to get back into a normal routine and not be so torn apart by the absence of Jake, she'd discovered it was impossible.

She bathed, spending time on her hair and nails, and finally got dressed in the green silk half an hour before it was time for Jake to appear. She wrote out a check to repay Jake all she had borrowed in Missouri, having already moved money from her savings account to her checking account to cover the costs.

She was waiting at the door when he came up the walk to her brown frame apartment building; she knew it was like a dozen others in the same complex. A shiny black Lincoln was parked at the curb with Jamie in it, but Molly barely saw her for looking at Jake.

His appearance, in a navy suit that made his silvery eyes look lighter, took her breath away. The dark tie and white shirt were businesslike, professional-looking, yet the smile was Mr. Soundmaster. To her eyes, he looked more handsome than ever!

"Jamie's in the car or I'd want to stay right here tonight," he said, his eyes devouring her.

"Go back and get her and let me show you my apartment. Oh, here, this is yours," she said, and slipped the folded check into his coat pocket. He took it out and smiled as he read it.

"If you're going to be Mrs. Cannon, this is a little beside the point," he said as he tore it up.

"Jake! That's a lot."

"You're worth it," he said and kissed her lightly.

"Thank you. Go get Jamie; she'll like Ming and Chan, my cats."

"They'll be a match for Alfred." He hurried down the walk, and Molly watched every step he took. He came back with Jamie beside him, wearing an ice blue ruffled organdy dress with matching sandals. She looked so perfect, so doll-like, that Molly wondered if she could ever relax and play. Alfred was tucked under her arm, but she held another fluffy white bear in her hand.

"Hi, Jamie," Molly said, going out on the porch to meet them. "I wanted you both to come in and see my apartment. Do you have a new bear?"

"See," Jamie said, holding up the white bear. "Daddy gave him to me today."

"And what's his name?"

"Bach."

"Bach Bear. How nice," Molly said, smiling at Jake. "Did your Daddy name him?"

"Yes. But I liked it," Jamie said, squeezing the white bear and then giving Alfred a hug.

"I think you'll like my cats, too," she said, holding the door as Jamie went inside.

"The cats are in the kitchen. Come on back." Jake stood looking around her tiny apartment. It seemed cozy with its colorful throw pillows and prints on the walls and the second-hand furniture made it easy to keep. They entered the narrow green kitchen, where one cat sat on a chair and another lolled in a corner on the floor. Both blinked lazy green eyes at Jamie.

"Meet Ming and Chan. Chan's on the floor. They're very friendly. They like to be petted." Jamie moved to kneel down by Ming and carefully touch his head. She looked in uncertainty at Molly.

"He doesn't mind. You can pick him up if you want." She glanced at Jake. "She isn't allergic to cats, is she?"

"No. Can I see the rest of the place?"

An innocuous question, but the rest was her bedroom and bath. She led him across a short hallway into her red and white room. A vase of silk poppies stood on the dresser beside her water bed. Jake moved around the room, glancing at the deep red throw rugs and the polished floor.

The room had always been adequate for her, but Jake diminished it. He was too tall, too broad-shouldered, and too male. He looked as out of place as if he were standing in a doll house. Molly felt his presence had been indelibly stamped in her bedroom. "It's nice, Molly."

"Thank you," she said, and began to imagine where he lived, what his bedroom looked like. She knew him so well in some ways, but so little in others. He picked up a picture on the dresser. "Who's with you and Ivy?"

"Mom."

"Your mother's pretty, too."

"Thank you."

He set the picture down and glanced over the dresser. In minutes Molly had put Chan and Ming outside and the three left for the restaurant.

Jake took them to a quiet French bistro with a stone floor and rough wooden beams. Through a leisurely fish dinner, Molly had a chance to talk to Jamie at length, while Jake sat quietly. Then he told Jamie about Molly getting him to walk across the beam between rooftops and how he had dangled from the roof. He emphasized the humor and omitted the danger, and Jamie covered her mouth to hide her giggles. But her laughter was infectious, and Molly thought again about what a precious child Jake had. In her heart, she knew she would welcome becoming a mother to Jamie, but she remembered her conversation with Jake and still wondered if he had been prompted to ask her to marry him by the idea that Jamie would have a mother.

After dinner Jake turned to Molly. "Come home with us, will you? You can meet Vera. She stays when Jamie's home so Jamie won't be alone when I go out."

"I want you to see my room," Jamie added, slipping her hand over the car seat to tug gently on a lock of Molly's hair.

"I'd love to," Molly answered, curious about Jake's house. They all sang while Jake drove; he taught them some lines in German from Humperdinck's *Hansel und Gretel*. Molly enjoyed Jake singing with enthusiasm, lowering his voice so he wouldn't drown out Jamie.

It was dark, but Molly could see from the street lights that they were driving into an elegant residential area. Finally, Jake turned into a curving drive that wound up a slope past lighted, well-landscaped grounds to the house. As Molly studied the large, two-storey stone house, far more elegant than anything she had pictured in her mind, some notion inside her changed; the mental scales that weighed her decision whether to accept Jake's proposal tipped to the negative. For she admitted there was an issue she would have to bring up. That evening, another chasm had widened between them. Already she loved Jake and was growing to love his daughter. If she were to marry

Jake, she had to face reality. Molly knew she couldn't bear to watch Jake send Jamie away. Just as strongly, she knew she wouldn't be able to bear parting with the little girl either.

Jake stopped at the back door. Ahead was a two-car garage with both doors closed. A high fence hid the back yard. Jake took her arm to enter a kitchen with oak cabinets and white counters. A white-haired woman sat at the kitchen table. She was reading a magazine, but she looked up and smiled when they entered. Jake introduced them, saying, "Molly, this is Mrs. Majors. Vera, this is Miss Ashland. I told you Vera stays with Jamie when I'm away." They talked for a few minutes. Then Jamie insisted on showing her room first, so Molly climbed wide stairs, her footsteps silenced by the thick beige carpet.

Jamie tugged on her hand as she went down a hall lined with framed oil paintings. The room looked like Jamie; neat, a little girl's dream room, with a white provincial bed, pink spread and canopy, pink roses in the wallpaper, and shelves and chests overflowing with toys and books, dolls and bears. Molly suspected Jake tried to give Jamie everything he could. When Molly detected the love and pride in his expression as he looked around Jamie's room, she was convinced Jamie shouldn't be shuffled around. Jake shouldn't have to go through the heartache of separation either.

"Show her your room, Daddy."

Jake draped his arm across Molly's shoulders and the three of them walked down the hall to a big master bedroom done in dark blue and beige. Besides the king-size bed, she took in a desk with neat stacks of papers, paintings, a rocking chair, a dark blue leather sofa. Molly wondered if Jake had had the room redone because it looked so masculine. She moved to study framed pictures on one wall; baby pictures of Jamie, photos of Ben and Jake, a wedding portrait of a younger Jake. Molly felt a twist inside as she looked at that shot, but she turned and smiled. "This is very nice."

"Thanks," he said, shedding his coat and tie. "Come see the downstairs."

"I'm going to put Alfred and Bach to bed," Jamie said.

"And Jamie, too," Jake said. "Get on your pj's and I'll read you a story in a little while."

As they walked into the hall, Vera came up and went into Jamie's room with her, the two of them talking about bedtime stories. Jake smiled at Molly and pulled her close their hips touching, the slight contact stirring Molly's memories.

The familiar scent of after-shave was inviting and she slid her arm around his narrow waist. He grinned down at her, his lashes thick and slightly curled, his mouth so sensual. Her lips tingled and she ached to be alone with him, to have the privacy and intimacy they'd had in Missouri.

They went downstairs and walked through the wide hallway green with potted plants. Then he led her down a step to a large, comfortable family room with chintz-covered furniture, bookshelves on the walls, and a wide fireplace with an antique clock above it. While Molly made herself comfortable on the sofa, Jake opened paneled doors that revealed an elaborate stereo system. He selected a tape and in minutes slow, soft, country love songs came on. Molly realized he must have acquired the tape particularly for her. Then Jake crossed the room to the bar and poured two glasses of wine. He returned to sit on the sofa, and faced Molly.

"Now, we take up life in the real world, don't we?" he asked.

"Yes, we do," she said, swirling the pale wine.

He took the glass from her fingers. "Jamie and Vera are upstairs and will be for another twenty minutes." His silvery eyes watched her, his mouth so close, so tempting. Molly forgot problems and closed her eyes, wanting only to be kissed.

Jake pulled her onto his lap, his hands drifting over her as he kissed her deeply. She shifted her hips closer, feeling his hard maleness, and wished they had absolute privacy. Her hand slipped beneath the collar of his shirt to caress warm flesh, and Jake's hand floated over the thin silk as his fingers stroked her breast. Finally he paused, and her eyes opened slowly. He was watching her as he held her against his chest. "I love you," he whispered. Her heart pounded; she prayed they could work everything out, because she wanted to be Mrs. Jake Cannon more than she had ever wanted anything in her life.

He moved her beside him. She turned to face him, picking up her glass of wine and taking a sip. "You have a wonderful home."

"And something is terribly wrong," he said quietly.

She was startled that he could tell so easily. "There's something we need to discuss," she said, trying to find the right words. "You told me that you didn't ask me to marry you because you need a mother for Jamie."

"I meant it," he said solemnly. "I'm not taking a wife for that reason."

Although her heart was already committed, Molly realized she would have to fight Jake's fear of failure before they could share their lives. Taking a deep breath, she searched his eyes, wondering if he had looked closely at his motives. "If I were to marry you, I would be Jamie's mother. She's a precious child and she adores you."

He sat waiting and listening, thinking Molly looked more beautiful than ever. But her green eyes were troubled and from the moment she had stepped out of the car, she had been subdued and solemn. He didn't know if his house bothered her or what had happened. He wanted to carry her upstairs to his bed, but he knew he couldn't. They weren't alone and besides, Molly had withdrawn, putting up invisible walls between them. Jake had a panicky feeling that he was losing her.

She ran her fingers on her knee, choosing her words carefully. "If I were Jamie's mother, I couldn't live in Detroit and let her go off to Arizona."

He drew a deep breath. "I've explained to you why I do."

"Jake, look at this house—I didn't know you were this successful. Take a chance! Keep the stores here and open another in Phoenix. You're successful enough that you can take a chance!"

"Hell, Molly, *you* won't take a chance on what your heart tells you!" She blinked at him, her face becoming pale. He reached out to stroke her cheek. "Trust your heart."

Her breath caught. Days ago she had taken a chance on what her heart wanted. Now she was struggling to keep what she had found. "There's more reason than ever to say no," she said, trying to make him stop and look again at his values. "I couldn't watch her go to Arizona and I don't see how you can! You can live in a smaller house, drive a smaller car, and give her the daddy and the love she needs and wants!"

"Damn, you don't know what it's like to fail and lose everything!" he snapped, shifting away from her. "I have to be able to pay her medical bills, to send her to good schools. I want her to have the best of everything I can give her."

"Then give her what you can and what she wants most of all—you!"

"My dad was always starting over and always failing."

"You're not going to fail!"

"Look at Ben. He hasn't made anything of himself; he couldn't take care of a daughter the way I take care of her."

"Jake, teddy bears and fancy clothes aren't what puts the sparkle in her eyes."

Jake stared at Molly, hurt. After losing Sheryl, the separation from Jamie had been the most painful event in his life. He had finally adjusted, and Molly was opening up old wounds all over again. There was no way to make Molly understand what kind of childhood he'd had, how he'd hated it and been determined to get out and have a different life from his father's. "It's so damned easy for you to say because you're a gypsy and you didn't grow up without anything!"

"Well, we didn't have much, but we loved each other!" she said, his accusation painful, even though he had called her a gypsy before. "And I know you had some family love, too."

"Yes, we did, but it was bad at home when I was a kid."

"It's not like you have to throw all this away and start from nothing. If you go to Arizona and fail, you'll have some of this to come back to."

"Molly, the people who have followed that line of reasoning and gone broke are legion."

Voices came from the hallway and Jake stood up, as Jamie came into the room carrying a book. "You said you'd read me a story." She paused to look at Molly wistfully, and Molly had to smile.

"And then you'd like it if I'd read a little while, too," Molly guessed.

Jamie nodded and ran to sit in the center of the sofa. "Come sit down, Daddy," she said, patting the sofa beside her.

He did, settling Jamie on his lap and moving next to Molly. While he read from *Winnie-the-Pooh*, his mellow voice a rumble that lulled and enticed, Jamie looked alternately at the occasional drawings and at her daddy. Her eyes began to droop as he read in a deep, furry voice that became softer and softer. Molly was reminded of moments she'd spent in his arms, listening to him talk in the same quiet tone after they had made love. Jake was wonderful with children, she decided. She wondered if he'd ever wanted more. Finally Jamie was breathing deeply and evenly, her eyes closed in sleep.

"Guess you're excused from reading tonight," he said to Molly, closing the book. "I'll take her upstairs and be right back."

Molly took the book from him as he stood and carried Jamie up to bed. When he came downstairs, he closed the door and crossed the room to pour more wine. When Jake was settled comfortably, beside her again, he asked, "How's Ivy?"

"Fine. Worried about what Ben thinks about her career. He doesn't approve of her dancing."

"I'm not surprised at that."

"Everything's changing," she said sadly, tempted to kiss him, but sensing the gulf between them had widened to disastrous proportions. They were quiet, and for the first time, it wasn't an easy silence.

"If I thought I could manage it, I'd move in a second," Jake said tersely, and Molly began to understand that she had brought up an old issue he had fought with by himself. "But I went over and over it and I'm afraid I'd lose everything. It would take a hell of an investment, more than opening a store here. I've had one store here begin to lose money and I closed it fast."

"You have savings, I'm sure."

"Yeah, but you'd be amazed how quickly money can go when you're buying inventory."

Molly felt hemmed in, upset over his attitude. She waved her hand. "This marvelous house—how wonderful is it, Jake, when there's no one here except you?"

"Dammit, Molly, you don't understand because you don't have anyone to be responsible for! You can move on a whim. You don't have that much to lose if you start over, and it won't hurt someone else if you fail. And you don't know what it's like to see your child have an asthma attack. I have to be able to pay her medical bills."

She stood up. "I'd better go home," she said. In the back of her mind, she had feared this moment would come since their first kiss.

He stood up, shaking car keys out of his pocket. "You make it sound as if I don't love her," he said hoarsely. Molly hurt as if she'd received a blow.

"That's not true, Jake!"

"It's because I love her that I stay here!"

"It's because you love her and she loves you that you should go."

"Oh, hell, Molly. I know what I have to do. It's hard enough to leave her without having someone tell me I shouldn't!" With an angry set to his jaw, Jake took her arm and walked through the house. He left Molly a moment to go down a hall and tell Vera he was leaving. Then he returned and they went to the car. They were quiet. Jake stared at the road; he had a ring in his pocket he'd planned to give Molly, but he knew he would have been rejected so he hadn't brought it out. He glanced at her. She looked wounded and vulnerable and he hated that he had caused her to be that way, but she was going over old ground that he had covered thoroughly before making his decision to send Jamie south.

In Missouri, Molly had been right—their differences were monumental. He'd thought their points of contention had diminished to nothing, but this one issue had become an ever-widening rift. And he knew they never would agree. He felt as if something were slowly crushing him, taking his breath.

He gripped the steering wheel and stared stonily at the road, sure he was in for another big heartache. At Molly's apartment, he walked to the door with her. The moon was full, shedding a silvery brilliance on the tiny lawn, throwing the small porch into shadows.

Jake waited while Molly unlocked her door and shoved it open. "Want to come in?"

He nodded, knowing he should have said no, knowing he should turn and go and save himself more pain. But he couldn't. He followed her inside, closed the door and reached for her. She hesitated a second, looking at him with wide, accusing eyes, then let him pull her close to kiss her.

His embrace was brief, and then he immediately turned to go. "'Night, Molly."

She followed him to the door. "'Night, Jake," she said, remembering how they had said good-night when they had shared adjoining bedrooms in the Ozarks. He went down the walk, his distress evident in the stiffness of his gait. She was equally miserable, but she had told him the truth. She couldn't marry him and send Jamie away with her grandparents. Jamie adored Jake, and if he'd just settle for a simpler lifestyle, take a chance on starting a new store, he would be so much happier.

Molly leaned against the door, letting tears come, hating the thought of Jake and Jamie being parted— and of herself being parted forever from both of them. She knew she was ending the relationship with Jake. He wouldn't be back. The stubborn set to his shoulders and the pain in his eyes told her that.

She moved woodenly, getting ready for bed, her hand drifting over the green silk dress as she hung it up. She recalled the look on Jake's face when he had first seen her in it, and remembered how he had peeled it off her. She cried, wanting his arms, his laughter, his companionship, his wild kisses and lovemaking, wanting him beyond anything she had ever known.

The next few days were no easier, but she saw she had been right. Jake didn't call or come by. Ivy stopped on the way to the studio one morning. As they sat at the kitchen table over cups of coffee, Ivy stirred cream into her cup and said, "Ben called last night."

"That's nice."

"He's going to apply for a teaching job in a high school. It doesn't pay real great, but he would be teaching history—what he wants to do."

"That's nice."

"He's coming to Detroit this weekend."

"That's good."

"Molly, are you sick?"

"No."

"It's Jake, isn't it?"

"Yes. We're not dating anymore."

"I'm sorry." Ivy waited. When Molly didn't say anything, Ivy said, "You really love him, don't you?"

Molly looked up into Ivy's curious blue eyes. "Yes, I do," she said, convinced to the depths of her heart.

There was another long silence before Ivy asked, "Is there anything I can do to help?"

"No, thanks."

"Gee, I feel funny. You always help me and let me cry on your shoulder and listen to my tale of woe. Now, you're finally really in trouble, and I don't know what to do."

Molly smiled. "I'm okay. I'm glad you're here."

"Yeah. You want to talk about it?"

Molly shook her head. "Not yet," she said, sure that if she did, she would break down in tears.

"I better go. I'll see you at the studio."

"Sure."

THE DAYS PASSED, not getting any better. The weekend was endless and unbearable and Molly wondered how long it would take her to get over Jake—or if she ever would. Monday evening she went out with Ivy to eat at a new fish restaurant—art deco posters, green walls, and balloons for decorations. In a booth, Molly

sat and toyed with steaming shrimp creole, listening to
Ivy talk about Ben.

"He thinks he'll get the job and he's so excited about
it. He's invited me to Ames next weekend. Look." She
stretched her arm across the table. A thin, gold chain
was fastened around Ivy's wrist, and her blue eyes
sparkled.

"That's lovely," Molly said, nodding when the
waitress asked if they were finished.

"Ben gave it to me," Ivy said, touching the brace-
let. Molly was mildly amused, remembering wryly that
Ivy had been showered with gifts from males since
she'd had her thirteenth birthday. For the first time,
Molly noticed that Ivy wasn't wearing much makeup.
She had on a simple white blouse and blue shorts like
Molly's.

"When will you leave for Ames?" Molly asked,
picking up the check.

"Here's for mine," Ivy said, handing Molly some
bills. "I bought a plane ticket and I'm flying down. I
wanted to ask you if I can get off early from the studio."

"Of course," Molly answered, taking a last drink of
coffee.

"I have to tell you....I'm sorry now that you and
Jake have broken up," Ivy said, hesitating, excitement
radiating from her voice, "but Ben asked me to marry
him! I get a ring this weekend."

While it wasn't surprising in some ways, it startled
Molly to hear Ivy announce Ben's proposal. Before she
could say anything, Ivy began, "I know how you feel
about rushing into another marriage, but this time I'm
sure. You know Ben's different from Willis and Drew."

"I know he is. What about your dancing?"

"I'll give it up," Ivy said matter-of-factly. "I can take courses in Ames in accounting and get my degree. Molly, I love Ben. I have more fun with him than any man I've known, and he's more considerate and he's more intelligent."

"I'm glad," Molly said. Maybe Ivy had finally found the right man. With a twist of pain, she realized that now her life would be forever linked to Jake's and she would hear about him constantly. Ivy would be Jamie's aunt. Molly felt tears threaten, and she didn't want to dampen Ivy's joy. "I'm glad," she repeated and looked down to get her purse.

"I'm so happy you said that," Ivy said, relief obvious in her voice.

"Ready to go?" Molly asked.

"Sure."

Molly slid out of the booth and turned toward the front. Her gaze drifted over the people waiting to be seated, and she was suddenly riveted, unable to breathe or move as she looked into Jake's gray eyes.

CHAPTER EIGHTEEN

HE STARED AT MOLLY a moment, his dark brows narrowing. He looked as handsome as ever in a navy blazer and gray slacks. And then Molly's heart suffered another jolt. His hand was on the arm of the blonde standing beside him. Molly's gaze returned to Jake and he smiled, but it was fleeting and stiff.

Molly became aware of her plain clothing, aware she would have to walk past him. She didn't have on makeup, her feet were in sandals, and her pain was compounded by knowing he was out with someone new.

She walked rigidly toward the door. It seemed a mile from the booth to the entrance. Then when she was only a few feet from him, Ivy spotted him.

"Jake!"

Molly knew the moment Ivy realized Jake had a date. Her voice changed and she mumbled, "Hi," hurrying past him with a glance at the blonde, who was watching them with curiosity.

"Hello," Molly said uncomfortably.

"Hi," he said, his voice at its deepest level.

She passed him and was out the door, welcoming the cool night air. She felt dizzy with shock and hurt; she'd known he would go on with his life, but hated to see that he had.

The parking lot was full and crowded. Cars were parked at odd angles and when they neared the three-year-old red Renault Ivy had just purchased, they found someone had parked too close on Molly's side for her to get to the door.

"I can't get in."

"I'll back it out," Ivy said, squeezing between the cars to get in on her side.

Molly's gaze drifted over the tree-shaded and lamp-lit parking lot. Right across from them she spotted the shiny, black Lincoln, larger than most cars in the lot—Jake's car. She stared at it, moving out of Ivy's way, remembering the last time she'd been in his car, reflecting that another woman would ride in it tonight.

Ivy backed out and swung the Renault around. Molly came out of her reverie. "Ivy!" she cried, waving her hands.

The Renault banged into the fender of the Lincoln, and Molly wanted to run away and avoid the next few minutes.

Ivy emerged. "Oh, lordy! I hit someone."

"Ivy, how could you! How could you!"

"I just didn't see the end of that car. Look at it—it's as big as two cars and it's sticking out in the lane. Oh, lordy, I'll have to go find the driver. Let me get the license."

"Ivy, it's Jake's car."

Ivy's head reappeared above the door of her car. "Jake?"

"You just hit Jake's Lincoln! He'll think we did it on purpose."

"Now why would he think something like that? Oh, thank goodness, it's Jake! He won't be mad at me."

"Well, I am! This is embarrassing."

"I'll pull out of the way and talk to him."

"I'm waiting in the car, and I don't want to face him."

Ivy pulled alongside the parked cars, and Molly climbed into the Renault. "I'll leave the keys in case you need to let someone out," Ivy said.

Molly didn't want to have to look at Jake or talk to him. She was embarrassed beyond words. When he emerged, walking beside Ivy, Molly looked down at the purse in her lap, toying with it. She refused to get involved.

She waited for Ivy and time stretched to eons. Then the door opened and she looked up to see Jake lean down on the driver's side.

"I wasn't even in the car," she said awkwardly, feeling her cheeks grow hot.

"Ivy told me you weren't. It's not bad, and I told her I'd take care of it, because she'll have one claim from Ben's car. You might suggest a driver's ed course."

Molly looked at him, curious as to why he had come over to talk to her. Was he trying to be funny with his remark? He didn't seem angry.

"Ben's asked her to marry him."

"She told me tonight," she said, beginning to grow more intrigued, her embarrassment fading. Jake stood in the shadows, yet there was enough light to see his features. He was so handsome, and so near. Longing swept over her like a tidal wave, and she wanted to reach out and grasp his hands and tell him to forget the woman in the restaurant.

"Seems as if we can't get into the same neighborhood without disaster."

"I didn't cause this."

"I know you didn't."

Why didn't he go? He had a date waiting. Molly's heart began to beat faster. "Where's Ivy?"

"She went inside to wash her hands. Are you okay?"

"Yes," she lied; she had never felt worse in her life.

"Say, buddy," a man's deep voice said, "would you move your car, please?"

Molly glanced up to see a couple waiting to get to their car. She started to move over as Jake slipped behind the wheel.

She bumped him, only the slightest touch, but it was like fire. She drew a sharp breath, seeing his eyes flicker as he turned the ignition and closed the door to ease the car a few yards farther along.

He cut the motor and turned to look at her. "I'd better get back inside," he said, not making an effort to move.

She couldn't say a word. She could only stare at him and want to touch him.

He glanced out the front window and drew a deep breath. "Here comes Ivy. You take care, Molly," he said. He climbed out and was gone.

Watching him as he walked back to the restaurant, Molly wanted to run after him to be with him. She knotted her fists together and sat silently as Ivy got in to drive.

Finally Ivy asked, "Did you and Jake talk?"

"Not about anything important. Some guy came along and needed the car moved out of his way, so Jake moved it." It was difficult to talk. Molly had been jolted by the brief encounter, as well as by the knowledge that he was going out with others.

Why had he stopped to talk at all? She mulled it over until Ivy dropped her off. Her sister turned to her.

"I'm sorry about Jakes's car, but he was really nice and I told him you didn't have anything to do with it."

"I know. I'm happy about Ben."

"Are you really?"

"Yes," Molly said and meant it, acknowledging that the changes for the better in Ivy had been brought about by Ben.

"Good. It feels so right, Molly. It's different than with the others."

"I'm glad. 'Night, Ivy." Molly smiled, went inside and then quietly fell apart, crying, watching the hands on the clock, anguished that Jake was with someone else each minute of the evening. As she had so many times already, she went over again and again the thought of accepting his proposal. But she always came to the same impasse. She wouldn't be able to leave Jamie and she couldn't bear to watch Jake suffer with missing her and with not knowing her as she was growing up. It wasn't necessary. At least to Molly it wasn't necessary.

She decided that night that it was time to move on, to leave Detroit and avoid painful encounters with Jake. It would give her something to occupy her mind and her time, she decided, glancing for the hundredth time at the clock.

A WEEK LATER on Monday, Molly wasn't one bit closer to making a move. A dull lethargy had settled on her, and she couldn't shake it off. She didn't want to eat, and she had lost interest in moving from Detroit. Ivy had come home from Ames with a small diamond ring and excitement enough to generate a fire. She and Ben planned to be married in a simple ceremony at the end of July. They would wait for Ivy's divorce to be final and for her to get moved. It would be another occasion when Molly would have to face Jake, and she doubted she would get through the event without bursting into tears.

She locked up the studio for the evening, having stayed behind until the sun was almost below the horizon. She made her way through the shadowed alley behind the long, one-storey building where she rented space for the studio. Then she turned toward the parking lot and stopped as she glanced up and saw Jake leaning against his car.

CHAPTER NINETEEN

"I'VE BEEN WAITING for you," he said quietly, and her heart thudded so violently she was afraid he could see her pulse beat. He was wearing tight, faded jeans and a T-shirt, and dimly her mind registered that he was definitely in shape now.

He came toward her. "Can you come eat with me, and we can talk?"

"Sure," she said, thinking that at that moment she would have said yes to most anything he had asked—except to the one big question between them. "I'll have to change," she said.

He held the car door and she climbed inside the Lincoln, again self-conscious about her appearance. She was without makeup and dressed in navy leotards and ballet slippers. Her hair was looped and pinned on top of her head. During dancing, tendrils had escaped and fallen, curling around her face.

Jake climbed in and turned to face her. "You look great."

If Molly hadn't been so sad, she would have laughed. Instead, she merely smiled. "Thank you, but I've been dancing all day. You look as if you've kept up your exercises," she said, trying to keep her gaze from drifting over him.

"Yeah, I have," he said, reaching across to take her hand.

Molly thought she would melt from the touch as his strong fingers locked with her slender ones. What was he doing? He was acting as strangely as he had the night Ivy had hit his car.

"I wished you loved me enough to marry me no matter what the hell I do," he said suddenly, words running together.

"I do love you! And I can't bear to see you and Jamie both hurt needlessly..." Molly couldn't control her emotions and she turned her head quickly, embarrassed at the hot tears that stung her eyes.

Jake pulled her into his arms. "Stop crying," he said gruffly, crushing her against his chest and running his hands over her back. It was all Molly could do to keep from bursting into sobs. "I flew to Arizona this weekend to look at locations."

It took a second for the words to register. "Jake!" she exclaimed, stunned over his announcement.

"I'll take that chance, Molly," he said with a stubborn thrust to his jaw. "I have to. Now, how about you?"

Life had turned upside down as the full significance of what he said and asked dawned on her. She flung her arms around his neck, startling him so that he fell back against the door as she kissed him. His momentary surprise was brief. His arms crushed the breath out of her lungs and it was long minutes before either spoke. She looked at him, tears sparkling on her lashes and to Jake, she looked like the most beautiful woman in the world. He tingled with wanting her and wished he'd had sense enough to wait until they were home to talk. "Will you marry me?"

"Of course!"

He grinned, feeling like shouting for joy. He folded her in his arms again. "You got over your damned reluctance about commitment?"

"Completely," she said and smiled at him, her fingers drifting over his cheeks and throat. "I've been totally committed since one sunny afternoon at a lake. I've just been fighting for our future happiness."

He kissed her throat. "Can we go inside that office of yours and be undisturbed for a few minutes?"

Her green eyes darkened as she said yes.

They both hurried inside, Molly's fingers shaking in her haste to unlock the door until Jake took the key and finished the job. Inside, she started to lead the way to her office, but he caught her arm, kicked the door shut behind him and listened for it to lock. As he pulled her to him, he reached into his pocket. "I'm doing this all wrong. I wanted it to be perfect and take you to dinner to ask you to marry me and give you a ring, but I can't wait."

"This is perfect," she said, watching him open the box to reveal a gorgeous diamond. His fingers shook, and Molly closed her hand over his, feeling tears of joy sting her eyes. He paused, looking at her.

"If you cry again . . ."

She stood on tiptoe to kiss him, salty tears mingling with their kiss. He pulled her away a moment. "Will you put on my ring?"

She laughed, trying to stop crying, feeling a giddy happiness as they both fumbled with the ring, and finally slipped it on her finger while the box fell unheeded to the floor. And then she was in Jake's arms while he kissed her and pulled her against him, spreading his legs as he leaned back against the door and cradled her hips against his. Molly felt his throbbing arousal straining against the tight jeans; her hands drifted over him, wanting to touch and touch.

His hand slipped beneath the leotard, stretching the elasticized material to peel it away as he kissed her throat. He trailed kisses to her breast as he displaced white lace underthings, his hands and arms dark against Molly's pale flesh. Then he flung his T-shirt aside and Molly's hands caressed his muscled chest, slipping down to the buttons on his jeans. Clothes were discarded with trembling eagerness. As Jake leaned down to flick his tongue across a trembling pink nipple, he whispered, "Where's your office?"

Molly pointed and he swung her into his arms, carrying her the short distance to her tiny office. Its brown carpet would never again be drab in Molly's eyes.

LATER, MOLLY LAY IN HIS ARMS, their bodies beaded with perspiration, hearts beating together while she stroked his chest and trailed her fingers down over his stomach and leg.

"I don't want to stop touching you."

"That's nice, but you're not the one stretched on this scratchy carpet. Let's eat and go home. Or go home and go eat."

She laughed and sat up. He came up too, pulling her to her feet and hugging her briefly before they began to dress. In minutes they were in the car. "Jake, I need to shower and change if we're going to eat. Let's go to my place first."

"Anything the lady wants," he said happily.

She studied the ring. "Did you find a location in Phoenix?"

"Yep. I think it all looks great."

"Have you told Jamie?"

"Nope. I want to do that when you're with me," he said, dropping his hand to her knee, his thumb drawing circles on her leg.

"You'll never know how I felt last week when we saw you."

"Forget it, hon. Except maybe that precipitated events."

"What are you talking about?"

"The lady with me that night works in one of the stores. I thought maybe it would help if I went out with someone. And it did."

Molly looked at him sharply and saw his smile. "It made me realize that I couldn't be happy without you," he explained quietly, his smile fading.

"Oh, Jake, I've been so miserable," she said, scooting closer to hug him.

"Hey, wait! I can't see to drive."

She cuddled against him, keeping her hand on his leg. "I wondered why you kept talking to me in the parking lot."

"I couldn't bear to leave you. I wanted to pull you into my arms and take you home with me."

"Not half so much as I wanted you to. I wish you'd told me how you felt that night."

"I'm sorry, Molly. I just get chills thinking what I'd do if I couldn't provide for Jamie." After a moment he laughed. "Ivy would hit my car! Don't tell me you aren't disaster! I'm going to take out a whale of an insurance policy; house, car, me..."

"Nothing has happened to me except when I've been around you!" she protested. "And maybe when we marry, everything will be peaceful. No more disasters."

"No more climbing on rooftops either!" He sobered as he said, "I knew that night, after seeing you again, I'd have to rethink my life, and I did. In Missouri and back here at the hotel, I was gone almost two weeks from the stores, and they clicked right along, making steady profits, so maybe I don't have to hover over them. You know I'd rather be with you and Jamie than anything else on earth," he said, his voice dropping down. "And in Phoenix, if I fail—"

Her hand clamped on his lips. "Don't say it. You won't fail. Don't even think about it. And if you do, I'll teach you to dance and we can have a dance studio." He laughed, dropping his arm around her shoulders as he slowed and parked in front of her apartment. "Just get on television in Phoenix," she said, "and let them hear your sexy voice and see your sexy bedroom eyes and you'll sell stereos just like you have in Detroit!"

"I think we may have to postpone dinner for a little while longer," he whispered as he opened her door and waited for her to enter.

Two hours later, Molly stretched and sat up in bed. "Are you hungry?"

"Famished, but I have to go by my house, too."

"Is Vera with Jamie?"

"No. Jamie's with Mom for the night. I had plans," he said in a husky voice, reaching out to cup her full breast in his large hand. His callused thumb flicked lightly over the nipple, bringing the bud to tautness, making Molly draw a deep breath and close her eyes as she lay back down.

"There goes dinner," she whispered, her tongue flicking out to touch his throat.

Later, Molly emerged from the shower to find Jake dressed in his jeans, peering inside her refrigerator.

"Molly, this is the most revolting bit of nothing—"

"I haven't been hungry," she said quietly.

His expression changed and he closed the door, crossing the room to her to squeeze her shoulders. "That's over, and I'll spend my life telling you how happy I am you've made me willing to take the risk to move and start somewhere else. I adore Jamie and want to be with her..." His voice trailed off and his eyes became red as he pulled Molly closer, stroking her hair. "Thank you, love. I've been too afraid, but you gave me no choice in the matter. I'll make a go of it," he said, with all the stubbornness she knew he was capable of.

She laughed. "Good mulish attitude."

"So, you've turned me into a gypsy, too."

She shook her head. "Only temporarily. I suspect we'll put down roots pretty deep."

"Can you round up your relatives by next weekend so we can have our wedding then?"

"Yes," she said, confident she could and as eager to be married as Jake.

Pleased by her response, he toyed with her hair. "Let me pay the expenses for the wedding."

"You don't need to, but thank you. I have savings and since you tore up my check for our time in Missouri, I have plenty."

"Okay."

"Jake, I'd like to have a dance studio in Arizona. I wouldn't have to work long hours and Jamie could go with me some of the time, and then she'll be in school—"

"Hon, you do whatever you damn well please after you say 'I do'. I've never asked," he said, "but do you want children?''

"Yes", she answered. "Do you want more?''

"Absolutely," he replied, his gray eyes changing as he leaned down to kiss her. "In a little while. Not right this minute.... I want you all to myself. I've rented a villa in Puerto Vallarta for a week for a gypsy sun dancer.'' His mouth covered hers and his hands pushed the towel between them away as Molly stood on tiptoe to kiss him.

CHAPTER TWENTY

THEY EMERGED from the airport at Puerto Vallarta and headed toward the taxis. Jake paused to get a map from a vending machine and Molly walked ahead. Sunlight was bright and Molly's eyes sparkled. Jake couldn't take his gaze from her long legs as she walked, and he noticed that the green cotton suit she had changed to from her wedding dress brought out the green in her eyes. She wore the emerald pendant he had given her as a wedding gift, her cheeks were flushed, and a smile continually graced her face.

His pulse raced at the thought of being alone with her in only a few more minutes. He caught her arm and started across the expanse of paving toward the taxi stands.

Nearby a crowd began to gather and someone screamed as a purse snatcher broke from the crowd and ran.

"Jake, look—"

"Molly, close your eyes!" he commanded, scooping her into his arms and sprinting in the opposite direction toward a taxi. He was thankful he had been exercising. "We're not going to witness anything!"

Shouts could be heard behind him and a whistle blew, but Jake kept running without glancing back. He reached a cab and a wide-eyed driver opened the door for Jake to set Molly inside. Jake turned to flash money at the driver and give his destination. When the man nodded, Jake added another bill and sat down beside Molly. He slammed the door, and the taxi began to move.

"Close your eyes," Jake told her, leaning over her to kiss her and block her from seeing the furor. The driver honked; the taxi careened around a curve, racing from the airport.

Molly was laughing too hard for Jake to kiss her, so he paused, grinning at her but not moving out of her way.

"Jake, the driver—"

"For what I paid him, he should let me rape you back here and never say a word. We are going to a fully stocked villa. We don't have any reason to leave it or our private beach, so we can't witness or be a part of anything that involves anybody else."

"Sounds good to me." She slanted him a look. "You are in shape, running across the pavement like that while you were carrying me. My, oh my, what biceps you have, darling," she murmured, running her hands up his arms to his chest. "What luscious pectorals...mmm..." Her fingers trailed down. "What hard...thighs..."

"Molly!" He slid away from her quickly and drew a deep breath as they wound up a narrow road with tropical forests on either side. "It's damned hot here," Jake mumbled, wiping his brow. Molly laughed.

He grinned at her and began to sing; Molly joined in. Warm wind blew through the open windows and tangled her hair, and she was sure the driver was thinking they were crazy Americans. But when Jake changed to something in Spanish, the driver began singing with him, grinning over his shoulder to the extent that Molly wished he would turn around and keep his eyes on the road.

After Jake had paid him and thanked him, the taxi roared down the road, and finally quiet descended. They entered a walled villa, which was silent except for the fountain in the courtyard, the bird cries and the faint sound of the ocean. "Jake, it's so beautiful!" Molly cried.

"We could have had it with servants or without," he said, opening the door and carrying her inside. As he set her down and closed and locked the door, he said, "I asked for no servants. Means you have to pitch in and work."

"That's your standard procedure—off to the woods and work," she said playfully. She'd glimpsed the elegance of the villa and the sparkling sand and blue water beyond, but was more interested in Jake now.

"But first—" he leaned down to kiss her "—sun dancer, I can't wait..."

Molly closed her eyes, raising her mouth to his, her heart bursting with joy as Jake's arms tightened around her.